RAMPAGE

CALIBER
BOOKS

Also from ALAN CAILLOU

CABOT CAIN Series
Assault on Kolchak
Assault on Loveless
Assault on Ming
Assault on Agathon
Assault on Fellawi
Assault on Almata

MATTHEW TOBIN Series
Dead Sea Submarine
Afghan Assault
Congo War Cry
Death Charge
Swamp War
Terror in Rio
The Garonsky Missile

MIKE BENASQUE Series
The Plotters
Marseilles
Who'll Buy My Evil
Diamonds Wild

IAN QUAYLE Series
A League of Hawks
The Sword of God

DEKKER'S DEMONS Series
Suicide Run
Blood Run

The Charge of the Light Brigade
The World Is Six Feet Square

Rogue's Gambit
Cairo Cabal
Bichu the Jaguar
The Walls of Jolo
The Hot Sun of Africa
The Cheetahs
Joshua's People
Mindanao Pearl
Khartoum
South from Khartoum
Rampage
A Journey to Orassia
The Prophetess
House on Curzon Street

RAMPAGE

For further information visit the Caliber Comics website:
www.calibercomics.com

Cover Art by Chris Lincoln

CHAPTER 1

The desk clerk beamed affably when he went into the hotel.

He said, "Otto von Abart. You know him?"

The clerk blinked at him, touching his face with a thin finger. "Von Abart? You know the address, Mr. Stanton?"

"Over on the Starnbergersee." Fumbling in his notebook, he said, "I've got the address here somewhere."

"Ah yes, of course—the hunter." The clerk was smiling. "You wish to telephone?"

"Please."

"It will take a few minutes."

"In my room. Do you have any American whisky?"

"I can get you some."

"Bourbon?"

He watched as the clerk ran his finger up and down the edge of his pointed jawbone. "Bourbon is a little difficult. If you will wait until this evening, I'm sure we can find some."

"Good. A couple of bottles if you can."

He went up the wide oak staircase, feeling the smooth texture of the carved handrail that was as sleek as a woman's skin, and when he reached his room he took out his map-case and spread a large-scale map of Malaya on the floor, standing above it and staring down on it as though his escape lay along the bright red lines which were the route he had marked before coming here. He lit a cigarette and took a file of notes from his briefcase, and when the phone rang he took it over to the bed and lay down comfortably before answering it. The disembodied voice was deep and rich.

"Hallo?"

"Herr von Abart?"

"Ya."

"Stanton. Harry Stanton."

There was a brief moment of surprise.

"Herr Stanton? But—why, when did you get here? We were expecting you tomorrow. I made arrangements to meet your plane."

The English was easy, precise, comfortable. Stanton said sourly, "I came a day early. I wanted to get away."

"But where are you? At the airport?"

"The Bayerisch Hotel."

"But this won't do, Mr. Stanton. Wait, I will send the car for you at once. No, I will come myself. Did you have a good trip?"

"Fair. Too damn fast, no time to collect my thoughts. How are you?"

"Now that you are here I am looking forward to meeting you. The Bayerisch? I will be there in half an hour."

"I could take a cab."

"I wouldn't dream of it. In half an hour."

"All right, I'll be waiting."

"It's good to know we are beginning."

"That's how I feel too. In half an hour then."

"Even less."

"*Auf wiedersehen.*"

"*Auf wiedersehen*, my friend. We look forward to this."

He put down the phone and sat on the edge of the bed for a while, thinking, and then took a mildewed book that was bound in heavy Germanic leather and read the gold letters of the title, stumbling over the unaccustomed Gothic.

The Art of the Hunter. And under it, in smaller type, *Treatise on the Trapping and Destruction of the Predatory Animals. By Otto von Abart.*

There was a photograph for a frontispiece, showing a darkly sunburned face with pale cold eyes and a wide forehead. A handsome man, slightly balding, with the first slight vestige of a double chin under a square-shaped face that seemed to show an authority, a competence. Searching for the right word, he said to himself, *An aristocrat.* The book had been published thirty years ago.

He put his book and his map away, splashed some water over his face, called for the boy to take his bags, and went down to the bar to wait, and when von Abart came, he was surprised, knowing that there was no surprise in the passage of time but not ready for it, to see that he was much older than he had imagined, with the sunburn paled and the hair quite gone and the line that was under the eyes now resolved to dark shadowy pouches. But there was still that air of aristocratic good looks, matured now to an almost monarchical power.

Unconsciously, he put on his boyish charm as he stretched out his hand. "Herr von Abart? This is a great privilege. I've been wanting to meet you for a long time."

"It's good to see you, Mr. Stanton. They told me a great deal about you."

"I just finished reading your treatise."

"Oh yes? Then you speak good German."

"I speak lousy German. It gave me a bad time. I must confess I skipped the hard bits. Plenty of them."

Von Abart's teeth were white and firm, and his smile was composed, reserved. *An aristocrat,* he thought again.

"I am mortified that you did not let us know when you arrived. I would have met you."

7

"At one o'clock in the morning? It didn't seem right. Besides, I wanted to...well, to walk around for a bit. It's a beautiful town."

"Your first time in Munich?"

"Yes."

"Then perhaps we'll have time to show you the city."

"Perhaps."

"And I'm anxious for you to see my trophies."

"I hear it's a fine collection."

"The best in the world, Mr. Stanton. The best."

A brief moment of distaste quickly passed. He said to himself, *Well, he's an old man, he's at the end of his career, nothing but trophies to show for it.*

Von Abart was saying, "...and a pair of tusks, more than two hundred and fifty pounds. That's a big tusker."

Stanton said politely, "It's a record that's never been broken."

"Yes. In twenty years, no one's ever shot a bigger one."

"In Somalia, I believe it was?"

Von Abart was delighted. "Just over the border. Of course, on the other side, in Kenya, I'd have been in trouble. That's the advantage of undefined frontiers, isn't it? No pettifogging civil servants to say what a man can and what he can't shoot. Well, shall we go?"

The clerk was putting the bags in the car, bowing and beaming his pleasure, and when the gun-case went in, von Abart said angrily, "Be careful with that, confound you. Those are precision instruments."

There was quite a reception committee waiting for him at the house. There was Herr Mendel, Director of the German Zoological Foundation, accompanied by his bustling assistant, Herr Schlock, and Herr Schlock's lumpy daughter who was acting as his interpreter; there was Frau Bruhle, Director of the Parks Association of Bavaria; and there was Herr Kaltenberg, who was the Chief Accountant for the City's Sub-committee on Zoological Affairs.

Mendel had prepared a speech. With the others standing by and looking satisfied, he said pompously, "On behalf of the City of Munich, of Bavaria, and of the German people, I have the honor to extend to you, Herr Stanton, the heartfelt welcome of more than one million people to whom our most beautiful Zoo, one of the finest in the world, is a reflection of the Germanic culture and the Bavarian love of all that is...that is most beautiful. We are very happy to see you here, and we know that in selecting the team for this endeavor, we have made a most...most felicitous choice. The greatest hunter in America, and our own famous Herr von Abart, We know that with such highest competence we cannot fail to get that which we all want, which is that our Geo-Zoological Garden should once more occupy the high esteem of the whole...the whole zoological world. And now, I will translate what I have just said for the benefit of my good friends who are present."

Watching von Abart, Stanton saw his sly smile, and he repressed a sudden desire to wink. When it was all over and the clapping was finished, he said simply, "I am delighted to be here in your beautiful city, and I am grateful for the honor you do me. We'll do our best to satisfy you."

They all went into the house.

It was one of those old mansions that border on the sumptuous edge of a castle, with lawns, ill-kept now, that ran down to the cold river-waters of the rushing Isar, and tall hedges that kept out the bourgeois world of the pedestrian without masking the high mountains that rose like a purple Valhalla in the far distance, topped here and there with snow that still lay white and cloudy on the summits. There was a wide hall that was plastered over with stucco between the timbers, and the frieze that ran round its high walls was a rococo sculptor's nightmare, But when they went into the library, Stanton pulled up short and stood in the doorway while the others crowded about him, pleased with his astonishment.

It was an enormous room, and it was crowded tight with hunting trophies, a sudden transition to a savage world that was familiar to him but yet seemed farcically out of place in these stolid surroundings. At the side of the massive doorway, there was an elephant's foot that served as a doorstop. Above the door itself was a Masai shield crossed with Danakil spears which were flanked by two eight-foot-long Sakai blowpipes, their crisscrossed designs worn smooth. A stuffed tiger's head glared at them from over the huge fireplace. There were leopard, sambur, wildebeest and seladang, the wild buffalo of Malaya. The grey mask of a rhino protruded grotesquely from the wall beside him, inviting him, he thought irreverently, to stick his hat on its gigantic horn. Instead, he touched the hard grey hair of it with the tips of his fingers, feeling the death in it. He said slowly, "The longest horn I've seen. Must be over four feet."

"Fifty-three and a half inches precisely," von Abart said.

"A record?"

"Of course. Everything in this room is a record. Every single one of them. That tiger there...four hundred and twenty pounds in weight, and six feet nine from his nose to the tip of his tail. That's quite an animal. Wouldn't you say?"

"Quite an animal."

He stared about him, overwhelmed in spite of himself by the massive obtrusion of trophies. The long, dark-colored floor, highly polished, was scattered with skins of tiger and leopard, their teeth horribly bared, and almost every panel in the massive, musty room was covered with spears and arrows, with krises and blowguns, with javelins and with knobkerries. There was no relief at all.

It was a room, Stanton thought, to which a man might

retire when he felt the need to impress himself with his superiority over the animal world, or to convince himself, at last, of his own greatness. He wondered if he himself would ever come to this. Turning away abruptly, he went over to the map-stand that stood across a corner. He pulled the sheets down slowly, while von Abart's voice droned on behind him. "You see? Two hundred and fifty pounds of the finest ivory in the world. Look at the way it's matured. I tracked him for two months before I caught up with him. And I got him at four hundred yards, can you imagine that? An elephant at four hundred yards? A Magnum .405, a Mauser, the best gun ever made."

The maps were all of Malaysia. Siam, Borneo, Java, Sumatra and New Guinea...the wild, dank jungles, he thought. He pulled down, at last, what he was looking for, a large-scale map of Malaya. Laying a hand across the spine of hills with his fingers touching Pahang state, he said, "Here—this is the area we want. This is where we want to go."

Von Abart left the tusk he was fondling and came to stand beside him. He said enthusiastically, "Good shooting country."

"We're trapping, Herr von Abart. Not shooting."

The German corrected himself gently. "Good hunting country. Almost the only place that hasn't been hunted out. But it's hard country."

"That's why it's the best place for us. Don't you think so? Herr Mendel?"

Herr Mendel spread his hands wide. "I...we are perfectly willing to leave the choice of locale in your...in your capable hands. All we need are the best specimens that can be captured. We want the Munich Zoo to be once again the best in the world. And that means not only many animals. It means also the very best. Not so?"

"Of course."

"Then you must go, Mr. Stanton, where you will find the best."

"Good. You know this part of Malaya, Herr von Abart?"

"I know it well. Some of my best trophies...The black leopard over there."

It was half concealed in the shadow of the curved arch that supported the roof. Looking at it, Stanton thought he had never seen such evil in stitched-in eyes of glass; they seemed to burn in the semi-obscurity, and only the black spots glistened in the black, black skin that seemed tinged with a magic gold. He muttered, "A beautiful animal. From Pahang?"

"Right where your hand is now. The rest of his skin—it's part of a fur coat now. This is what they all come to, Mr. Stanton, in spite of their stealth and their silence and their treachery. Fur coats to beautify our women."

Stanton said nothing. Von Abart went on, "And you, Mr. Stanton? You've been there too?"

"Yes. The last time I didn't do much, There was no time."

"Time is the enemy of the hunter."

"And I wasn't alone."

There it was, the recurring image of Cora, the wife he was trying to escape from.

She had had the greatest contempt for his skill with the animals, and yet she was an animal herself, as sleek and as cunning and as beautiful as the best of them. Sometimes it had seemed to him that she had goaded him deliberately, using her feline movements on him and laughing at his discomfort, taunting him with the knowledge that here was one animal over which he was powerless.

There was one thought that gave him comfort. He said aloud, "But she was a lousy hunter."

"I beg your pardon?" It was von Abart.

Startled, he said sheepishly, "I was not alone. I had a

lousy hunter with me. Women on shikar, they ought to stay back home."

He saw Mendel look at von Abart, and wondered if his daydreaming had been so obvious. He said brusquely, forcing himself back to the business in hand, turning again to the big map, "Here. We fly in to Singapore, take the railroad up country, strike into the jungle at Kepak and go north of the rain forest."

Von Abart frowned. "What about the monsoon?"

"Porters can move our heavy stuff ahead of us as soon as the north-east monsoon finishes about February. We should be able to meet up with them somewhere. Here, beyond this range of hills. Set up our main camp in the clearing and put up tents or palm-leaf houses. It'll be damp, of course, but the heaviest rains will be over."

Looking at von Abart, he wondered about his physical capacity. He said, worried, "I suppose we can get through the jungle. It's pretty rough country there."

He was conscious that von Abart's pale grey eyes were cold and hard. "I can go on foot where you can go, where a tiger can go, where a leopard can go."

"Of course. I didn't mean that at all." He said lamely, "I was just wondering how much equipment we can carry, and how much we can send on ahead with the porters—that's all."

Von Abart brushed it aside. "A matter of logistics," he said, "and nothing else. I see no problem at all. We need our rifles, our water bottles and maybe a blanket. Shelter and all the other little luxuries—we can manage without them if we have to."

"Yes, of course. We'll keep our cages at the main camp until we've trapped the animals that we need. Then we can send them to the east coast and ship them from there."

"It will have to be Singapore. There are no suitable harbors on the east coast."

Stanton bit his lip and said nothing. Feeling the sudden

awkwardness, von Abart turned away. "It's no problem," he said affably, "do whatever you think is best. But I've got some facts and figures ready for you if you'd like to see them."

It was over already; the momentary anger had gone. Stanton, smiling, said, "Well, good. We could manhandle the cages through the jungle and pick up the railroad, then ship them straight down to the harbor. Certainly, once we've struck camp, we'll want to get our charges back as soon as possible."

"Of course." Von Abart was jovial again. "Not to mention ourselves. A breath of good Bavarian air after the heat— some good Bavarian beer, eh?"

Somewhere in the house a gong sounded. Rubbing his hands together cheerfully, von Abart said, "Well, shall we eat?"

They all trooped into the dining-room. At the doorway, as Mendel and the others stood aside to let them pass, von Abart said, confidentially, "And later on, I'll show you the figures my secretary got together for us. She's done a good job. She'd have done well in the army."

"Your secretary?"

"Yes. I had her do a little research. Boats, trains, supplies. She's a bright girl, you'll like her. Now, will you take the head of the table, Mr. Stanton? If you watch through the French windows, you'll see the moon rise over the crest of the mountain there. It's a splendid sight, splendid." Looking at his watch, he added, "In about twelve minutes from now."

There was a discomfort in the smooth and polished excellence that surrounded him. They talked in a mixture of German and English; of animals, about which he knew a great deal, and about cloisonné, about which he knew nothing, and of the Frankish kingdom of Lewis the Child, of whom he had never heard.

Once, when Mendel made a recondite remark about the

Wittelsbachs, there was a sudden surge of laughter, and he himself, a little late, grinned broadly in appreciation of a joke he had not understood but knew was there somewhere; and looking at him with an assumed affection, von Abart had said gently, "We should be talking English, you know, although Mr. Stanton's German is really quite excellent. I must congratulate you, Mr. Stanton. You come from a monolingual people, and yet...really quite excellent."

He had said to himself, hiding his anger and smiling with the same falsity, I wish he wouldn't be so goddam patronizing. We live in a democracy, Jack, and don't you forget it.

And ten minutes later, they were all talking about the margravate of Burgau. In German.

CHAPTER 2

The meal lay heavy in his stomach and seemed to drug him into a yawning lethargy, into an acceptance of so much that was completely foreign to him, He tried to reason with himself, explaining carefully that the foreignness was the strangeness not of another country, which would scarcely have dismayed him, but of another world, another age. It was a world in which fine wines stood proud in exquisite glassware that had survived a thousand delicate handlings since a devoted craftsman had formed them more than a hundred years ago; it was an age in which *this* was proper and *that* was just not done. In spite of the courteous deference that was shown to him, it caused him to assert himself a little more than he would have done, and he knew that they would note this down as an arrogance. He was on the defensive, and for no reason at all.

Now, the others were gone, and they were seated, the three of them, round the low table in the library on which one of the maps had been spread out. The smoke from their black cheroots hung in the dusty air. It seemed to cling to the dry skins of the animals. The timber ceiling above them, anciently vaulted, was almost in obscurity above the scattered circles of yellow light. In the ashtray—held in the curved claw of an ostrich—the stubs were piling up in an untidy brown heap of wasted leaf and ash, and the floor beside them was littered with their papers.

16

Reading from the file Mendel had prepared, von Abart said, "Tiger and leopard—these are the real reason for the shikar. We need a seladang, some lemur, tapir, and the sondailus."

Stanton nodded. "The white rhino. It's supposed to be extinct, but I myself have never believed this. I'm glad the Zoo agrees with me."

Mendel raised a didactic finger, waving it in the air.

"No, Mr. Stanton, it is not extinct. We have word, of course, from our...contacts?...in Singapore. And what is more, we learn that black leopard have been seen in the area north of these mountains here—big ones, very big. We would like to have one. For the rest, an elephant, some barking deer. The list is quite detailed."

Von Abart went over to his tusks and fondled the smooth yellow surface of them. He said scornfully, "The Indian elephant. A dull creature. But his African cousin now...Did you ever see tusks like these, Mr. Stanton? Ever, anywhere?"

Stanton picked up a heavy file from the table; in fine ornamental lettering, it was inscribed: *The hunting-grounds. Maps and notes. Compilation—Otto von Abart.* He heard von Abart say cheerfully, "Africa—the ancient land of the elephants. There, he's still the proud creature he used to be, he hasn't degenerated into a beast of burden. The Indian elephant is an overgrown donkey, no more. But this one—two months on his track, and he knew I was after him. He led me through the deserts and up into the dry mountains. It became an obsession, a challenge. Even the Somalis had given up. They said I'd never catch up with him. And you know? When I began to get closer, he turned south and headed for the border. It was almost as if he was like a wanted criminal fleeing the country, knowing that once he crossed the border there was protection to be found. It was as if he knew that the Ogaden were no longer safe for him because the best hunter in the world was after him, it seemed as though he knew it. He led me a chase in his own territory, and when he found he couldn't shake me off his tail he headed for sanctuary." He laughed coarsely, jubilant in nostalgic triumph. He said, "And it did him no good at all. At four hundred yards, right through the opening in the skull, a Magnum."

Looking at him, feeling the weight of the heavy file like a solid exemplar of competent persistence, Stanton said coldly, "Over the border. In the Game Reserve?"

Smiling, von Abart shook his head. He said stolidly, "The Association cleared me. It was still in the Ogaden.

"Since then, they've been a little more careful with border delineations."

It was meant, almost unconsciously, as a jibe. Von Abart ignored it. Or perhaps, Stanton wondered, did he really discount altogether the fact that he had poached it? That he had made his kill on the wrong side of a hopelessly undefined frontier? Didn't it worry him at all that there'd been a minor scandal about it, with all the old Germanic hatreds of East Africa aroused once more for the sake of a wandering elephant? Or had he, instead, convinced himself, as he'd convinced the Hunters' Association, that he'd really been over the border in the vague, ungoverned areas of the Ogaden where a man could kill what he liked, human or bestial, and no one to worry him about it? There was an autocratic contempt on those square, firm features that would not tolerate the petty regulation of men whose stature was less than his own. It was a contempt that was beginning to worry him. None the less, looking over the maps von Abart had prepared, Stanton was forced to admire his solid and precise workmanship. There was not a hunting area in the world that had not been meticulously annotated. Flipping the pages he read aloud:

"Mijertein: easy access by truck from south or west. All types of antelopes including rare species such as Dibitag. Lion, cheetah, and desert leopard, but thick thorn bush in patches suggests skins may be spoiled by too much scarring.

"New Guinea... headhunters... Dyaks... Borneo... Java...

Zanzibar." A complete gazetteer compiled with Teutonic thoroughness, he thought.

He said, "Your information's pretty solid."

Von Abart was visibly pleased. "A matter of research. My own notes, those of others before me—they've all been collated."

"I must congratulate you."

"It's not easy for a man of my experience, Mr. Stanton, to take the role of second-in-command. I wanted to make it clear, from the outset, that I would do the best I could for you."

Well, there it was. Glancing quickly at Mendel, noticing the alarmed embarrassment, he said smoothly, knowing that it was essential not to start off with any misunderstandings, "Yes, I know that. When Mr. Mendel wrote and said you'd be coming along too, I can't tell you how happy I was. He put me in charge of the operation, but...well, you've had thirty years longer at this sort of thing than I have, and I'm counting heavily on you. I'm sure we all know that."

"The old must move over to make way for the young, Mr. Stanton."

"Don't hold my youth against me. I've been hunting for ten years myself. I know my job too. And I know Malaya." He was smiling broadly, making a joke of it. Mendel came to the rescue.

"It's a matter of—of politics," he said apologetically, "The relationship between our two countries...A great deal of the post-war financing of the Zoo was done—indirectly—with American money, did you know that? So it seemed only courteous..."

"There's no difficulty, Herr Mendel," von Abart said. "My respect for Mr. Stanton could not be higher. He even reads my books. I'll admit that, at one time, I rather hoped...Well, it comes to all of us in time."

"Yes. Of course. Now, where were we?"

The subtle anger had passed again. He said to himself, *Am I as touchy as this Bavarian aristocrat who can't see that he's on the skids? A man who spends his solitude surrounded with evidence of a once-great past?*

"We were in Malaya, Mr. Stanton."

He brought the meeting, with conscious effort, back into focus.

"Well, once we have escaped from the orderly life of tea and rubber estates, the jungle will tie us close to the animals we want. Getting a seladang is one of the problems."

"No problem, I assure you," von Abart said. "You dig a hole, and they fall in." He said drily, "We should not really speak about these things in front of Mr. Mendel. If he realized how easy it is to catch an animal..."

Mendel caught the changed mood at once. He said cheerfully, "Ah, for the experts, yes. But if I were to go there I would be terrified. I am a city man, Mr. Stanton. I must feel hard pavement under my feet." He pulled a map towards him and laid a pudgy hand on it.

"Here," he said somberly, "if you get well away from the coast...The whole population still lives on the banks of the rivers or by the sea, and once you get up here we feel that some of the heavier jungle will give us the kind of animals we want. We have had long and detailed conferences, Mr. Stanton, and you will see the reports we have had from a man out there who works for us sometimes. He is a trader, an Armenian, I believe. His name is Hadjian."

The pudgy finger was exploring the low mountains of the Thailand border. "The Sakai people...They still live deep in the jungles, like animals. Geographically, I suppose, they are not very far from the civilized world, but in time...They are animals, hiding in the darkness of the trees, naked, savage, unpredictable. It is here, Mr. Stanton, that we feel you will find what we want." He added diffidently, "But of course, the choice is up to the experts."

"This Armenian," Stanton asked, "he's been up there? I know the Sakai well. It's not easy to deal with them. A man who trades with them would be useful."

"Yes, he spends a lot of his time there. Herr von Abart knows him, too."

Von Abart was pouring brandy into tissue-thin snifters watching the play of light at their edges. Passing them around, he said, "An Armenian. A race like the Sondailus; they are supposed to be extinct, but if you look hard you will find them, in unexpected and inaccessible places. He deals in tin, in rubber, in orchids, in skins—and in arms. In short, he deals in anything that will make a profit." He could not keep the scorn from his voice. For von Abart, Hadjian was a survivor from Musa Dagh, a man who had escaped the genocide. The prospect brought Stanton vivid memories of the war and that other genocide, Not wanting to make an issue of it, he said, "There's a great fear among the Sakai—among the Senoi, that is. They hate and fear the rest of the Malayans. It makes them dangerous. But if this man moves about among them, he's probably in a position to give us a great deal of help. Guides, trackers—we can't move without them. Does he know anything about animals? If he trades in skins, he probably does."

"To him," von Abart said, "an animal is a hide, no more, a hide that can be measured in terms of dollars. To this extent, he knows about animals." He warmed his back at the fire, and went on:

"He showed me a black leopard skin once. Nearly a foot longer than my own record. It was badly scarred, but he said they grew bigger up in the hills. And I think I believe him."

"Well, might be worth looking into. No problems with labor there?"

"No, none. We can get all the help we need. They know what they're doing and they'll stick with us."

"What about personal servants?"

"That can be arranged. City dwellers don't usually like to go into the jungle. Probably some Chinese Malayans."

"And Sakai trackers for the jungle. They live in the jungle, so their eyes are used to the half-light, but out in the sun their sight isn't too good. We could get Tamil Malayans for other tracking."

"Whatever funds you need..." Mendel said. "There's plenty of money behind us, and there'll be a letter of credit at the Hong Kong and Shanghai Bank in Singapore, I fear we have given you a long list of animals, Mr. Stanton. But when you come back with them, we shall once again be very proud of our Zoo."

Stifling a yawn, Stanton studied the figures, grateful that so much of the dull routine work, the research and the logistics, had all been done for him, wondering how quickly they could get out there where the animals would be alive and virile and panting, with the fiery, unspoiled animation of Malayan reality. How long would it be before he felt the soft pliancy of the undergrowth at his feet? Singapore first, but briefly. A city bright with the kaleidoscope of the East, its streets filled with Sikhs and Tamils and Pakistanis and Chinese. Then, the tea and rubber estates that had always looked to him like gigantic, orderly, domestic gardens. At last, the jungle, green and dark and damply frightening, smoking, like a smoldering fire that was ready to engulf, as though in protest, the domestic life that clutched at its skirts.

He remembered the bamboo houses on their tall stilts and the hum of mosquitoes; and he remembered the Sakai people, the dangerous, primitive, somehow terribly competent Sakai. And he remembered, above all, the cheerful make-do-and-mend that served always as a reminder that civilization was a long way behind them. The beat-up old trucks with grinning natives working the carburetors over with hammers, repairing gasoline leaks with chewing-gum, stuffing blown-out tires with grass, keeping the vital trucks somehow, by every turn and trick of ingenuity, on the road. You need a washer for the gas pump? Cut it out of the felt of your hat. New contacts for the distributor? Break a pencil and use the graphite, but get the truck home somehow. There was pleasure in the reflection of inadequacy; it was almost a cult. A cult, he said to himself, a cult of make-do-with-what-you-have.

And now? Now it was different, there was money behind them, and more when that ran out, and official business to be attended to, and a high degree of organization already achieved before he arrived by a precise and methodical German professor of zoology to whom an animal was a skin to put on a woman's back, or a trophy to hang on his wall. He wondered if he'd have trouble over von Abart's obvious dispassion towards the animals he loved so well, and, reflecting on it, he thought, *Well, at least he knows I'm the boss.*

A lamp went on behind him somewhere near the door, and he saw the other two look up, getting to their feet and smiling, and when he turned his head, a cigarette drooping from the corner of his mouth, he saw her in the light that fell from the ceiling in an amber wash over her bare shoulders, and for a startled moment he thought that she was naked. Then he saw that she was wearing a dress of sorts that clung to her body as tight and smooth as a skin, leaving the upper half of her breasts completely exposed and molding the lower, and then slipping tight down her hips to a point very high above her knees, so that when she came forward, the thought that was uppermost in his mind was a sort of wondering preoccupation with the question, Can she possibly sit down in a dress like that or does she have to stand all evening?

He quickly pulled himself together, a slight feeling of oafish shame touching him, and stood up with the others. He wondered if they'd noticed that his mouth had been momentarily open, and when she stepped into their circle and held out her hand he was in command again, with all the youthful charm and the good teeth, and von Abart said, smugly, "May I present Mr. Harry Stanton from America. Fräulein Annaliese Kruger, my secretary."

Mendel was bowing over her hand, kissing it, and receiving no answering smile. Her eyes were on Stanton, and he felt suddenly uncomfortable again as though she were getting rid of Mendel quickly in order to meet the important guest last instead of first, and he thought again of Germanic thoroughness. It was a small thing, but it seemed a calculation on her part that was deliberately meant to impress him. When she turned to him at last, the perfunctory business with Mendel done with, he took her hand and said, "This is a great pleasure, Miss Kruger." And he was thinking, hoping it would not show on his face but not much caring if it did, *Brother, imagine a woman like that in the jungle on a hot night with the sand soft under her back. A pity she's not coming along with us; I'd do something about it.*

It was only then that the word "secretary" struck him.

So that's it, he thought, *that's the way the land lies. Well, good luck to him, though why the hell he lets her dress like that with other people around...If she were mine...*And then, looking at von Abart's complacent expression, seeing that even Mendel was breathing faster, he began to wonder.

She said, smiling at him, "We've heard a great deal about you, Mr. Stanton, a very great deal." And he said, making conversation, trying to keep his eyes off her breasts, "I've been going through some of the figures you prepared for us—was it you?"

"Yes, it was I." Her English was fluent, precise, correct, and her voice was a little throaty, deep and soft. He was conscious that she used it carefully and studiedly, like a singer in a Berlin night-club.

He said, meaning it, "Well, you did a good job on them.

24

There's everything there we have to know. A pity you're not coming with us."

He spoke almost jocularly, feeling the need to keep talking, and then, in the little silence, there was a sudden awareness that Mendel and von Abart had exchanged glances again, and that she was smiling at them both, ready to start laughing, as though something extraordinarily funny were about to happen. It made him uncomfortable, and he was quickly thinking of the answer to von Abart's next question, knowing now that they had been planning together behind his back, when von Abart stalled him by saying easily, "Well, now's as good a time as any, isn't it? I was going to suggest to you that Miss Kruger join the expedition. She'd be invaluable."

He wanted to say, "She'd be more at home on the pages of *Harper's Bazaar*." Instead, he said slowly, "Well, let's discuss it in the morning, shall we? Of course, it would be delightful, but, well, it's going to be pretty tough. It won't be a picnic. Shall we talk about it later?"

It was very hard, with her there, to come right out and say no. Von Abart said smoothly, "Why don't we settle it now? Of course, if you'd rather just the two of us...But I should tell you, Anna is one of the clan."

"The clan?"

"She's an expert hunter. An expert."

"A hunter? He said incredibly, "You mean you've been out there before?"

She wore the easy smile of tolerant amusement, but her grey eyes were steady and alert. She said gently, "But, of course. Otto and I...many times..."

"I see."

He said to himself angrily, *Well, how the hell do I get out of this one? They chose their timing well, late at night, at the last minute, with an entrance straight out of the Deutsches Theater.* In the silence, Herr Mendel said, awkwardly, "I must confess,

Mr. Stanton, that Herr von Abart had already suggested to me the advisability of permitting Miss Kruger to accompany the expedition. I told him that it was a decision you would have to make yourself. Certainly, you will need clerical assistance—the records, the tabulations..."

Yes, *let's be methodical about it all.* He said aloud, "I agree that there'll be a great deal of the work that Miss Kruger obviously does so well, but the point is...The privations of a shikar...It's not easy for a woman, even for one who is used to it."

Damn her, he thought, why the hell doesn't she say something herself instead of just standing there looking at me as though I'm a slavemaster about to dispose of her? The idea that came to him with the term slavemaster made him uncomfortable, and he looked briefly at her body and quickly away from her, wondering if he could really convince himself that she'd be a nuisance. Then he thought, the hell with it, making up his mind already but determined not to give in without the semblance of a fight. Looking at her directly, he said slowly, "You really know how to live in the jungle? The heat, the dangers..."

"Danger? There's very little danger, Mr. Stanton. Otto and I have hunted many times in Malaya. In Thailand, in Burma, in Borneo, in Africa. I have lived among wilder tribes than your Sakai" She added slyly, "Or we should really call them the Senoi, shouldn't we? The name Sakai has a connotation of contempt."

He knew that she was flaunting her knowledge. He said brusquely, "No amount of armchair expertise will soften the pain of a snake bite."

She said calmly, "We have identified fifty-six different varieties of reptiles in this area. Only twelve of them are poisonous. Believe me, Mr. Stanton, the jungle has always been kind to me. I have no fear of it."

"Well, that's half the battle. But dammit, I just can't

imagine you out there."

"I've crossed from the source of the Perak river to Kuantan on the China Sea. On foot. With nothing but a rifle, a mosquito net, and a bottle of iodine. Don't be misled by my—my penchant for pretty clothes, Mr. Stanton." Was she speaking at von Abart, he wondered. "The life I lead here demands a certain attention to—to grooming, is that the word? But in the jungle..." She laughed and said, "You wouldn't recognize me. You probably wouldn't even like me. But you will not dispute my competence, of that I assure you."

He wondered if she were making the point deliberately, and if so, how she had guessed at the root of his objections. It was not, he knew, the toughness of a woman that would dismay him; it was her femininity, her need for the little amenities. Her denial of them, casually thrown off as of no consequence, seemed to him to be an effort to force him into an admission that his acceptance of her would be as a person, and not as a woman. It was a subtlety from the strange world that was meant to make him, the naive intruder, a party to their scheming.

But the fight was lost. Putting up a show of a rearguard action, he said, "And you can really use a rifle? With some degree of safety?"

He felt that she was laughing at him, and then the amusement was gone from her eyes, as though he had unknowingly touched on something that caused her secret and grave concern, and he wondered, with a vague feeling of anxiety, what it was. It occurred to him that she was building herself a reputation in an unlikely field, and he knew that with a hunter of von Abart's stature at her side, a little deceit would be easy. He was sure now that he had found her weakness.

There was triumph in the discovery. The image was clear in his mind. He could see her handling her rifle, diffidently, with an avuncular Otto by her side, saying perhaps, "Steady, now, keep the left eye open, squeeze, don't pull." In a hasty moment he almost made his point out loud, and then he thought better of it, telling himself that he was being gracious too, that he wasn't the boor they thought him, that he too knew the niceties of good manners. Seeing the inexplicable anxiety that came into her eyes, he smiled at her, letting her see that he was really on her side and that, if the deceit were there, then he would happily be a party to it.

And then, in the instant of his certainty, he was unsure again, and when he looked at von Abart he saw a grave, controlled awareness in the pale cold eyes as though there were a secret there that had been close to elucidation. He thrust the problem away from him, knowing that he did so because he could not solve it, and at the same time telling himself that it was of no consequence—who cared a damn anyway? He said to her again, "You can really shoot straight?"

The trepidation was gone. She answered his smile and said, "I'm a crack shot. I'll show you my trophies one day."

"Would you mind showing me your hands?"

The battle was over now, and he knew that she knew it, They were only humoring each other, making a show of it. She held out her hands, and when he took them, feeling the touch of her flesh for the first time, he said good-humoredly, "I'm supposed to believe that hands like these can hold a Magnum?"

"In a week they won't be like that anymore, Mr. Stanton." She did not pull them away from him. "In a week my nails will be broken, the skin torn. But it's not irreparable damage, is it?"

"No, but you think it's worth it?"

"I'm quite sure it is."

Von Abart, preening himself about her, said pedantically, "The care of her physical beauty is only one facet of Anna's many-sided character."

Well, that was the hell of a way to put it. He said, "And you're not afraid of the predatory animals?"

"I can handle any animal, Mr. Stanton."

He dropped her hands quickly and held out his own in a gesture.

"Well, what can I say? I'm one against three. I think it's a bad thing in principle, a woman on shikar. But if you're all convinced...Certainly, we'll need trained assistance. Collation of records, that sort of thing."

"And I'm a Fellow of the International Zoological Society, Mr. Stanton."

He knew that it was thrown at him to make his acquiescence more palatable, to make this defeat seem more logical. Defeat? Did he really want to keep her away? Was he secretly pleased that she'd be there, in spite of von Abart's obvious ownership of her? Did he really care so little for the complications that could arise between them on her account? He thought angrily, *Well, it's his own damn fault, letting her walk around like that, with a neckline down to her waist.*

Mendel was relaxed again, glad that agreement had been reached. He said placidly, "I am glad, Mr. Stanton - a decision I had hoped you would make. Fräulein Kruger has a very complete knowledge of zoology, very complete. I know that she will be very useful."

He said, smiling at her, "You just don't look like the outdoor type, that's all. Forgive me if I seemed reluctant."

"I'm very grateful to you, Mr. Stanton." Looking at him with bland innocence, she said deliberately, "And I'm sure that you'll find my presence an asset."

Having said that, having firmly established the delicate touch of coquetry so that he would be well aware of it, she moved over to von Abart and slipped her arm under his. When he sat down, she slid into position on the arm of his chair and took a cigarette. His hand at her back, von Abart said, "And how was the party?"

"Dull." Turning to Stanton, she said smoothly, "Otto

phoned me that you had arrived a day early, but I couldn't really get away any earlier. One of those things."

And yet he knew that she had delayed the introduction until von Abart should have sold him her capabilities. "I had her do a little research," he had carefully said at dinner. "She's a bright girl." And then, over their coffee, he had piled up the annotated maps, and the notes, and the figures, and the documents. He had laid them out to be admired, saying nothing and knowing that the impression they would make would be sufficient, carefully refraining from talking any more about her, carefully not saying, "She's my mistress and I'd like to have her along on the trip if you don't mind."

Stanton made a mental note of the methodical deviousness, of the careful guile, and with that awareness there was the offhand determination that if anything went wrong between them, if he found himself casually exorcizing the heat of his loins on that lovely body, then her lover had only himself to blame.

It was a purely adventitious thought, put away without further consideration almost as soon as it came to him.

Later, when Mendel had gone, looking at his watch, worrying about the late hour and fussing over his exit, assuring them of his willingness to help in any way he could, they had climbed the wide staircase together, the two men side by side and the woman a little ahead of them, moving her body as though conscious of their presence behind and below her. She had gone to her room, next to von Abart's, and von Abart had come with him to show him his own room on the floor above.

Sitting on the edge of the bed, a glass of brandy in his hand he had said, "I noticed, Mr. Stanton, of your awareness that we had...we had tried to force your acceptance of Fräulein Kruger. But I beg of you, please do not feel badly about it."

Gesturing with his broad hand, he insisted, "I assure you, you will be glad she is with us. She's a fine hunter, a very fine hunter. She knows as much about animals as I do."

"That's high praise. I don't mind, really. If I seemed hesitant..."

"Of course, of course, I understand perfectly."

"On a deal like this...it's an important one, it's not like a guided tour through the National Parks. We'll have to get into some pretty inaccessible terrain if we're to find the specimens we need. And if the going gets too rough, it may not be easy."

"Take my word for it, she's very competent in the bush."

"It's hard to believe that she can handle a rifle. I had the impression she'd be more at home in an expensive night-club." He was smiling consciously to make it sound affectionate, "She's really a good shot?"

"Excellent."

There had been a momentary hesitation, and he wondered if von Abart were telling the truth. He added casually, "As a matter of fact, one of those trophies downstairs is really hers, the lion over the bay window. A neck shot at three hundred and fifty yards. That's not bad, you know."

"A neck shot at that range? If she'd missed the spine, she could have been in trouble."

"But she doesn't miss. And she knows it."

"That's extraordinary."

Was it imagination, or was there a trace of jealousy there? Consciously getting away from the discussion of her, he said, "You've a beautiful house here. Beautiful."

"It's very old, Mr. Stanton. My family have owned it since 1702, when they bought it from Max Emmanuel. Karl Albert, after whose wife the Amalienburg was named, used this very room on his wedding night. Cuvilliés was a guest here while he was designing the Court Theatre, and he built the new staircase for us. It's a house with a proud history." He added

ALAN CAILLOU

quickly, "But our plumbing is modern. I believe that's considered very important in America."

Stanton looked up sharply. He said easily, "But of course. Any fool can be uncomfortable. Have you been to America, Herr von Abart?"

"Yes, I was there once. I saw very little except broad prairies and...barbed wire. I was a prisoner of war."

"Oh. Oh, I see. Well, those times are a long way behind us."

"Yes, they are. And there's a great deal ahead of us. Shall we go over to the Zoo tomorrow? You'll see the changes they're making."

"A good idea."

"They're getting ready for the new stock we shall bring them."

"Splendid. Herr Mendel seems a very competent man."

"He is. We must do a good job for them. Now, I expect you're tired."

At the door he turned and said, "And again, thank you...the matter of Fräulein Kruger..."

"I'm glad she's coming along."

"If you are not now, you will be, later on. You will see."

"Sure. You bet."

"Is there anything you need, Mr. Stanton?"

"No - nothing, thanks."

"Then let me say again how glad I am that we are together. The three of us."

"Good night."

"See you in the morning."

He lay back on the bed and closed his eyes. *The three of us*, von Abart had said.

CHAPTER 3

The snow had fallen gently during the night, and turned to slush when the rain had come in the morning, so that when they drove down the bank of the river in the big Mercedes, the muddy water splashed up against the passing, unheeding pedestrians who walked with their heads bowed against the wind and their shoulders huddled.

The Isar was running fast with the icy torrent that came cascading down from the cold high Tyrolese Alps as though searching desperately for the warmer cornfields that it would irrigate and bring to sunny life. The trees were stark and bare against the sky.

The Zoo was deserted, and only the blue-coated keepers were at work, cleaning away the leaves and the refuse, bringing new warm hay into the compounds, carting the hodded bricks for the new buildings. The wide sluices that separated the compounds were scattered with twigs and dry winter leaves, and in the Malaysian section only the barking deer stood forlornly outside their shelters, grouped together and staring blankly over the ditches that defined their habitat. Inside the buildings, the heat was stifling and the air was ripe with the sour smell of manure. A young keeper, not more than eighteen years old, showed them over the wide, winter-empty park, splashing through the mud beside them in his high rubber boots. The

Director of the Zoo, a tall, heavy man in a grey Bavarian cloak and a green felt hat, waved affably at them from the baboons' compound, and the young keeper, whose name was Pfund, swung the metal gate open for them. The Director, crouched down over an animal, beckoned them over.

Von Abart made the introductions, and the Director said, his voice heavy and labored, "He's dying, you see? Dying. And there's nothing we can do."

The young baboon he was tending was whimpering, its sad eyes wide and uncomprehending. "You see? Dying. They killed him. We give them everything they want, and still they fight, just like men."

Stanton stared at the group of apes that stood chattering on top of a stone mound.

"A female?"

"Always the same thing, Mr. Stanton. It's the only thing they fight over. Exactly like men, eh? Only sometimes we fight for less important things. And now, what can I do? There is nothing I can do except bury him. A good specimen; young, friendly, and all he understands is that we can do nothing for him, he's lost too much blood and he knows it. They know more than we give them credit for."

"We plan to bring you some new ones, you know."

"Yes, I know that. But these, Mr. Stanton, these are the ones I love. They've been here a long time. Well, life passes, life changes. Only the trees are the same." He sighed and stood up, a tall man, heavy with age and sorrow. "So you are the famous Harry Stanton. I've heard much of you. I am glad that you are helping us. Our Zoo will once again be the best in the world. And when do you leave?"

"In two days' time. We've settled on Pahang."

"Good. Bring me back a good orangutan. We badly need female."

"We'll bring you all of them. It's a long list, and a good

one."

"Have you seen our tiger? Let me show him to you. Come."

The Director stood up and spoke to the young keeper, "Stay with him until he's gone. In half an hour he will be dead."

"*Jawohl, Herr Direktor.*"

"And be careful when you take him out. Don't let the others see. Shall we go?"

They turned away, and then a frightening incident exploded among them suddenly. It began when von Abart, looking up at the group of apes on the hill, said contemptuously, "They don't like him."

Startled, Stanton said, "They don't like whom?"

"The boy. Look at that old baboon up there. Look at the hate in his eyes."

As Stanton watched, the old baboon, the wide mane of his head grey and shaggy, came ambling slowly towards them, swinging his crouched legs in wide arcs, his long hands dangling. The young keeper, kneeling down over the dying animal, looked up in slow alarm, and the Director, standing quite still and talking softly, said, "Just stand up and back away slowly. Don't hurry."

The keeper, strong in discipline, nodded, stood up, and moved slowly towards the gate, and then the old baboon rushed forward, snarling, and seized his arm, The keeper screamed as the baboon sunk his sharp yellow teeth deep into the flesh, and the Director, an elderly man knowing that only his great knowledge could be of help now, shouted urgently for a water-hose. Outside the compound, some laborers dropped their work and came running, and then von Abart stepped forward and clouted the baboon on the side of the head with the flat of his hand.

Again, the Director shouted, "Get back. Leave him to me." But the old baboon had already dropped the keeper's arm and had turned on von Abart. Standing to his full height now, his teeth bared, his barrel chest at full expansion, he slashed out with a lightning arm and ripped his paw into von Abart's face, and as he moved in for the bite at the throat, von Abart, ignoring the blood that streaked down his cheek, struck out with his booted foot, straight at the animal's head. It fell back, screaming its rage, and von Abart said coldly, "Get out...everybody...get back."

He picked up a stick and struck again at the baboon's head, and as it screamed again, other apes came pouring out of their grey plaster caverns, and von Abart stepped back through the gate that Stanton was holding open for him, pulling the young keeper with him and slamming it shut as a dozen of them, screaming viciously, hurled themselves at the fence in violent anger, leaping up and down, pounding the rock of their enclosure, showing their fangs and snarling abuse.

Von Abart dabbed at his face with a handkerchief and the Director pulled off the keeper's bloody jacket and looked at the wound on his wrist, saying again and again, "The poison. We must get the poison out. Run over to my office, tell the doctor." And young Pfund, recovered from his fright now and ashamed of his own screams, nodded and said again, "*Jawohl, Herr Direktor.*" And when he had gone, the Director turned to von Abart and said slowly, "I must thank you, my good friend. That was a very brave and foolish thing to do. Let me look at your face."

"It's nothing."

"There will be infection."

"I will let it bleed a little. If you have some iodine..."

"Of course. In my office. And perhaps a little cognac too. A friend bas brought me some from Paris."

As they walked over, Stanton said slowly, "He's right, you know. That was a very dangerous thing you did. You could easily have been killed."

"By baboons? They are foolish, unskilled animals."

"They can kill a leopard."

"Only because a leopard is afraid of them. I am not."

"Then you ought to be. A little intelligent fear is a very healthy thing. But I must admit they could have killed that keeper too. There's nothing more terrifyingly vicious than a pack of angry baboons at work."

Von Abart, holding a white handkerchief to his face, was smiling, pleased with the exhibition of his prowess; and later, when he sat in the office while a fussing secretary pulled the edges of the wound together and fastened them with plaster, Stanton watched him with a kind of awe. He was thinking *If the other baboons had come to the rescue a split second sooner...All of us were at the gate except von Abart, and with a stick in his hand he was ready to go for the lot of them, ready and anxious to move among them and kill them all. Yet he knows that one ape could tear his arms out of their sockets as easily as a man dismembers an over-cooked chicken. He knows their strength, he knows their ferocity, and he knows of their dreadful competence, and yet...yet he walks in among them with a stick and without a trace of fear on his face. Not even the intelligent fear that keeps a man alive when the danger is too great for easy survival.* Aloud, he said, "I watched a pack of them go for a leopard once. The dry season. The game had moved out into the desert to look for water, and there were only a few apes left in the dried-up bush, and a leopard that didn't know any better had killed a young baboon and was making a meal of it when I came up. The leopard scurried for cover, but the other baboons were waiting for him, and they moved in on him like a company of commandos. He killed five or six of them before one of them got a grip on his throat, and then they systematically tore him to bits and scattered the pieces of him over a couple of acres of bush. By the time they'd finished their work, there wasn't a limb that hadn't been shredded. It was frightening."

"Your intelligent fear, Mr. Stanton, is a good thing to

have, I agree. But you can't force it into your understanding. Neither should you try to."

"But we won't take chances like that in Malaya."

"In Malaya? Of course not. In Malaya there will not be a kindly Herr Direktor ready with his iodine and a bottle of French brandy. In Malaya, we will dig some holes in the ground, some animals will fall into them, and we will take them out and bring them back to the Herr Direktor. It is as simple as that."

"If only it *were* as simple as that!"

"Ah yes. If it were really so easy, they would send a young boy by himself. As it is, they have to send an old man along too, because the old man knows more about animals than anyone else alive, yes? This is why we will work well together, my friend." He said jocularly, "The old man and the new. How old are you, Mr. Stanton?"

"Thirty-two."

"Ah, thirty-two. When I was your age, Malaya had not been hunted out as it is now. And in a few years' time, it will be a place for couples on their honeymoons."

There it was again. The vision swung into his focus once more and he was with Cora on a white clear night with the Pahang river rippling up reflections from the clear, bright moon, and their marriage was new so that the enmity between them had not yet begun to solidify. He had gone out by himself very early the next morning, long before the sun was up, to sit in a blind, and at dawn he had shot a tiger, bringing it back to the camp slung from a heavy pole carried by a chanting group of Sakai.

Just awake and still sleepy, but contriving to look delicate and lovely, she had watched them sling it up for skinning. Angrily, watching her silent contempt for him, he had said, "Dammit, it's a man-eater. It's been troubling the Sakai—they asked me to shoot it for them. It's taken three or four women from their tribe. A young boy last night, too." She had said softly, "You're a good man, Harry, a good man with a rifle."

This was where it had all begun, and when they had got back to the States, there had been a rapid succession of other women, some furtive and some not so furtive because she didn't seem to care too much, or so he thought. Till one day she had gone and the next thing he knew was that an affable, cheery lawyer came round and gave him some papers to sign and talked about a property settlement, and now the decree was in his pocket and he was broke but he was through with her. And thank God too, he said to himself.

Well, he had survived even Cora. He had survived a dozen other women too, and he thought, *This is the company I belong in, the company of men who know what they're doing, and to hell with the women.* Looking at von Abart, he thought, *and to hell with that long-legged bitch he's tied up with too, poor devil; I bet she leads him a dance.* Thinking again about the tight-fitting dress and the carefully groomed semi-nudity, he thought again, *And how come he lets her dress like that so that a guy takes one look at her and thinks of bed automatically?*

His good humor was back again, and seeing von Abart grinning at him, he slapped him on the back and said, laughing, "We'll dig some holes, and they'll fall into them."

He was glad that von Abart had shown his spirit; there was something contagious about courage.

She was waiting for them when they got back to the house.

Standing at the desk and locking back at them over her shoulder, with her long Nordic hair left loosely to hang down her back, she was wearing a modest-seeming dress with a high collar that flared out at her neck, standing stiffly up behind her, with a skirt that flounced out at the waist in a design that he supposed was a dirndl of some sort; and then, when she turned and came to greet them, he saw that the neckline went straight down to the waist so that he waited for her, almost unconsciously, to hunch her shoulders forward. She was holding out a file of papers, saying, "The schedule. The charter plane leaves at ten o'clock in the morning, and we refuel at Istanbul. We'll need to spend a night at Bombay and then to Singapore with a brief stop at Colombo. It will take us about a day in Singapore to make the final arrangements there, and then we move up-country by rail."

Von Abart stood beside her, slipping an arm casually round her waist, taking the papers from her and looking at the first page. He said, "I don't want to waste time on an overnight stop. Can't we just refuel and go on?"

"I can't get a relief pilot and our own will need rest."

"Who's arranging our kit to go up-country?"

"I sent a telegram to a trader, named Hadjian, who'll take care of the luggage. He'll have an agent at Kepak meet us and supply transport to the edge of the jungle."

"How long will it take to get to the camp site?"

Anna shrugged. "It's difficult to say. Four, six, eight hours — it all depends on the thickness of the forest. But the clearing should be established."

"Porters, last-minute supplies — what about them?"

"Porters will be waiting, and we can get any supplies we may need from shops in a small village near the edge of the forest. There won't be much available, but we can shoot for the pot. Medical supplies will go with us, and the camp headman can take charge of some of them for the trackers and servants. There's a list in the file of the things I've ordered. There's only one thing I didn't know about. Mr. Stanton's clothing — whether there's anything special he needs."

Looking at her, trying to keep his eyes on her face, Stanton said good-humoredly, "No, I've got everything I need."

"Spare boots?"

"Yes."

"You have your own guns, of course. Do you need

ammunition?"

"More than enough. We won't do much shooting. Just the food game we need."

"A revolver? I don't think it will be necessary, but just in case. It's possible we'll have trouble with remnants of the Communists and the bandits. As far as I can make out things are settled now, but it's better to be on the safe side."

"I don't think I'll need one. We can't afford to do anything with trouble of that sort except run from it."

"Vaccinations — smallpox, typhoid, cholera?

"The works."

Watching the two of them, standing there almost like a married couple, he wondered briefly, *What does she need him for, a woman like that who could get anything she wanted just by clapping her hands?* He wondered what her background was, whether the fine old house and the aristocratic nucleus that was the shell von Abart lived in...He wondered if this musty milieu really appealed to her so much, or whether it was the impact of von Abart's casual nobility on a peasant who had been blessed with a long slim body instead of the dumpy pudding that would generally be her lot? Was it the feudal story over again? Or had she, as a hunter, been drawn to the acknowledged expert in the field? Mendel, a stuffy, fussy, bourgeois Bavarian, had obviously accepted the relationship as a normal one, though von Abart had said offhandedly, my secretary, as though he would not, in front of an American, immediately admit to a relationship that was anything but proper. He would not admit it, but also, he would not attempt to hide it. And here again was evidence of his essential distinction: to the von Abarts, nothing would be more natural than a supreme contempt for what the other fellow thought. A polite glossing over at first for the sake of the niceties, and then no more about it; just mind your own damn business.

He's right, Stanton thought. *It's nothing to do with me.*

Just as long as she doesn't get in the way out there.

And yet, at the back of his mind, the anxious nagging was coming through again, the fickle fear that had been on him when the subject had first been broached: could he comfortably lie awake on his celibate cot at night and listen to their whispered love-making? The heat and the excitement made an animal out of a man, and out there in Malaya, with the confines of civilization left a thousand miles behind them, anything could happen.

He was suddenly conscious that she was watching him, amused at the distant blankness that he knew was in his eyes. He turned away in confusion, and heard her say, "Don't worry about the details, Mr. Stanton. Or were you out there ahead of us?"

He turned it to his advantage. "No, I wasn't dreaming. I was just hoping that you'd be all right out there. I just can't get used to the idea of you in boots."

Von Abart patted her affectionately and stood back to admire her. Holding out an elegant hand, he said cheerfully, "She has the happy facility of being able to wear clothes well, even trousers. She's beautiful, isn't she? Eh? Don't you think so?"

It was as though he were admiring a horse. Stanton, the foreigner in a strange country, prepared now to accept the informalities of a society he did not understand, hid his distaste. He said easily, "And very efficient, too."

"Worth her weight in gold, Mr. Stanton."

"I've always disliked having women on shikar. They clutter up the place too much, and they always worry about mildew on their clothes, or silverfish, As long as you realize that it won't be easy."

Delighted with the point he was going to make, von Abart wagged a finger at him. "Let me tell you a story," he said. He bent down quickly and rolled up the leg of his trousers. There was a long scar at the base of his calf, surmounted by a hole so deep that it seemed to go right through the muscle. "You see that?" he said. "A lion. A big, stupid, clumsy lion. I was sleeping out in the bush one night, in Somalia, and a lion blundered into the camp, half asleep with a stomach overloaded with fresh zebra. You know how they are when they've overeaten. He walked right over me, and as I jumped up, wondering what the devil was happening, he took fright and grabbed with his teeth at my leg. Both of us, the lion and I, half asleep and suddenly alarmed. He dragged me a dozen paces and I yelled my head off because I couldn't reach my rifle, which was under my sleeping-bag, you understand? So Anna swings her gun by the barrel and cracks him a mighty blow across the top of the head, and the lion dropped me and ran. And with one quick shot she brought him down at fifty yards, in the darkness, just a bright moon to see by. I thought she must have cracked his skull wide open, but no, it was the rifle. Split right down the stock, a fine Mauser I'd given her just a few weeks before. That's no way to treat a good rifle, is it?"

He threw back his head and roared with laughter. She stood there watching him in tolerant amusement, smiling gently and turning her eyes on Stanton, seeming to say, *Let him have his fun, Mr. Stanton, just so long as you don't underestimate me.* There was a feline look about her, too, in the way she moved, slowly and with infinite control, more like a cheetah, he thought, or a leopard that moves in slow motion but is always ready for lightning impulsion. He looked at her breast, half exposed by the deep neckline, and then looked back at her eyes and saw that her amused expression had not changed except that now, behind the amusement, there seemed to be a calculating appraisement, as though she were thinking about him in the same way that he was thinking about her, and then she hunched her shoulders and turned away slightly, and he knew that it was a deliberate attempt to goad him because he had been looking at her like that, He said aloud to von Abart, seeking to put her in her place as a chattel, "Yes, she's very beautiful, isn't she?"

It was the most casual exchange of trivia. Von Abart,

smug and proud and secure, was still overpoweringly cheerful. In Stanton, a faint distaste was building into an enmity, an enmity that lessened its danger every time he looked at her and realized that her only weapon was her body, and that a woman's body was an easy battlefield for him to work on because it was a field he knew well and could trample as he pleased and then withdraw at will. And between them, she rested, waiting, accepting, smoldering.

He sat back in the big armchair, crossing his long legs and flexing the muscles in his shoulders, feeling the restless impatience that he always felt before a trip to the hot, wet hunting-grounds, unsatisfied with the soft luxury that was all round him, eager for the hardship and the toughening that came with it.

An obsession, von Abart had said about the elephant. It was an obsession he could clearly understand. There were forces that drove a man out of an unsatisfactory environment that he called civilized, and into the darkness and mystery of an unchanging jungle; it was a rebellion against progress, an insatiable demand for a return to the primitive, where the enemy was on a lower plane and the challenge was a bodily one. And yet, the craving for escape had come to him almost casually, a great dark cavern opening before him and slowly being flooded with a light that explored its most subtle intricacies.

At that time, there had been other pressures, the pressures of fear and of hatred and of bewilderment, with aircraft screaming their terror over the humid forests, and bombs bursting around his foxhole. His rifle, then, had been a weapon for protection against men who were strange, as he was, to this world of the animals, and he had sensed, in a moment of compassionate perception, that the animals too were cowering in fright from unaccustomed impulses; he had almost become one of them. And when his unit had gone and there was nothing left but the sour smell of death to remind him that they had been there, when he had found himself alone and lost, a solitary survivor in an immensity that should have terrified him, he had found only comfort in the sudden solitude.

He had wandered through the hot, wet jungle, learning to use a captured Japanese sword as a machete, hacking his way through the tough, wet vines, drinking from moss-covered pools in which slimy animals stirred, eating lizards that he caught with his bare hands, learning to cook on a fire started with the lens of his binoculars that had been smashed by a sniper's bullet, staying alive at first by the exercise of will power and later by the application of the knowledge that came to him with practice. He had learned to stay alive and to be grateful for the jungle that hid him from the ubiquitous enemy. He learned to love it, so that when they came back one day with more bombs bursting and shells raking the forest that had become his home, he had hidden out until they had gone again, living alone and existing from day to day, like one of the animals himself. And then, many years later, when the war was over, he had gone back again and found that the jungle was the same as it always was. And somewhat to his mild surprise, he had found that he was an expert, a hunter, a man who could shoot straight even when his eyes were filled with sweat and the malaria was vibrating inside him.

There had been many journeys after that, to Malay, to Africa, to Brazil. A hunter, an expert among the animals because he could easily become one of them. He had found that he could sell his knowledge, and slowly his reputation had grown. He was no longer Lieutenant Stanton, missing in action and miraculously found alive at the end of the war; he was Harry Stanton the hunter, on his way up fast, soon to become the top man in his field.

And now, there was von Abart, sitting across the room from him, looking at his poached yellow ivory and at his golden young mistress. Von Abart, lately the top man in his field.

Move over, buster, I'm on my way there.

CHAPTER 4

They were alone together at last.

Von Abart, the second in command, had gone off in the rented truck to get the kit on board the plane, a chartered Bonanza. He had been up all night supervising the checking of the supplies, and at midnight he had insisted, "No, no, you two go off to bed, get some sleep. There's nothing to do here but make sure we've got everything." All through the day the loads of kit had been coming in and were laid out neatly in a big garage for packing. Sleeping-bags, folding cots, water-bottles, medicines, ammunition, spare clothing—he was a competent quartermaster preparing for a military operation, checking and rechecking and ticking off the list that Anna Kruger had meticulously prepared.

They had climbed the wide dark stairway together, and as he went on up to his own room he was thinking, *Sleep? Tomorrow we'll be on our way and the soft wet snow will be a memory.* He had slept badly and woken in the morning red-eyed and tired, but once he had felt the cold morning air on his cheeks and had seen von Abart just finishing the last load, with his chauffeur and another man roping the bundles, he had begun to feel better, and when the pickup arrived he had said cheerfully, "Well, if you go and wake up the young lady, I'll get this lot over to the airport and you can follow in the car."

Von Abart had brushed the suggestion aside with a wave of his hand. "Give her another hour in bed, it's only four o'clock. I'll go over, get the loading done, and then you can both join me there, about half past five."

"No, let me do it. You've been working all night."

"I'm an airman myself, Mr. Stanton, I want to check the plane out."

"All right then. I needn't ask if there are any last-minute chores."

"None. All the kit's checked out. Everything as it should be. Come out at five-thirty and we'll take off at six."

"As planned."

"Precisely. Anna will be up at five, but just in case..."

"Of course."

He had gone off then, and Stanton had eaten the breakfast the early-rising cook had prepared for him, and then gone slowly up to Anna's room to knock on the door, wondering vaguely why the servants hadn't been told to wake her. He tapped twice, quietly, and she called out, "Come in."

He hesitated and, not opening the door, said, "It's me, Stanton. Time to get up."

"Come in, then."

He opened the door and looked at her, the yellow light from the bedside lamp falling across her hair. Standing at the door, not wanting to go any closer, he said again, "Time to get up, I'm afraid. How did you sleep?"

She yawned and stretched her arms, pulling her shoulders back sleepily, "Where's Otto?"

"He's gone to the airport already. To load the plane."

She was suddenly wide awake and alert. "Oh? Well, that's nice, isn't it? Did you have breakfast?"

"Yes, thank you. Shall I have them send up something for you?"

"When I come down. A cup of coffee, that's all I need."

47

"Well, I'll see you downstairs." He backed away awkwardly, knowing that there was no reason to feel embarrassed but somehow expecting her to slip out of the bed in front of him. He closed the door quietly and went downstairs to wait for her, vaguely troubled and not really understanding why. It was something to do with the offhand manner in which von Abart seemed to say, "Go and get her out of bed." It was as though he could not bring himself to suspect that any little intimacy might get out of hand, as though his flaunted trust in her—or in Stanton?—were so complete that there could never be any danger in letting them be alone together in a bedroom in the demanding hours of the very early morning. He was conscious, too, of her sudden wariness when he had told her that they were alone, that her Otto had gone to the airport. Was it distrust? Or was it a latent excitation?

She came down soon, in a belted jacket and slacks, with an open-necked shirt and a scarf round her throat, looking incredibly fresh and wide-awake, and they stood alone together, quite at ease in a house that seemed, in spite of the servants, to be deserted and empty, sipping their coffee and watching the faint white flakes of snow that were settling on the dark window-panes.

When the chauffeur slammed the door of the Mercedes on them and the servants bustled round beaming and waving and being *gemütlich*, they settled back together under the rug he had put over their knees, and for a moment there was an intimacy between them that was at the same time comfortable and displeasing. With a heavy wool coat loosely wrapped about her, she looked unexpectedly fragile and delicate. She said nothing until they were clear of the house, and then, staring out of the window at the trees and the mountains, just taking form now with early-morning grey, "Well, Mr. Stanton. It begins at last."

"Yes. I'll be glad to get there."

"Have you convinced yourself yet that I will not be a

nuisance to you?"

He smiled at her. "I never thought you would be. Not after the first few minutes. I hope you didn't think I was being...well, discourteous in not wanting to have you along. I was thinking of you, really. I still am."

"But you're not worried anymore?"

"Not really. We'll find plenty of work for you."

"To keep me out of mischief?"

"There's not much mischief you can get into out there."

"No? Really?"

"Well, there's not the time, either. We'll all be pretty busy."

"Yes. Yes, of course." She waited for a moment and then said slowly, "What do you think of Otto, Mr. Stanton?"

There was a taste of unease again, at the thought that she would discuss him behind his back; it seemed to be a deliberate attempt to align themselves against him. He said easily, determined to overlook it, "I like him very much. That incident yesterday with the baboon...He could have been killed, you know."

"But all he got was an honorable scar on the face. More evidence of his mastery."

He said uncomfortably, "He saved that young keeper's life. God knows what would have happened if he hadn't done what he did?"

"Yes, I suppose so."

"Of course he did."

"He likes you, you know; did you know that?"

The moment of anger had gone. He said, surprised, "He likes me? Did he say so?"

"I can tell. I can tell exactly what goes on in his mind, all the time. And he thinks you're good company for me, too."

"Well..."

"He thinks I need good company. He thinks I get tired of

49

that empty, ugly house, that I need a change once in a while."

He did not like the way the conversation was going, but putting on an expression which he hoped was rather paternal, he said tolerantly, "But he's obviously very fond of you, Miss Kruger."

She said sharply, "Oh, for God's sake, call me Anna."

"Of course, if I may."

She was suddenly smiling again, and she put out a hand and touched his, and said, very gently, "We'll all be together for a long time, won't we? By the time all this is over...We needn't stand on ceremony."

"And you're really not worried about the difficulties we're going to find? I still don't believe you realize how hard it's going to be."

"I know that we're in good hands."

"It's not only a question of fatigue. We might easily run into trouble with the tribes. Malaya is not as safe today as it was a dozen years ago."

"I packed a revolver for you after all."

"I told you I didn't need one."

"I know. But there was room, so...if it's not needed, it won't be used. But if it should be, then it's there. Did I do wrong?"

"No, of course not,"

"Good."

"On the contrary, you've done a very good job. We'd never have got away so fast without all your preliminary work."

"Oh, I'm a very efficient young woman. I've heard Otto say so a thousand times."

"At least he appreciates you."

"He gloats over me. That's not the same thing, is it?"

"It's a free country, Anna."

"Yes, it is. One day, I suppose, I'll get tired of being just another trophy."

"I'm sure you do more for him than bolster his ego."

"You mean that he's in love with me? Is that what you mean?"

"It seems to me that he might be."

"Love is a two-way deal, Harry. Lovers have the benefit of individual choice; trophies don't."

"It seems to me that you mean a great deal to him."

"So do those ghastly heads."

He said carefully, "We're not...I hope we're not going to have any...any difficulties on this trip, are we?"

"Lovers' quarrels?"

"Er, yes. Sort of."

Her good humor was back again. She said cheerfully, "No quarrels, I promise you."

"Good. It's very easy for things to get out of hand. We'll get tired, exhausted. Tempers begin to fray."

"No quarrels. That's a promise."

"We've got a job to do, and I want to make sure that it's done just as well as we know how."

"It means a lot to you, doesn't it, Harry?"

"Well, of course. It's my business, trapping animals. This is an important assignment for me. The biggest I've ever had. Anyone in the trade would give a million dollars for it."

"For the prestige, you mean?"

"Hell, no!" he said, smiling, "I didn't put that very well, did I? I should have said it's worth a million dollars to me. And that comes at a very handy time. I was getting kind of broke."

He did not know exactly why he was speaking to her so frankly. He reflected, momentarily, that this was something he could never have said to von Abart. He went on, speaking freely, "I had a little trouble at home. My wife divorced me. In America, that's an expensive proposition."

"It is anywhere."

"In the States, brother! The man always pays. It's a

derivative of our pristine morality."

"And you still love her?"

"I'm glad to be rid of her. Is that unkind? I suppose it is. But she led me a dog's life, she really did. No. No, I don't love her."

"She was a hunter, too?"

"No. She had too much contempt for the animals. And that included me, too. She was beautiful, and cold, and contemptuous."

"And now?"

"Now what?"

"Now will you marry again?"

"Like hell! This is the best thing that's ever happened to me. He was surprised at his own vehemence, aware that she was amused by it. He said, "She took me for everything I had, and still I got the best of the bargain." It was the first time, he realized, that he had been able to joke about Cora, and in the half-hour it had taken them to reach the airport, he knew that they had each shown the other a glimpse, no more, of the grubby little pains that twisted and turned inside them.

They had mapped their course down the green and blue Italian littoral and over the Greek islands of the Ionian Sea to Istanbul. When the sun came up they were high over the Alps of the Austrian Tyrol, watching the bright gold colors of the snowline, with the trees in the deeper shadow of the valleys covering the lower slopes darkly.

In the small, tightly crowded cabin of the chartered plane, bundles of the equipment obtruded everywhere. The hum of the motors was a soporific. Von Abart yawned, patted Anna lightly on the knee, closed his eyes, and fell asleep. She looked across at Stanton as she slipped her hand under her lover's arm, and he thought again what an oddly assorted couple they were.

In sleep, von Abart's face was heavy and lethargic, and the smoothness of her skin so close beside him made a sharp and saddening contrast as though the older man were saying, *This is what the slow persistent years will bring you both to.* The scar across his cheek where the baboon had slashed him was still covered with its strip of plaster, and he wondered again about the cold contempt of a man who could challenge a pack of angry apes with a small cudgel. In the stuffy, overheated atmosphere, Anna had taken off her coat and her jacket and put her long legs up on a bundle of tentage, letting her head lie against von Abart's broad chest. Her bright green shirt was open at the throat again, and she pulled it away from her breasts, letting the air reach her body, looking at Stanton with her eyes half-closed, not smiling, just looking to see if he was watching her. Stanton turned away and closed his eyes, and when he opened them again she had fallen asleep too, a hand at her throat and her long hair falling down over her shoulder.

He looked down below and watched the long thin line of the beaches through the gaps in the clouds, wishing they had a faster plane, worrying about their plans and wondering what they had forgotten; and then realizing that all the administration had been done for him with precise Germanic competence and that everything would turn out just as they had planned it.

But there was a worry at the back of his mind, too. At the house, the casual relationship between von Abart and his mistress had seemed an orthodox, straightforward matter of two people living together in relaxed and satisfying amity. He had a habit, von Abart, of putting a hand to her side when he spoke to her, of touching her flesh as though to feel its warmth and assure himself of his ownership of her. And for her part, she accepted the seigniorage without visible emotion, as though it were part of a bargain she was perfectly prepared to keep. And yet, when she had said to him in the car (the first time they had been alone together, he noted), "Love is a two-way deal, Harry," it had seemed that there was a great deal of bitterness there, as though the manifest acceptance were merely for the sake of the proprieties. And when he thought more about it, he realized that he could, at first, have recognized a mistake in his judgement of their relationship; that he could have taken too much for granted. Is a pretty woman living in the house necessarily a mistress? Perhaps not, but...And then, as though to make it plain, she had said, in effect, "I'm only a trophy, Harry, like those ghastly heads." She wanted him to know, he was sure, what her position was and that she was not entirely satisfied with it.

Well, the hell with it, he thought. As long as she doesn't make a mess of the shikar. And she won't do that because von Abart won't stand for any nonsense. And neither, come to that, will I.

He slept for a long while then, and woke suddenly when he felt her hand on his arm. She had leaned across the intervening space and woken him, pointing to the ground below them. Straining to look down, he saw the broad white stretch of brilliant sand, dotted here and there with clumps of green bushes, that he knew was the Turkish coastline. The plane tilted over as the pilot swung round to the east, and she said quietly, "Istanbul, Harry. We refuel here."

He nodded and reached for the ventilator to try and coax more air into the stifling cabin, and von Abart woke up and said, blinking, "Where are we?"

Stanton pointed below. "He's turning in to Istanbul."

"Good. How long do we stay here?"

"Just time for a cup of coffee. Are you tired?"

"No. I slept for a while. And you?"

"Tired of waiting to get there. I'm anxious to get to work.

Anna was slipping off her shoes and getting her sandals on, and he noticed the incongruity of her bright-red toenails, wondering how long the fashion-model polish would last when the trek through the jungle began. When the pilot flung open the door for them and they jumped on the hot driven sand, she braced herself against the wind and let the biting grit beat against her face, wrinkling her eyes and brushing back her hair with a gesture. Von Abart said, "For God's sake!" and they all began to run for shelter as the windstorm swept over them.

The pilot stood there with his feet wide-braced as the Turkish assistants leaned into the fuselage and pushed it towards the hangar, and once they were under cover they sipped their thick black coffee impatiently and waited only for the refueling before they swung wide up into the hot blue sky again, sandstorm or no sandstorm, knowing that in half an hour it would be too thick to fly through. Far above it all they banked round to the south, and they all stared out of the tiny windows, watching the great red cloud below them and grinning because they had escaped its fiercest intensity.

Looking across at Anna, Stanton said cheerfully, "Munich's along way behind us."

She smiled at him. "It won't be long now. The bush and the jungle, and a million years of undisturbed history."

Von Abart leaned in towards them. Gesturing broadly, he said, "And the animals are waiting. A million years of history, and this is what they come to. They'll finish in our nets and our pits and our cages."

Looking at Stanton, Anna said, "And as trophies."

Now, as he lay listening to the dulled rumble of the wheels under his aching body, feeling the stench and the hot wet clamminess closing in around him, he knew that he should have foreseen all the trouble that was to come to him; he knew, too, that this was where it had begun.

"As trophies," she had said, and there had been a calculating thoughtfulness in her look that had made him smile – a detached, supercilious sort of smile that had come to him easily because he had not then known the force of the power that she could exert on him.

Bombay, Colombo, Singapore. There had been no time to stop and reflect. They had adhered with meticulous thoroughness to the tight schedule which they had prepared—which she had prepared, he thought. And his awareness of her as a woman had slowly become sharpened by his knowledge of her competence.

And now, as the train pulled shakily in to the tiny whistle-stop that lay like a symbol at the edge of the jungle, he wondered that in so short a time they could all have come so close together.

CHAPTER 5

The damp and the heat came at him as he stepped from the train, and the sound of the whistle in the silence was a scream of agony. The ground, even in the heat of the day, was wet under his feet, and it seemed that the lianas draping tenuously over the wooden shack that was the station were pumping the overflow of the jungle down into the clearing, seeking to flood it again with its primeval slime. Momentarily, it was a shock.

And then all the memories came pouring back to him with the sounds and the smells and the humidity cloaking him and hiding him from the civilization that lay at the other end of the railway track, no more than a day or two behind them, but seeming to be discarded as no longer of importance.

A cluster of bright yellow berries hung from a tree close by, and he looked at them and said to himself, remembering, *I ate those once, and I nearly died.* Beyond them was a tall straight vine that curved back on itself like a monstrous thorn, and he thought, *And in there, if you draw your knife across it, you will find clean water without the slime and the larvae and the stench of the pools. And the pigs will root at the bamboo there, and if you wait patiently, with your knife and your hunger ready, then you can drop from the branches faster than he can move out, but watch for the tusks because they are needle-sharp and yellow and they will rip you open if your knife is not in the neck at the first sharp stab. And then, with the optic glass, you start a fire.* And with the phrase, he said aloud, "New lands, rivers or mountains in her spotty globe."

He looked at the others, then, conscious of von Abart's amused stare. He grunted cheerfully and said, *"Paradise Lost"*. He laughed and added, "The torrid clime smote on his sore behind, or something..." and suddenly they were all laughing together, and when Hadjian came up, panting and beaming at them, von Abart said loudly, choking over his laughter, "This is my poetic friend Harry Stanton. Mr. Hadjian, Fräulein Kruger, of course, you already know."

He was plump and happy, a fat little trader who was on to a good thing and knew it, and he spread his arms effusively and welcomed them with broad gestures, smoothing the creases out of his white silk suit and apologizing for the weather as though he had personally caused it. Tugging at the too-tight collar of his silk shirt, he said, "But in my house it is cool; there will be ice for me on the train." They walked over to where the trucks were waiting, and Hadjian stood back to admire them, saying happily, "Good trucks, old but good, with very good drivers, Tamils both of them. They know mechanics, not too much but something. Is better, I think, they know mechanics." Peering at them shrewdly, he said, "Of course, cost little bit more, but maybe worth more, what do you think?"

The trucks were built like open-sided buses, with three seats running across the width, and rifle-racks fastened to the teak pillars that supported the roof. There were no doors, Clambering clumsily aboard, Hadjian said, "You will stay at my house, I think, for a little while, no? Your head-boy is there, waiting, his name is Talib, a very good boy, maybe the best we have. I have maps, supplies, everything you need, it is all ready. How many porters you need? Maybe twenty, thirty?"

"Twelve, Mr. Hadjian," Anna said promptly. "Twelve will be plenty. If we need more I'm sure we can recruit them locally."

He looked at her uncomfortably. "In Sakai country? Your telegram said with the Sakai."

"It's Sakai we shall need, Mr. Hadjian. The others will be useless once we get into the area we hope to work."

"Yes. Yes, of course, but I beg of you. You must be careful. They are very difficult people. Like animals."

Von Abart yawned and said loudly, "If you mean you've been selling them unserviceable firearms again, I assure you they will not hold it against us."

Hadjian said nothing.

The jungle closed in around them. Their truck bounced over the dirt tracks, slipping into the deep ruts, ploughing through wide patches of water where the white lilies lay like dropped handkerchiefs, lumbering heavily over rotted vegetation that squelched under the wheels, and soon Hadjian recovered his good spirits and said cheerfully, "There—where is the orchid, you see my house. Not very big, but good, you know? Comfortable. We have little drink first, no? Then to eat, then I show you all the maps I have for you. The place you wish to go, this is not very—how shall I say? Not many people go there, only me sometimes. Better you take my maps, you will find them very useful, I think."

The scent of the jasmine and jacaranda was ripe in their nostrils when they swung through the wide timbered gateway into a clearing where the house had been built. It was a low, many-roomed bungalow of bamboo and palm leaf, and a thousand bright flowers were running rampant all over it. A Malay girl was standing there, watching and smiling at them, and a group of noisy children scampered around, dressed in brilliantly colored sarongs. Hadjian looked apologetic and said diffidently, "My wife, Mr. Stanton, and some of my children." He turned and shouted at the driver of the truck that was behind them, and in a moment it swung round and drove straight across

ALAN CAILLOU

the tamped earth of the patio to where an old bathtub had been set in the shade. A Tamil servant clambered down from the back and tipped a sack of ice into the bath and then went running for the beer bottles, and the children crowded round shouting at each other and clapping their hands. Hadjian shooed them away happily and turned to Stanton.

"And now," he said with an elaborate gesture, "my humble home is yours."

Later that night, sitting on the edge of his cot and poring over one of the maps Hadjian had given him, Stanton could not recall a time when he had eaten so much food in one sitting. There had been chicken and pheasant and partridge and roast lamb (or was it goat, he wondered?) and round balls of some indeterminate cheese in olive oil. There had been Japanese beer and Greek wines and tiny cups of bitter Turkish coffee scented with crushed cardamom seed that would keep him awake, he knew, till the early hours of the morning.

The yellow light of the single bulb was flickering, trying to muster enough strength to glow, and he walked over to the window and turned off the electric fan that was playing over a long block of melting ice to cool the room down. The light leaped up immediately, and he wondered what prodigious feats of engineering had been necessary to bring the solitary cable here from the railway line, more than three miles through the jungle; wondered, more precisely, just whose palms had been greased to bring the luxury of civilization into the depths of the jungle where a man could take all the land his servants could keep cleared of the ever-encroaching growth.

He went back to his map, and soon a pretty young Malay girl came in, a girl from the village, dressed in a yellow sarong that was wound tightly over her young breasts, a smooth-skinned girl with her long, black, polished hair, set with ivory pins, piled

60

high on her head and her body gleaming. She carried a tray on which was a bottle of brandy and a tumbler, and she set it down on the table beside the bed and looked at him and waited, and he searched his mind for half-forgotten phrases and said at last, smiling at her, "*Gehel*," meaning tired, and when she sat on the bed he remembered that it also meant to rest, to sit down, to lie down, depending on what dialect you were using. He shook his head, touching her arm gently, making a motion to indicate that he wanted to sleep, and when she lay down, instead, he stood up and spread his arms wide hopelessly and shook his head again, not knowing what language she might speak. She got off the bed then, and said in English, "If the tuan is tired..." Her eyes were wide and solemn and sad, and he watched her go and thought, *The perfect host, all the comforts of home.*

He poured himself a drink and swallowed it quickly, then poured another and began to sip it, taking out his pencil and making careful notes on the border of the map, wondering how accurate it was. He worked for an hour, and then there was a knock on the bamboo support of the door, and when he said "Come in!" Anna was there. Standing in the doorway in a housecoat, smiling at him, she said, "I couldn't sleep either. I saw your light. I thought if you were working, perhaps I could help."

"I was just making a few notes. I think I had too much coffee."

"May I come in?"

"Of course. Sit down."

She closed the door behind her and came over to sit on the edge of the bed beside him. She showed him one of Hadjian's maps which they had been studying earlier, putting it on the bed between them. She said, "Here...there's a track marked. I wonder if we could manhandle the trucks up the slope here? It seems to be sandy soil, and if we could get through there...What do you think, Harry?"

He passed her a cigarette and lit it, looking at the line she was indicating with her finger. "I don't see why not. It might get us there a day or two earlier. On the other hand, we don't want to lose one of the trucks."

"We can always run it down again, don't you think? It might be worth trying. If we don't do that we're going to have to bridge this ravine here."

"Uh-huh."

"Well, shall we try it?"

"All right. We can send a runner ahead of us to take a look at it first and report back to us."

"Good, that's settled then."

"What does Otto think about it?"

Folding the map, she said carefully, "I didn't ask him. He wouldn't be able, right now, to give us a decent answer."

Surprised, he said, "Oh? How's that?"

"He's drunk, Harry. Didn't you notice?"

"Drunk? I don't believe it."

"It's not very obvious, really. But he did have a little too much, you know."

"Well, it didn't seem to show on him."

"Oh, he can hold it as long as he has to. But then, once he gets on his back, he's out cold."

She folded the map and turned towards him, holding the map lightly in one hand as though to indicate that she was just going. She stretched past him to knock the ash off her cigarette and he could smell the scent of her hair. There was that old stirring again deep inside him, and he put a hand on her knee trying to make it no more than a slight affectionate gesture. He said, "Well, it's our last night of civilization. Of relative civilization. Will he be all right by the morning?"

"Yes, He'll be all right as soon as he has to be. It's all part of his makeup. What he has to do, he can do."

"And you, Anna. You're not worried? No problems?"

"Problems? Nothing I can't handle."

"If there's anything I can do to make it easier for you..."

"I know. But you needn't worry on my account, I don't think you'll find I'm the weakest member of the expedition."

"Oh?" He wondered what she was trying to say. "I'm quite sure Otto's not going to find any difficulties. A man of his enormous reputation..."

"It's a thirty-year-old reputation, Harry. He hasn't lost all his craft yet, but..."

"When was the last time he was out here? Two years back, wasn't it?"

"Nearly three. He was already showing signs of wear."

"He's not as old as all that. He's not even sixty yet. And he still looks tough."

"Oh, he's tough all right."

"Then we should have no problems."

He began to move his hand slowly on her thigh, feeling the firm flesh under her housecoat. She stood up abruptly, smiling at him, knowing that what she had come to find out was now a matter of certain knowledge for her. She went back to the door and said, "This is a young man's shikar, Harry. There's a lot to be done that an old man can't do. That's why Mendel insisted on putting you in charge. Didn't you know that?"

"Well, I guessed as much." He knew it was time to withdraw, making a game of it and going along with her. He said, "I'm still glad he's with us. He knows more about animals than any ten men in the business. And I like his spirit."

She said, "Aren't we all nice people? Good night."

She closed the door gently behind her and left him staring after her. He lay on the bed and closed his eyes. He was thinking, *Well, we'll see what happens. It's not going to be too difficult, I can see that.*

* * *

They set off by truck before sunrise, leaving Hadjian, plump, prosperous and beaming, waving them off from the rest-house and nodding his head as though to say, Well, that was a good bit of business.

The jungle lay ahead of them, beneath and over the Cameron Highlands in the distance. Everywhere the greenery seemed to be stretching out to meet them, fingers of forests reaching out to clutch at and to menace them. Wide banyan trees flamed in red with hanging roots and vines that anchored them to the ground. Palm-frond huts sat shakily at the edge of the road, where wisps of smoke from cooking fires gently disappeared into the blue sky. A rusty bicycle frame gleamed like a wound in the green grass of a ditch. Between the road and the wall of the forest, a Tamil, his long black hair tied in a knot on top of his head, stood knee-deep in a rice paddy-field. Brightly colored butterflies fluttered over the tops of the tall grass, finger-painting the dark green background.

They left the tarmac and lurched drunkenly along a narrow dirt road, with the truck lumbering now, unsteadily, over the broken ground. Then the track came to an unexpected end, and some boys jumped down and sliced at the vines ahead of them, while the drivers shouted encouragement, and soon they were through the thick tangle and on to hard ground that was broken with clumps of bamboo too heavy to cut. The trees about them were tall and heavy with foliage, knit close together, with the high green branches of one clutching at the tops of another so that there was hardly any sunlight filtering through at all. A dark-red bird fluttered out of their way, squawking angrily at them, and a startled deer, no bigger than a rabbit, stood frozen with fright close to the wheels of the truck, its tiny legs splayed out wide. They could see the quivering of its flank where its frightened heart pounded. The steam began to hiss from the radiator, and soon they passed the tidy edge of a rubber estate, the cleared jungle opening incredibly for it but standing rich and luxuriant on its borders as though waiting for the overseer to relax his vigilance so that it could close in again and cover the neat estate as though it had never been there. It seemed alive in its waiting intensity, as though governed by an intellect that said, *Our time will come again and all this will be impenetrable jungle once more.* He noticed that the barbed wires strung from posts along the confines of the estate were curled and hanging where they had recently been cut, and he pointed and said, "The Sakai ... wire bangles for their women." He fancied he saw one of them when he looked back, hiding deep among the bushes, silently waiting till they should have passed, cowering like animals in naked patience, their shining flanks mottled by the patches of chiaroscuro that came through the leaves, their long blowpipes ready to resist the unexpected invader.

Then the estate was far, far behind them and the heat of the day had turned into the damp oppression of the night. They wiped at the sweat on their bodies, swatting at the mosquitoes, listening to the raucous sound of the frogs, and once, when they stopped for an hour while the Tamils cut their way through a tight skein of liana that barred their way (with the head servant quickly seizing the opportunity to make tea), they found that the leeches were waiting for them, creeping up unobtrusively and fastening their tiny teeth insidiously on their legs.

They moved on again until the darkness became as impenetrable as the jungle itself, and the headlights would show only a wall of black-green humus that seemed to glisten with its humidity. Then they camped for the night, too tired to talk, eating quickly from the old-fashioned aluminum pots, one fitting into the other in a tall tier, that had been brought from Hadjian's house for the first meal out on shikar, finishing off the first bottle of brandy and then sinking on to their canvas cots, slung over with mosquito nets that draped like ghosts from the branches above them, to sleep without thought for the morrow, exhausted by the sudden transition from one world to another.

They set off again at sunrise, refreshed again and beginning now to feel the essence of their purpose, watching the trees change color as they climbed higher into the foothills, feeling the clearing of the air as they left the valley, forcing the truck through paths that had been worn by elephant or by the secret Sakai. Sometimes, they would see a *kajang* hut in the distance, just a framework of poles covered over with palm fronds, and there would always be a thin spiral of smoke beside it. Once, a group of frightened children, quite naked, scurried away from them in terror, scuttling under cover and leaving behind only a frightened silence. They saw a crumbling stone fortress that was covered over with vines, a forgotten heap of stones built there by whom? And why? Staring at it as they went slowly past, Stanton heard von Abart say, as though reading his thoughts, "Built by the Portuguese to fight off the Dutch. And then destroyed by the Sumatrans. Three hundred years ago, Harry. Here, that was only yesterday."

Two tiny Semang women, both clutching babies to their naked breasts, stood and watched them, unafraid, staring and wondering. They wore short bark-cloth skirts and their bodies were scarred where they had drawn the sharp edges of sugarcane leaf over their skins, rubbing charcoal into the wounds to raise and beautify them.

Looking at them, Anna said, "Semang, Harry. They have a woman chief, did you know that? Matriarchal."

He nodded, remembering the pigmy-like men, remembering the caves they lived in, remembering how one of them had taught him to make a shelter by covering fallen tree trunks with branches of palm to keep out the poisonous damp that made the dreadful green moss appear overnight on the soft flesh of the forearm; to hide himself, too, from the prowling Japanese, as they themselves now hid from the foreigners.

Now their speed dropped to a crawling pace as they climbed higher and higher, and when they came to the top of a short rise, the forest had opened up and there was a high plateau ahead of them where the treetops were purple under a bright hot sun that seemed to broil their curled branches, though the evening was not far off. Far in the distance, the mountains were covered with haze, and a white cloud stood high over a peak that might have been an extinct volcano. Everything was silent.

They stood and looked at it for a while, and feeling the need to break the monotony, Stanton said, "All right, we'll spend a few hours here. Stretch our legs, make camp for the night. The drivers can work on the trucks."

He called the head-boy over, and said, "Talib, isn't it?"

The tall plump Malay nodded gravely, silent, courteous, waiting, "All right, we'll camp for the rest of the day. I want the drivers to go over their trucks. We won't get them much farther, but as far as we can. You can set up the tents. Don't let them, light fires near the trucks. You know what has to be done?"

"I know, Tuan." His eyes were grave and solemn, his cheeks smooth, his long black hair piled high on his head.

"Good." Kicking at the drier earth under his feet, he said, "It's dry here, there should be good water. Better get the cans filled too. Over there, perhaps." Pointing, "Over where the flowers are." They were bright in the sunshine, huge orchids that splashed crimson against the dark edge of the trees, high among the topmost branches. He watched Talib go over with some of the boys, their water cans dangling from their shoulders and soon he was back, alone, holding out a huge red flower with both hands, offering it to him. He took it and gave it to Anna, and she looked at it and said, "We're home, Harry, this is the only place to be."

He watched the servants gathering wood for the fires, and saw that the drivers (reluctantly, because they would rather have slept) were checking the undersides of their vehicles, scraping off the hard-caked mud and tightening up loose bolts, testing the pressures of the big, worn tires, seeing that they would serve until the last minute when they would have to wait for the shikar to continue on foot, knowing that the secret of success lay in nursing the equipment by means of every possible device, knowing that the machines suffered more than the men, because their enemy, the jungle, was alive and they were not.

He watched them set up the tents, knowing, too, that these would not last long in the mildew, that they would rot into shreds very quickly, but grateful for their friendly shelter while they lasted.

Von Abart took his rifle and inspected it. Standing there with his bush-jacket open to the waist, the streaks of red mud and dust on his face making his eyes paler than before, filling his lungs with the cool air of the foothills, making a symbol of it, feeling again the escape from the confines of a noisy city, bathing himself in the sybaritic excellence of the wilderness, he said cheerfully, "One more day of this, I think, and we shall be starting the hunt, no?"

Stanton was taking a compass bearing on the high peak ahead of them. He took his binoculars and handed them over.

"The mountain there," he said, "that's where we have to be. And to get there, it's not going to be easy. Look at the vegetation."

Von Abart stared through the glasses. Shrugging his shoulders, he said, "Two valleys to cross. We can bridge the rivers at the bottom of them. If we have to leave the trucks, it's still not more than a day's hard walking."

"It would be quicker to go all the way on foot now. But if we can get the trucks there, it will be just that much easier to get the animals back."

"Your problem, Harry," von Abart said. (Was there a note of diffidence there?) "But why don't we set up a permanent camp right here, where we are? All the trapping we need to do can be done within—what, two or three days' march from here?"

"You've got a point there. But I think we'll go a little closer to the mountain."

"Yes, of course." Von Abart handed back the glasses brusquely and patted his rifle. Changing the subject deliberately, he said, "Well, if we're stopping for the rest of the day, we might as well hunt for the pot. There'll be partridge here, pheasant, some wild boar, venison—take your pick. They're just beginning to come out from their nests and their caves and their lairs. What shall we have? Guinea fowl? Antelope? Mouse deer?"

Stanton saw that there was a shotgun barrel lying under the rifle-barrel of his gun, an over-and-under combination of .300 and 12-gauge. Taking off his shoes to tip the sand out of them, he said, "You're the hunter. As long as we have some food."

"Good." Von Abait hoisted the rifle on his shoulder, looked at the setting sun, and went off into the bush.

Anna came over and stood beside him, watching the sand trickling out of the shoes in a fine red stream. Tall and slim, her long legs apart and her arms akimbo, she stood over him where he squatted on the cooling earth, watching him, standing there with the yellow sun on her and casting a long shadow that seemed to tie her to the soil. She looked up at the horizon, watching the sun go down below it, watching it sink quickly as though impatient with the day, and in a few moments the heat was gone and the earth was cold and damp-seeming to the touch, They heard a shot from the bush and knew that von Abart had quickly found his game, and Anna said, "The shotgun. That means fowl."

Looking up at her, he said, "Are you tired?"

"No. The first night in the bush I am never tired. It's like coming home. This is where I belong, Harry."

"You belong on the front cover of *Vogue*."

"Like this?" She held her hands wide, showing the dirt and the grime and the dust.

He laughed and said, "I must admit it makes a difference. When I first saw you, I just couldn't picture it."

"And now?"

"You're beginning to show signs of strain."

"And that is bad?"

"That's good."

She looked at him, and said, "You don't like...elegance? Is that the word?"

"Elegance? I like it very much. But I've been trying to forget."

"Oh?"

Not feeling the pain of his separation now that she was safely far away and almost forgotten, he said slowly, "Cora—my ex-wife. The last time I was out here, she was with me. She wasn't exactly the hunting type, and in the bush she was...well, let's face it, she was a bloody nuisance. She liked to stay elegant. It made life a little rough."

"And now?"

"Now she's in a night-club some place, draped across a corner seat. Elegantly."

"With her boyfriend?"

"No. It wasn't that. Quite the contrary. She'll be surrounded by a dozen admiring, handsome young men, and when the evening's over she'll hold them off with an elegant gesture, say she's too tired, and go to sleep alone. That's the kind she is."

"And that was the trouble?"

"That was the trouble." Looking at her, he knew that this was her choice of conversation, not his. He said lightly, "That was always the trouble between us."

She turned away from him and took her rifle from her hut, sighting it carefully, and in a moment she sat down on the ground beside him, resting her elbows on the raised knees with her legs spread wide, like a man's, and took slow aim at the broad branch of a bamboo tree. When she fired, Talib, knowing at once what she was doing, ran over and placed his finger over the bullet hole, saying, "Here, Memsahib, here," and she nodded and said, "It's shooting to the left a little," casually dismissing the inaccuracy with expert nonchalance.

Stanton took the rifle from her and looked it over. "A nice gun. You want me to fix.it for you?"

"Don't bother. Just as long as I know."

"They always get knocked about a bit, no matter how carefully they're handled."

"Otto would be horrified. A precision instrument."

Somewhere in the forest another shot sounded. He said, "He's not going to be pleased at hearing your gunfire while he's trying to find supper."

"Out there? The game is thick. A couple of shots won't scare it away. Tell me about your Cora; was she beautiful?"

"A porcelain figurine. As beautiful and as cold. And as fragile."

"Children, Harry?"

"No. Goddammit, I'm not surprised! She hardly ever gave me the chance. Let me fix this for you."

"I can do it."

He slipped the bolt back and fired carefully at the same tree, then squinted to find the mark. Talib, grinning, was still there, his finger pointing again. She went over to the truck and brought back a pair of pliers, handing them to him, and he twisted gently at the front sight, then fired three shots in succession while Talib stood close by, watching and grinning and saying, "Good, good." He handed it back to her and without trying it she put it back in the gun rack and shouted to the boy to bring some water for washing.

Stanton took out his map-case and marked the mileage

they had covered, and took a compass bearing on the mountains that lay to the north of them, marking the next day's route on the map with a drawn pencil line, and then he too stood over the canvas washbasin they had put out for him, took off his shirt, and splashed water over his face and bare chest, and when he had finished, Anna, close by, was brushing at her hair, holding her head forward and down and grimacing and saying, "I should have cut it short."

Her sleeves were rolled up, and her arms were brown, and her shirt was open at the throat.

He said, "A scene of perfect domesticity. Are you glad to be here? You're not sorry you left the comforts of home so far behind you?"

"You won't believe me, Harry, will you? This is my home. The other—it's just a showcase to sit in for a while. But this is where I belong. Out here where the little niceties are not so damned important."

"Uh-huh. Tomorrow, the next day, that's when the niceties will have gone. That's when we start the hunt."

"Trackers?"

"Talib will go looking for them as soon as we make camp tomorrow. Seems like Hadjian sent a runner out here before we left. There's supposed to be a village over there somewhere."

"Senoi?"

"Yes."

"We'll never see them. They'll hide from us."

"We have Hadjian's good offices. Talib knows them, apparently. Some of them are here already. Didn't you notice?"

He pointed over to the edge of the trees where Talib was in earnest conversation with a Senoi. He was small and dark and somberly brooding, and he wore a piece of bark-cloth that hung from a string round his waist. He carried a spear and a blowgun, one of a silent fast-disappearing people whom the Chinese and the Tamils and the Sikhs and the Malays cordially hated, calling them contemptuously Sakai, the slave-people, refusing to mix with them and holding themselves aloof and (if the truth were known) in fear of them.

They lived deep in the hidden jungles, fearing and hating the progress that was slowly and surely coming to their country, not knowing, perhaps, that primitive peoples the world over were losing their ancient seclusion and going down under the march of what some of them called civilization. They lived in caves and huts and under fallen trees, like animals, being animals themselves, and using an age-old skill that had grown into their bones and alone permitted their survival, Their enemies were the tigers, in fear of whom they chanted propitiatory songs, and their friends were the apes whom they trained to find food for them. They could walk up the bare trunks of a tree with nonchalant ease, and they could bridge the streams with ropes of rattan, and clamber from tree to tree in the high branches, even in absolute darkness, moving in silence. But their faces all bore a trace of fear. They were hunted, bewildered, and strangely ready, always, for instant flight, because the memory of the sorak, the ancient war-cry of the Malays, was always with them. They, too, like the Armenian Hadjian, came from a persecuted stock. And thinking about it now, Stanton wondered if herein lay the strange affinity that seemed to exist between them.

The memories came rushing back to him, and he laughed and said, "You know how they scare off a tiger? They shout at him, telling him they know his deathly secret."

She threw back her hair, letting it fall down over her shoulders.

"Oh? What secret is that?"

"The tiger," Stanton said gravely, "has no navel in his belly. As every good Sakai knows, the navel is at the back of his neck, and the tiger is so humiliated by this aberration that the mention of it is enough to make him scurry back to his lair in shame."

She laughed with him, and said, "The tiger doesn't have a lair."

"More correctly, he has three. All temporary, perhaps, but none the less, they are lairs."

She looked at him quickly to see if she had correctly interpreted the faint touch of aspersion in his voice, but she saw that he was smiling still. He said, "Let's not quarrel over zoology. I stand aside before your expert knowledge."

She pulled her shirt out at the waist, smoothing the damp creases out of it, so that for an alarmed moment he thought she was going to take it off, and he looked round quickly to make sure that von Abart was still away. But she merely eased it at her waist and then tucked it back in again, casually, not turning away from him. He trembled slightly and found it hard to restrain the almost overpowering urge to put out his hand and touch her. She turned her back on him and looked at herself in a small mirror, touching her hair, and knowing the gambit he put an arm lightly at her waist, careful to show complete nonchalance, and said, carefully making small talk, "This time tomorrow we should be able to start building a permanent camp."

He slid his hand up to her breast and then moved it hastily away again as she turned to him, smiling. She said, seeming to be indifferent to the quick light caress, "More Senoi coming in. Over there."

"A good boy, Talib."

They were creeping carefully out of the jungle, six or seven of them, clutching their weapons fearfully, gathering round the tall plump Malay whom they knew to be their friend and not, like most of his people, waiting to drain their blood as a libation to his strange gods. Behind them, he saw three women come slowly forward, their cooking-pots on their backs in crude rattan carriers, and he saw Talib call to one of the boys who brought a skinned wet monkey to give them as a peace offering. He wondered when it had been killed, and by whom, wondering again at the smooth, unsupervised efficiency of the things that went on without his own prompting, knowing that this was the test, always, of a good head-boy. It was not the things that he had to do that mattered; it was always the things that could be left, without mention, to the others, upon which the efficiency of a shikar depended.

Voicing his thoughts, he said, "Nothing worse than a boy who has to be told what to do. Isn't it time for a drink?"

He shouted to one of the servants, and in a moment the bottle of brandy was brought, with two freshly polished glasses on a tray (polished, he knew, on somebody's sarong), and seeing the darkness closing quickly in on them, he said, "I hope Otto's all right out there, It's not hard to get lost in the jungle at night."

"Otto? He's got plenty of faults, but stupidity's not one of them. He won't get lost."

There was a faint annoyance with her again. He said sharply, "You don't have to be a fool to get lost out there. I've wandered about in the jungle for days, weeks, months on end. Half the time you just don't know which side is up."

She poured the drinks and said cheerfully, "Well, here's to sin, Harry."

His good humor came back quickly, and he said, "I'll drink to that." He began to think how quickly she could change his mood, molding it, it seemed, to take whatever form she wanted for the moment. Then von Abart came back carrying three plump pheasant and a small boar which was thrown over his shoulder. The Moslem cook took the pig from him reluctantly and handed it quickly to one of the other boys, a pagan, knowing that even the brief touching had defiled him, but fearing the scorn of the white man who would, he knew, laugh at him if he refused outright to touch it. Soon they could smell the sweet scent of its roasting over the hot wood embers in the open fire, and then the Sakai, happily mixing with the others now, were cooking the rats and yams they had brought with them at their own little fires and casting surreptitious glances over their shoulders to watch the white people eat their strange soft food and drink their strange hard liquids.

The night was cool now, and the moths were fluttering to their deaths around the bright white glare of the pressure lamp that was strung in the branch of a tree high above them, keeping the insects high up there where they would die in peace and not disturb the calm serenity of the camp below them.

And soon, the night was all about them.

CHAPTER 6

But it was three days later before they were able to make their permanent camp.

They had run down from the high plateau, weaving their way in and out among the clumps of bamboo and the thick clusters of rattan that seemed to reach out for them and hold them back, ripping savagely at the canvas that covered the stores on the roofs of their vehicles and gouging great gashes into the teak sides of the bodywork itself. The river that ran sluggishly at the bottom had presented no problem. They had filled it with earth and mud and sand, covering the dam with cut timbers and driving the trucks carefully over, and then the long haul up the other side had begun. They had cut down the trees that stood in their way, carving themselves a trail, forcing a track through the jungle, covering no more than ten miles or so till they came to the second valley, and here they halted.

A deep chasm faced them, its scarred sides densely covered with vines that flowed down to the water a hundred feet below them. Looking at it, von Abart said impatiently, "For God's sake! We might as well walk."

Stanton, looking up at the tall trees, had shaken his head stubbornly. "I want to get to the foothills," he said. "We take the trucks as far as they'll go. And that means a damn sight farther than this. We'll bridge it."

Anna was staring across the chasm through the binoculars. She handed them to him and said quietly, "Look, Harry, over there."

There was a group of men in ragged khaki, a little more than a mile away, standing under the shade of a tall casuarina and watching them. They carried rifles, and bandoliers were crossed over their chests. They were not Sakai, and he said shortly, "They could be Semang, Siamese, Kelantans, anything. Bandits, by the looks of them. We'd better move over to the east a little."

Von Abart looked at them for a while, and said, "Twenty, twenty-five or so. A few well-placed shots would soon move them."

Angered by the contempt in his voice, Stanton said sharply, "Are you out of your mind?" He called Talib over and said, pointing, "Over under the trees, Talib. Bandits?"

Talib stared at them for a while and nodded, not worried. He said cheerfully, "They come from north maybe, Tuan. No trouble. We shoot, no trouble."

Some of the other Malays were gathering round, and he saw that they carried rifles. He looked at Talib, questioning, and the grave concern was gone from the Malayan's eyes and in its place was a cheerful nonchalance, as though now he, too, knew that what Anna had called the niceties were far behind them and here, out here in the far jungle, he alone was competent to answer the many questions that would arise. He grinned and said, "Better we have bloody rifles, Tuan. We cross other side river here, plenty of trouble everybody, but no trouble us, we got guns."

"Uh-huh."

Talib tightened the sarong under his heavy, muscular shoulders. Pointing behind them with a huge hand, he said, "Place we come from, men go, men come, men trade all time. Place we go to, nobody go, only us. Plenty trouble maybe, but plenty tiger too. Leopard, rhino, all you want we got, but plenty bad people, too."

"Senoi? They won't hurt us. They'll just hide from us."

Talib shook his great head vehemently. "No, Tuan. These Senoi not like other Senoi. This place long way, nobody come, Senoi not frightened, Senoi fight us only we got bloody guns, is good."

"The village? You know where it is?"

"Other side river, Tuan. Better you not go there, I go. Big village, bad people. Senoi come to camp yesterday, you see? They from there, go back now, tell people we want porters, trackers, we give salt, ammunition maybe, they work for us good. They make trouble. I got kris, no more trouble. Best tracker, one man name him Baka. He come soon, from village, you see, good man."

"Well, right now we'll turn east along the river, see if we can find a better place to cross over."

"We go two three days this way, Tuan, we cross."

"Two three days' walk, two three days' drive?"

"Two three days' walk, Tuan."

"Good. Let's get moving."

They turned the trucks along the high cliff, searching for a way down, and when the evening came, they were now no more than twenty feet above the bed of the river. The chasm was narrower here, and scouting around they came across a rotted log bridge that had long ago collapsed into the water below. Stanton called to the others, knowing that this would be the best place to cross, and sent Talib to get the boys from the trucks with axes and parangs to cut down the trees and make a new bridge, watching them drag the heavy trunks up to the edge of the cliff. One of them climbed down to the water and waded over with a rope, and soon the logs were being dragged into position and covered with hard-packed red earth.

And before darkness fell, they were all safely across.

* * *

It seemed as though it were part of another world. Even the trees were different. The mud had given way to hard dry earth and the vegetation was sparser now. Huge ferns in brilliant greens towered over their heads, and a hundred different palm trees bent their trunks from the wind, They saw a big black siamang monkey, and they heard the trumpeting of elephant. A tapir, grey-and-black-patched and ugly, stared at them from the river and then plunged in fright into the water, and a herd of wild, black seladang grazed like cattle on the slope of the hill above them. Two green-and-crimson parakeets were perched on the yellow foliage of a bush from which hung great clusters of scarlet berries, and a tiny bulbul, the sunbird, stared at them unafraid from under its white eyebrows, In the distance, close along the edge of the river, two tigers were lying in the shade, and as they watched, another one appeared, dragging the carcass of a gaur.

Watching them, Anna said slowly, "In a place like this, all your knowledge means nothing. They tell me that tigers never band together."

"A good sign. It's tigers we want. The more, the better our choice."

Von Abart was rooting in his bag for the brandy bottle. He said sourly, "It's here that your knowledge is the true knowledge. In the jungle, among the trees. You'll learn nothing from books except rubbish." He drank from the bottle, wiped the top of it with his hand, and passed it with a gesture to Stanton.

Stanton, shaking his head, wondered if he were getting drunk again. He said cheerfully, making a joke of it, "That's a strange comment from a man whose books are standard works."

Nothing more was needed, he thought, than a joke, a cheerful word. Von Abart grinned and said, "Don't take any notice of me. I only write books in Munich. Here, I live them. We camp for the night?"

Stanton nodded. "Our last night out on the trail. Tomorrow, wherever we are, we make our permanent camp. We've come about as far as the trucks will go. Look at them. Poor old Hadjian."

"We're paying for them."

"Yes, I know. What a sorry sight."

They were covered with slime and mud and dust, their once neat redwood sides scarred and cracked. The last spare tires for one of them had already been worn through, and now one wheel had been stuffed with grass in lieu of the last good tube; another had been patched with strips of old casing that had been bolted firmly into place and miraculously held enough air to keep going. One of the main leaves from the springs had broken and had been replaced by a log of wood strapped into position with baling wire, and one of the headlights was smashed where a sapling, bent back as they had driven over it, had angrily whipped back its protest.

But they had arrived. They had crossed the mountain and the valleys and the rivers, and the kit and the supplies were still with them. Their nets and their ropes and their tools were still aboard, and the hunt would be simplified because of them.

They reached the camp site at noon next day.

They burst through a wide patch of heavy jungle, sweating and cursing and forcing their way through and into a broad cool clearing that dropped away suddenly, at its farthest edge, into an immense green plain below them. The tops of the trees down there were dark and vividly touched with bright flowers that had struggled through the hot wet oppression to find their way to the sunlight above, weaving their tenuous way upwards to the light and the cool air, bursting into bright reds and yellows and whites at the end of incredibly long vines that served, lower down, to bind the morass of the jungle into a tightly tangled skein from which the water dripped and oozed on to the rotting vegetation that lay, in parts, more than a hundred feet deep. It had piled itself upon itself, the humus, for century after century, undisturbed by man. The feet of the Senoi, whom the others scornfully called the slave-people, and the Semang, whom they called with greater scorn, *orangutan*, people of the jungle, were the only touch it felt of the breed that had grown from the animals it once had spawned.

The clearing, a mile or more across, was scattered with clumps of giant bamboo, and some of the thicker stems had been sharply cut where the Semang had been at work on the rafts they used to maneuver their silent way through the swamps and the fetid rivers. Huge ferns made dark patches of shade on the red earth. Tall casuarinas hung their whip-like branches low to the ground, and for a while they stood and stared at the beauty of it, feeling the cool breeze and the sun on their faces.

Then von Abart, pointing to the ground, said slowly, "We have come to the right place. Look."

Stanton crouched down beside the three-toed mark that was deeply imprinted in the hard earth. He spread his open hand over it, and seeing him, Talib came running over and knelt beside him, and said, grinning, "Rhinoceros, Tuan. Small one."

"Uh-huh. You know what kind?"

Talib shrugged his shoulders eloquently. "Rhinoceros."

It was a simple matter for them. He said gently, "There are many kinds, Talib. One-horn, two-horn, black, white, grey."

He was aware that Anna was standing beside him, Making a point of it, she said clearly, "White rhino, Harry. The lesser one-horned sondaicus."

"Are you sure?"

"I am sure, Harry."

Von Abart was watching them, feeling at the edge of the argument. He nodded. "Chances are she's right. If it's a female, it could be a sumatrensis, but here, I doubt it. Let's take a chance and call it an omen for our success."

The air of jubilation was catching. He stood up and said,

"All right, this is where we make camp. Our tents—over by the ferns there."

Talib was watching him closely, listening, thinking, his agile mind at work, "The trackers and the porters can put their shelters up by the bamboo clumps, with the fires well over to the side. I want a latrine dug for the men down at the foot of the hill there. Get stakes cut to ring the whole of the enclosure for the animals, you understand? A fence from the tall trees over to where the land drops away there, then round and back again to its starting point. I want the stakes not less than the length of a man's arm in the ground, and bind them with rattan, you know how to do it? Then, inside the enclosure, I want cages built, cages that we can manhandle when we have to. I want you to check these yourself, and I'll take a look at them when they're finished. Send a man down to the river and bring a sample of the water. The drivers can put up a compound for themselves over there, and you'd better give them two men to help clean up the trucks. Then, I want to see all the servants, the head porters, the head trackers, all right? Any problems with the help—that's your headache, not mine. I want three good gun-bearers to stay with us always, and I want a head-boy to take over from you, under your orders, to look after the camp here while we're out on shikar. You'll come with us. We'll trap the animals when we find them, and send them back in slung cages which we'll build as we go. The porters will carry our ropes and nets, and your head-boy will transfer them from the cages to the compound, and send the bearers back with the cages to find us again, wherever we may be, is that clear? You'll keep the keys to the supply boxes, and you'll issue the rations every day. A pound of rice to each man, some dried beans to those who want them, and ten cigarettes a day. There's whisky on board and if I catch you drinking it, I'll tan the hide off you, and the same goes for the others. They can make palm wine if they want it, but anyone who gets drunk when he's required to work will be in trouble. If anybody brings dogs into the camp, I want them fed. I don't want them rooting around the tents in the middle of the night. And when you select your head-boy, make sure you get someone you can trust. I don't want to come back and find that all the stores have been sold to some passing trader."

Talib roared with laughter, his great flanks quivering. He scratched at his ankle happily with the sight of his rifle and said, "No thieves here, Tuan, no sell to traders. No traders either, only Sakai, savage men like monkeys. Any man steal, I shoot him quick."

"And let me look at that rifle of yours."

Stanton took his long-barreled rifle from him and rubbed at the tarnished brass inlay of the stock with his thumb. It was an ancient Houiller, and the date was inscribed in flowing ornamentation: 1852. The barrel was so thick with rust that he could hardly see through it. He sighed, and said, "You mean to say you've got ammunition for this thing?"

"Yes, Tuan, plenty ammunition. Not plenty, some. Maybe two three boxes. Some people make it, Singapore, Jakarta, places like this. Not fit too good, but good, you know? Shoot pretty bloody straight some time, not always, some time just."

"And some of the others are carrying British Lee-Enfields."

"Not so good like this gun, Tuan."

Now, he knew, it was a question of prestige, of face. He said, smiling, "Well, behave yourself and I'll see if we can't find you something a little better some day."

The dark brown eyes were wide and solemn again. Talib said with great dignity, "Not for gun, Tuan. I do work good because I am good head-boy. Best head-boy in country maybe. You give me good gun, I show all my people, they know you know I am best head-boy. You see."

"Good. Now get the camp started and let me see all the

servants."

By evening, the building was well under way. The trackers and the porters were coming slowly in from the hidden village, thin spare men dressed in loincloths made from bark, with long thin spears and daggers made, he knew, from stolen bolts from the railway line back on the other side of the chasm which was their frightening link with a frightening world that served only to supply them with metals they did not properly know how to find for themselves. They stared at the trucks in terror, and some of them appeared only briefly, to scuttle back under cover to pluck up the courage to announce themselves. Talib, knowing that their fear could also erupt into danger, waited patiently, going about his work and waiting. He came over once and said, not feeling too sure of himself, "One man lose leg, Tuan, crocodile get. I think we gottim medicine, maybe use?"

Von Abart was running a pull-through into the barrel of his favorite rifle. Not looking up, he said coldly, "Send one of the boys to take him to his own *bomor*. We need our medicines. And don't worry me with your problems, you yellow savage, you heard the Tuan's orders."

Stanton stifled his anger, seeing the impassivity on Talib's face. He said smoothly, "I don't think a native doctor can do much for an amputated leg, not in these parts anyway. Let me take a look at him."

Anna was resting under the shade of a fern, lying on her cot and watching the cold night sky, the darkness gently closing in on them. She got up and said, "I'll go. There's sulfanilamide on the truck."

Von Abart looked at her briefly and said nothing. Stanton was conscious of the distaste there, momentarily, and then it was gone in a kind of vicarious suffering. This, he knew, was the old enemy. Stay well and fit and healthy, starve if you must, or tremble with the fever. Let the leeches suck your blood out, and watch the huge red swelling where the scorpion stung you. Suck the poison out of the snake bite, and cut out the worms that burrow under your skin with the sharp point of your hunting knife. But never lose a limb, because the blood drains out too fast and in the morning you are dead. And every week, every day, every hour, the crocodiles are at work, waiting and watching for the careless men who, not learning through years of suffering, still step unthinking into the dark muddy waters of the swamp where the long yellow teeth are waiting. And still they die, by the dozen, by the hundred, year after year and never learning.

It was all part of the struggle, man against his old, primeval enemies. He watched her go, knowing that she knew this, too, knowing that the yellow powder of the Tuan would bring him comfort and let him die less sadly, an unknown, unnamed savage to whom death was just another part of life.

The darkness dropped suddenly into a blacker obscurity, and all work ceased on the compound. The servants had been lined up, solemnly, their hands fresh-scrubbed for the occasion, their sarongs neat and clean and tightly wound. There was Suleiman, the cook, a Mohammedan Malay, quiet, courteous, efficient. There were Umat, the waiter, and Tokay, his assistant, and there was a pretty young half-caste girl named Chep who was dressed in a bright green Kashmiri shawl that some past lover had given her. And with them, hanging back in the darkness, was Baka the tracker, a silent, morose man who was part Sakai, part Semang, part Malay, and all animal. He had the long straight hair of a Malay and the dark brown skin of a Negrito. He carried not only the long lightwood blowgun, but also the old-fashioned bow which his ancestors had used, and two leather pouches of brown poison from the Ipoh tree hung at the string that was bound round his waist. He spoke in a guttural, monosyllabic language that even the polylingual Talib had difficulty in understanding, and he moved in absolute silence, his bare feet spreading over the damp earth in growing dimension, like those of a camel on the sand. The knife at his waist was intricately carved on its ivory shaft.

Stanton went over to the boys' compound and inspected the work they had done. Their huts were up already, flimsy shelters of bamboo and palm, and among them the women were moving silently about. He wondered where they had all come from so quickly, and knew that Talib had sent word ahead of the trucks, his runners moving faster than they could, through the jungle, covering fifty miles in a day, where they could cover only ten or twenty; tiny, slim runners who knew the clearings and the hidden villages and the secret scurryings of the people there, runners who would say, chanting in a sing-song monotony, "*Orang puteh suda sampai*...The white man has come," banging their town-crier sticks together and calling to the men in the jungle who would remain unseen until the runner was gone and then creep from their hiding-places to discuss the strange event, the narrow eyes alive with fear and a desperate yearning to see what the advent could mean. The runners would stop for a short moment to gulp down a mouthful of *blackan*—the paste made from rotting fish—that would sustain them through the night, and then run on again, chanting their song and slipping dexterously among the low, wet branches of the overhanging trees, broadcasting their news to a listening, silent jungle that was alive with unseen eyes.

The fires were burning brightly, and the women were tucking their waistcloths tightly about them, their ivory breasts shining in the red light, squatting down on their haunches to cook their evening meal. He watched some of them spreading the embers wide so that they would cool off quickly, and knew that these were the Negritos who were preparing the ashes for their men to sleep in so that the cold of the night would not kill off their naked bodies.

And all the time, a few respectful paces behind him, Talib followed.

Later that night, at dinner, von Abart said casually, "I told him to change our tents around, to put Anna's in the middle."

"Oh?"

"I don't know if you've noticed it, but apart from the savages we seem to have collected, the camp is surrounded by them. They're creeping up the trees to watch us, thinking we can't see them just because we are white."

"I saw. They won't give us any trouble."

"They'd better not."

Munching on a piece of venison, von Abart said, "That bastard overcooked this steak. And it needs some good German sauerkraut. Will we start hunting tomorrow?"

Stanton nodded. "Baka's going out tonight to the foothills there." He swung his camp chair round and gestured to the north of them. "The hills we saw when we crossed over the chasm. Consensus of opinion is we should find the big tigers there. I've told him we only want the big ones."

"What about that rhino?"

"The sondaicus? There's another tracker detailed to look for it tomorrow."

"Is the beer cold?"

Hearing the word beer, Umat, the waiter, moved silently over to the cooler and opened it. It was a makeshift box of wooden slats that had been covered with a four-inch layer of charcoal, kept in place with chicken-wire, and above which a can of water was dripping, drop by drop, through a nail-punctured hole to keep the charcoal wet. When he brought the cans to the table, they were ice-cold.

Speaking with his mouth full of meat, von Abart said, "And the leopard, that's going to be the trouble. We're in good tiger country, but leopard...I'm not so sure."

"If we get higher up the mountain we'll find them. The villagers have been told that we'll pay them for news of the animals we want. There'll be a constant stream of them coming in. The trackers will follow up. There shouldn't be too much difficulty."

The long cold night wore on slowly. The crickets were loud in the trees, and somewhere a parrot shrieked noisily. They stood for a while together out on the edge of the bluff, watching the pale sky and the brilliance of the moon under which the distant range of mountains was a dark cut-out cardboard laid across the horizon. Two half-wild dogs that had come into the camp with the Semangs were barking, and when von Abart picked up a pebble and hurled it, there was a sudden squeal and then silence.

As far as they could see, and beyond that in their own imaginings, the country was silent and vast and undisturbed, and they knew that out there, somewhere in the huge space of it, the animals they were seeking were prowling, themselves predatory, constantly aware of their own dangers from the ever broadening circles of civilization that spread like ripples into the far jungle and would one day engulf them.

But now, far from the sounds of the cities, there were only the stillness and a vast awareness of the distance that separated them from all concept of socialized comfort and behavior. It was here that, more than fifteen hundred years ago, the Indians from Madras had founded their Palavan Empire, where the warring Thais had been driven out by the invading Mongols, where the exploring traders had come for the spice and the gold and the tin and the hardwood from the distant forests that covered the slopes of the mountains.

Von Abart, yawning largely, went to his tent and slept, and in a little while Anna, too, left him alone there, standing still and quiet in the moonlight to remember the hiding and the running and the coming back again to turn his hard-acquired knowledge into pay dirt in the days when the war was over and the only battles were between man and the animals, as they had always been.

He dreamed in the darkness for a while, thinking of Cora, the cold, cold woman, and then went over to the fire where Talib lay asleep on his side, seeing the Malayan sentries that had been posted and knowing that the number one boy was doing his work well. He looked down at the slumbering form for a moment, looking at the bright patchwork quilt that had been thrown over the huge body, the bare feet sticking incongruously out in the night-time dew.

Talib's eyes opened wide in the darkness, and he was about to clamber to his feet, when Stanton said, "No, no, sleep."

"Everything all right?"

"Everything good, Tuan." He held up one edge of the quilt and showed the Houiller rifle underneath. "Everything ready. We got men watch all night. Best thing."

"Yes, I saw. That's a fancy blanket you have there."

Talib stood up quickly and held it out for him to take. He said, grinning, "My wife, young one, make for me. You like?"

"I like."

"You take."

Stanton shook his head. "You keep it. I have my tent. But I thank you."

"You want, you take."

"No, but you are good."

"By God."

"God will be kind to you."

"And to you, Tuan. If he is good to you, he will be good

90

to me."

"You speak good English, Where did you learn?"

"With soldiers, Tuan. Before that, in school. Mission School. Missionary come, teach me to be good Christian. But better I stay Muslim, go to Heaven maybe one day. Christian only got one wife, no good, better like Chinese man with teapot, he got one pot, plenty cups."

"You've got a point there. You like the school?"

Talib grimaced in the darkness. "No bloody good, Tuan. No smoke, no drink, no bloody woman. No good."

"The girl you got for the Mem, what's her name? Chep?"

"Chep, Tuan."

"Where's she from?"

"Come from Selangor, Tuan. Little bit Malay, Tamil, little bit Chinese maybe. All mix up, no father, maybe sailor some place come and go. I send her your tent maybe?"

"Not tonight, Talib. I'll let you know."

He could not easily identify the thought that was at the back of his mind. It was something to do with Anna, and with Cora, and with all the other women who had been there before her. The heat of the day had come and gone, and even in the cold of the night it was still on him. He said again, "I'll let you know, Talib."

"Yes, Tuan. We hunt tomorrow maybe?"

"When Baka gets back. Tiger first, rhino, leopard. We find leopard in the hills?"

"On mountain, Tuan. Big one. Men from village say big leopard, black like night, over on mountain. Not small like most, big one."

"Good."

Knowing the conversation was over, Talib waited for his dismissal. Looking at him, Stanton felt a sudden warmth of affection for him.

"Sleep in peace, now," he said.

Talib lay back on the sand, pulled the quilt up to his shoulders, and closed his eyes. Continuing his rounds, Stanton paused outside Anna's tent. There was a light inside, and he called out softly, "Everything all right in there?"

"Come on in, Harry."

He pulled back the flap and stood there, waiting and not quite knowing what he was waiting for. She was wearing her housecoat and lying on top of the cot with the mosquito-net thrown back. Her hair was yellow in the light of the kerosene lamp that stood on a box beside her. He said again, "Everything all right?"

"Sure. Is Otto asleep?"

"I don't know. There's no light in his tent."

He wondered why her light was on. He said, "Can't you sleep? There's a lot to do tomorrow."

"I'll sleep."

He was wondering how he could legitimately approach her bed. He said awkwardly, "I just wanted to say...well, I'm glad that you came along. It hasn't been easy, has it? And it's going to be a lot tougher."

"It's not been hard, Harry. I'm tougher than both of you if the truth were known."

"Yes, I believe you are."

"Have you got a cigarette handy?"

He came forward then and gave her one, and as he lit it for her, their faces were very close together; he could smell the sweet, feminine scent of her. He took one of her hands and said, trying to make it sound casual, "All the nail varnish gone?"

"The slow process has set in."

"Woman into hunter."

"It doesn't take very long. How quiet it is!"

He glanced involuntarily towards the entrance and saw that the flap of the tent was in place. He wondered if he had closed it as he came in or whether it had fallen shut. She saw the look and smiled, saying nothing. There was a constriction in his throat that was bothering him, like the beginning of a cough. He still held her hand, wondering why it seemed awkward to him, knowing that he knew what he wanted to do and had done it many times before, Thinking of his own expertise, he said easily, "You're a very lovely woman. I suppose you know that."

"I am glad to hear you say it."

Unconsciously, he was whispering, wishing he were sure that von Abart was asleep. He glanced at the flap again, trying to hide the look, but she said, "What's worrying you, Harry?"

"Well, I wouldn't want Otto...He might misinterpret. Sitting on the edge of your bed like this."

"I don't think he'd mind."

"No? Well, that's a nice thought."

"He likes me to be appreciated."

"Not exactly the word I had in mind, but..."

He bent forward and touched her lips with his, and when she did not fight him, he let his lips play against her cheek for a moment, not forgetting to breathe a little more heavily so that she should know that she really moved him. He touched her shoulder and she held his hand, though he was not immediately sure if this were a precaution she was taking or evidence of an affection, thinking he would soon find out and beginning to enjoy a recurrence of the game he had always liked so much.

And then there was the slightest sound outside, and he pulled back hastily and said, louder than he had been speaking up to now. "Well, if you're sure there's nothing you want. You need cigarettes?"

But she was looking at the entrance with a trace of alarm on her face, and then he heard Talib's soft voice outside, very quiet in the silence.

"Sir, we got trouble."

He went outside very quickly, just seeing that Anna had swung her feet to the floor and taken hold of her rifle, and he said, "Trouble? What kind of trouble?" Turning, he whispered to Anna, "Stay here."

Talib gestured silently towards the bush, "Three men. I go find out what they want, but first I say better tell Tuan, maybe trouble."

Stanton nodded, wishing he had not gone so far from his rifle on his first night. He said quietly, "Get my rifle. In my tent."

He saw now that another of Talib's men had silently come up behind them, a British Army 303 held loosely in his hand, and Talib gestured at him and spoke in a dialect he did not recognize, and the man slipped quietly away and came back in a moment with the rifle and a bandolier of cartridges.

Two more of their Malays moved into the circle of light, the flames showing redly on their yellow, somber faces. They moved like cats, quickly and silently, and Talib said, "I go talk to them."

He could still see nothing out in the bush there, but when Talib had gone over he saw a slight thin figure move from the shadows and he heard a soft, muted whispering, and in a moment Talib came back, not looking back over his shoulder, and said, "Six men, three in bush, three more other side little bit far away."

"Oh? What do they want?"

"They want our rifles, sir."

"Is that all? Tell them—tell them I'll shoot the first man that moves into the firelight. No, tell them I'll talk to them in the morning, but not now. Tell them I'll only talk in daylight, that I'm going back to bed now. Tell them."

Not moving away now, Talib called out twice, and in a moment there was an answer from the darkness, just a guttural grunt. Talib spoke for a moment, and then signaled with his hand and in a moment there were seven or eight of his men standing close to the fire. Talib kicked at the embers with his bare foot and stirred them into bright flame, and the fire leapt up to shine brightly on their faces and on the barrels of their rifles. He said, grinning, "I let them see we not all sleeping, sir. I tell them come back tomorrow."

Von Abart came out of his tent, rubbing a hand over his face standing there watching. He said nothing, but raised his rifle and fired two shots, rapidly, into the darkness beyond the campfire, and Anna came running out of her tent, her rifle ready, and Stanton said sharply, "That's enough. Leave them alone."

"The yellow bastards," von Abart said. "Shoot a couple of them and we won't have any more trouble. What the hell happened with the dogs? I didn't hear them barking, did you?"

"No, I didn't either."

They stood there in the firelight, wondering what would happen next. Stanton said, "Have they got arms?"

"Only spears, sir. Savage people."

"Did you tell them what I said?"

"I tell them good."

"Well, are they going away? Can't see a damn thing out there."

"No, sir, they just stand there. I think they stand there all night. But no trouble now, they see we not afraid. I tell them they come too close we shoot. I keep two three men stand guard, no trouble."

"Good. I'll be up and about during the night. And you'd better find out about the dogs, I've an idea...Well, go see what happened to them. Let me know in the morning." He said to the others, "No sense in everyone staying up. They know we're well armed, they won't cause any trouble. I only hope those bullets didn't find a mark."

Talib, standing stolid and huge in the firelight, shook his head. Turning to von Abart, he said slowly, "Better not shoot, sir, make trouble."

For a moment there was a flash of sudden anger, and then von Abart held out his rifle and gently touched Talib under the chin with its barrel. He said slowly, "Don't presume to tell me what's good, you yellow savage. And you don't call me sir, you call me Tuan. You understand?"

Not moving, Talib said stolidly, "I call you Tuan, Tuan."

"Just remember your place."

He lowered his rifle and turned away. Knowing the danger was past, not wanting to rekindle it, Stanton said mildly, "It's all in the point of view, Otto. The times are changing, we're not the great white race any more. It's a matter of prestige."

"Prestige," von Abart said thinly, "is a thing they'd better understand thoroughly. And for your own satisfaction, I fired up in the air. Nobody gets hurt. I'm not a fool." He looked at Anna and said nothing and then turned round and stalked back to his tent, Stanton said, "All right?"

She nodded, gesturing with her rifle, "A girl's best friend. Good night. See you in the morning."

"We'll get the boys off early. Just before daybreak, okay?"

"Sure. Good night, Harry."

"Good night." He watched her go back to her tent, admiring the line of her back and the way she walked, and thinking again, *Well, that's not going to be too tough. And the old man sleeps like a log. Good. Good.*

He went back to his tent, lay down on his cot fully clothed, and slept. Twice in the night he woke up and went outside. The Malay guards, sitting silent under their trees, stood up as he passed and he nodded at them because he could not talk to them, knowing that the camp was safe and feeling glad that they were there, and in the morning, when the first early light was in the east, before the red sun had come up, he went outside again and saw that the boys were getting the nets out and checking them under Talib's watchful eye. Talib came over and said cheerfully, "The dogs, sir, both dead."

"Oh? That's what I thought, They must have thrown some poisoned meat into the camp. Are they still out there, the

96

Sakai?"

The Malay pointed and he saw one of them, squatting on the sand in the open, a few hundred yards away, his long spear high above his head, motionless as statue, "All right, call him over."

Talib went off, and in a moment came back with three of them, the old man he had seen in the open and two younger ones standing rigidly behind him. Their lean bodies were taut and wiry, and they wore bark-cloth aprons around their waists and leather charms around their upper arms. Their hair, black and shiny, was piled up on top of their heads.

Stanton gestured to them, and they sat down on the ground, drawing their legs up in their favorite position so that the knees, incredibly, stood higher than their shoulders. They were a handsome trio, virile, alert, and very wary.

Sitting on the box that Talib brought him, Stanton said, "Okay, Talib, you know what to do. Find out what they want, tell them they can't have our rifles, tell them we're well armed, and tell them that we are not here permanently, offer them presents and see that they leave us in peace."

He sat there with his hands on his widespread knees, looking important, while Talib's voice droned on. They argued with him for a little while, and he used his hands to make firm, sharp gestures, and in a little while he sent one of the Malays to bring some salt that had been rolled into a tightly woven cylinder of palm leaves, and a big gourd of milk, The old man tasted the salt, grunted, and put it away, and then drank the milk, more than a gallon of it, and Talib sent it back to be filled again for each of the others, and looking at his surly face, Stanton knew that there would still be trouble from them. He pointed to the long knife the old man carried, and said to Talib, "Tell him to show me his knife."

The old man shook his head, and when Talib insisted, he took it from its leather scabbard and handed it over reluctantly, and Stanton went over to his box and took a small honing stone, the kind that can be bought in any hardware store for a dollar, and gently, methodically, slowly put a keen edge on the broken, ragged blade. The Sakai, peering intently, watched, and Talib nodded his head in satisfaction, and when he handed the knife back, the old man felt the blade with his thumb and looked startled and held out the bleeding tip of his finger to show the others, and they all burst out laughing suddenly, and then the moment of surliness was gone. They were chattering to each other, and Stanton said, "Tell him to keep the stone, not to break it, to be careful with it."

The others had crowded round, watching the conference, and one of the young Sakai was looking over the young girls who were standing in the background, and Stanton thought it was time to break it up, so he got to his feet and held out his hand. The old man stared at it, and Talib, holding both his hands together, showed him how to shake hands. Then they were turning away and Anna was there, coming out of her tent and walking towards them. The three tribesmen gave one startled look at her and burst into a run, and von Abart, laughing, said, "It's your hair—blonde hair. They don't believe it's real."

He looked across at her and smiled, and everyone was in good humor, and he said, "All right, back to work. The nets over to the hills within the half-hour. Over there, by the thorn-trees where the green patch is."

A little later, a long ragged row of porters left the camp, carrying the nets like limp bodies between them, moving at a slow, constant trot that would get them into the foothills by evening, Baka, the silent Sakai tracker, was with them, running lightly, untiringly, out in front, his long spear held lightly before him.

Stanton had said to him, talking through Talib, "It's tiger we want, but only big ones, you understand?" Making a mark on the sand to look like a tiger's pad, he had insisted, "Only the big ones."

Baka, silently, had nodded his head and moved off. And soon, the column looked like ants moving through the grass in the distance.

Watching them, the vultures were already circling overhead.

CHAPTER 7

The building of the camp went on apace. When they left in the middle of the afternoon, word had already come in that Baka had found the spoor of a group of tigers. Three big ones, he had said, accompanied by two cubs. He had marked their lair and was waiting for them out there in the bush.

They set out in the truck, the three of them, with Talib clinging to his accustomed place on the running-board, and by three o'clock in the afternoon they saw the tracker in the distance, standing motionless, leaning on his long blowpipe. And when he saw that the truck had stopped at the foot of a steep bluff up which it could not climb, he walked over towards them, the hot sun shining on his yellow face, his arms over his blowgun which he had laid across the back of his shoulders. His waistcloth was tucked up round his hips like a loincloth, and through it was thrust his fearsome broad-bladed knife that curved round to a long sharp point and had been drilled with holes down the blade so that it would cause a deadlier wound. He carried a leather water bag, and Stanton saw now that he wore four armbands, each one signifying an enemy killed, and round his wiry neck, on a string, were their four phallic trophies as mute and frightening testimony of his savagery.

They went down towards him, and walked with him to where a few flat stones had been carefully placed over a single pad-mark that was deep enough in the sand for them all to see. In the distance under a clump of acacia they could spot two tigers lying in the grass and swishing their tails at the flies, but Baka shook his head, meaning, "No, not these. This is a really big one."

Looking at the spoor, von Abart nodded his head in satisfaction. "A big one, eleven feet or more, nose to tail. Let's get after him."

"Where are the beaters?" Baka looked from Stanton to Talib, and when the Malay had translated, he gestured with his arm in a wide sweep to the hills. "Under cover," Talib said. "They wait, in bushes, not so hot. Lazy." The contempt showed in his wide grin, because only Sakai would seek shade and rest while better men were working. They followed Baka along the faint track, the pads showing in patches where the earth was wet, and then disappearing altogether where the soil turned to hard lava rock. But Baka, bent slightly under his spear, did not falter. He was the best man in his tribe, a man with an eye of astonishing perception who could tell from a bent blade of wet grass whether the woman who had trodden it down was carrying a load on her head or was merely pregnant. His old skin was dry and sweatless, dark like leather that has lain too long in the sun.

They walked behind him, not trying to find the invisible signs themselves, but leaving it to the expert, and once he stopped and talked for a while with Talib, and Talib told them that another tiger had joined him here and that they had gone off together towards the thicket that lay a few miles ahead of them.

For ten miles or more they walked, with the sun still hot on their backs and the hot air about them heavy with the silence.

Once, they saw a macmiss bird, and it flew to them and called, "Macmiss...macmiss...macmiss," meaning, so the Sakai said, "This way...this way...this way." They knew that it would lead them straight to the tiger and wait close by for the kill to be made, and that the hunters would leave it the animal's brain as a token of their respect for the perspicacity of a bird that would lead them so straight to their prey. They knew too, that when, in turn, the tiger made his kill, he too would leave the hunter's brain for the bird to pick at, because this exchange of services had been going on for thousands of years and not even the advent of civilization would ever change the old and settled ways of the jungle. And when the bird persisted in fluttering along beside them, Stanton bent down and picked up a pebble, and sent it spinning past its head, and the Sakai nodded their acquiescence, because they knew, wondering, that here was a man who could even tell the birds, "We do not kill today," in strict accordance with their own rigid custom.

They walked in silence, strung out across the track with their rifles loosely held. Out on the left, von Abart was moving easily, not tiring. In the center, Anna strode along with her gun held high on her shoulder, her arm swinging like a man's. And out on the right, Stanton was glancing from time to time at the long straight suppleness of her, seeing the erect carriage of the shoulders and admiring the taut prominence of her breast-line. She walked with a springy step, like a native, slowly and in perfect rhythm, without wasted motion, her head thrown back and her stomach arched under the cage of her ribs as though to accentuate the narrowness of her hips and the slim straight profile of her thighs.

The beaters were moving down from the top of the hill now, a dozen Tamils followed by a group of Sakai still carrying their nets, and in a little while Baka stopped, his work done, and pointed to a clump of rough bush.

"In there," Talib said. "Both of them. One very big, one not so big. Maybe others there too."

"All right," Stanton said. "Let's get set. I want the nets in among the trees over there, where the high grass is. The beaters can go through the thicket from the other side and drive him out here. I want two or three spearmen right beside us here, but I don't want him hurt. All right?"

Talib ran off, panting and sweating in the sun, and Baka sat down on the earth and took a bent and broken cigarette from his loincloth, rubbed his flint lighter with the heel of his hand until the touchwick glowed, blew on it, and lit up, his interest in the operation finished. The Tamils wandered over into their positions, and von Abart waved his hands at them, shouting, "Come on, you lazy bastards, get over there."

"Nothing for us to do now," Stanton said, "except wait." He turned to Anna and said, "You know they'll charge us, don't you?"

"I know that. I will not fire."

"Good. If it becomes necessary, I'll do it. But if they charge, let the spearmen drive them back."

They moved apart to fifty-yard intervals, and Stanton waved his hand to Talib for the drive to begin. In a moment they heard the first dull beat of the drums, as the Tamils moved into the thicket, occasionally picking up a stone and hurling it with unbelievable force into a clump of bush. The drive took on a V-formation as the center beaters waited for the flanks to move up, and the triangle closed with practiced competence as they enclosed the area where the tigers were, Then von Abart shouted and they saw the tigers, three of them, emerge from their cover, snarling and looking back over their shoulders. They could see the yellow muscles rippling along their flanks as they moved and then the first of the beaters came through, waiting carefully for the rest to catch up, and moving into a steady half-circle and then waiting for orders.

They were out in the open now, the whole group, it seemed, but Baka, taking an interest again, shouted something to Talib who shouted in turn for one of the beaters, and after a short argument two men went back to the other side and began to beat again, following the directions of Baka's pointed arm. And this time, the big tiger, an old male who had cunningly remained under cover, came rushing out in a savage temper, running over to where the rest of his group were and waiting with them to see what would happen.

They stood and watched for a while, watching the savage beauty of them as they milled around restlessly, snarling at the men who stood so close by, wondering whether to make a break through them and run back to their shelter, but fearing the vicious sound of the beaters' hollow drums.

Stanton examined them carefully with his binoculars, seeming to bring them no more than a few feet away from him. He handed the glasses to Anna and said, "Look. The one on the right, the big one," and then yelled to Talib, "All right, cut out the big one. Drive him to the nets."

Talib shouted an order, and the line of Tamils moved forward again, their drums silent now. The Malays had moved in beside them, brandishing their spears, and even the Sakai porters had drawn their knives and were thirsting for the blood of their common enemy, knowing that there were strange white people with them and that therefore the tigers, should they escape and remember the occasion, would not hold them, the jungle people, responsible for what was happening. This was important to them, for these white people had been so uncouth, so careless, so contemptuous of the tigers as to mention their name, saying the word *rimau* quite openly and in blatant disregard of the convention that demanded he should be called "His Excellency" when he was within hearing distance—which, in the dark green cover of the trees, might be anywhere around them.

One of the tigers, a young one, slipped snarling back through the circle and was gone, heading back to the wet hanging leaves that would stripe his body with their shadows as nature itself had striped it, hiding him completely while he watched, fearful that the escape had been made for him deliberately and not knowing what lay beyond it.

Von Abart shouted, "Watch out, behind you, mind he

doesn't come out again," knowing that the moment of careless relief was the moment in which he would summon his courage and dart back to attack them.

Now, there were only three of them, the big male and two females, and the encircling Sakai closed in, deriving courage from the others and fearful to let their fear show through, fearful of the huge number of them.

One of them lowered his great striped head and moved with slow deliberate pace at a group of the porters, and then suddenly, at a quick word from Talib, two Malays were there beside them, working in smooth accord with the contemptible jungle-men because the white man had told them to, brandishing their spears and waving their heavy clubs, The tiger moved forward, and a thrown club hit him at the side of the temple, driving him snarling back, not understanding why the men did not run from him as he had always learned they would do. One of the females made a break and was gone, back into the edge of the jungle, moving fast. Then the other female charged for a Malay who was standing tall and still and silent, waiting. As the animal reached him he dropped swiftly to his knees and held his spear high, and the tiger, seeing the sharp point shining in the sunlight, swerved away from it and was gone with an angry roar.

He was alone now, the big male, and it seemed that he knew his fight had become a personal one. He drew back, licking at his lips, looking over his shoulder at the jungle where his females had gone and where safety lay. He began to make short sharp rushes, his huge teeth showing his anger, but wherever he went the men were waiting, banging their sticks and their drums, waving their weapons, brave in number and deriving more bravery from the winning of the battle.

The half-circle was strong and solid ahead of him, and he backed away slowly, being driven, sensing that behind him, among the trees, where there were no men, there must be hidden danger, but not knowing, because this was virgin territory where tiger had not been hunted before, that the nets were there waiting for him.

Again he charged forward, and Stanton, watching, saw one of the Sakai hurl a spear that bit quivering into the ground close beside him, so that the tiger turned back from his charge and struck out at the spear instead, snapping it in two, like a matchstick, and then there were a group of Sakai there, several of them, beating their gongs in rapid succession, a discordant, unnerving sound of frightening insistence.

The tiger turned and ran, and at that moment, Talib, dancing on his great splayed feet now, yelled a single word. Someone pulled at a rope and somewhere a bent sapling sprang straight and the net went up with a swoosh and the tiger was an angry, snarling, frightened and furious captive.

Stanton looked at his watch: the whole operation had taken less than an hour from the time the drive had begun. Pleased, he turned to the others. "Not even six o'clock yet and we've got our tiger. Let's go over and say hello."

They went down to the clump of acacias and looked at him, doubled up in the restricting net, lying on his back and clawing at the nylon cords. Talib was already moving in with a loop on the end of a pole, trying to slip it through the mesh and over the animal's struggling feet.

It was a big one, with a skin that was quite unmarked. Von Abart nodded with satisfaction. "I told you, a good one, as big as I've seen. We have started well."

"Now all that remains," Stanton said, "is to get him back to the camp. A few days in the compound will take the fight out of him."

Anna was staring at the animal, fascinated by the sheer size and strength of it, saying nothing but once, he saw, licking her lips to take the dryness away from them. Was it fear? He wondered. Her eyes were bright and the sun had burned her face to a deep tan.

"First time you've seen a tiger trapped?"

She nodded. "Usually we shoot them. Then, they don't get quite so close. I would not have believed that you could drive them off like that, with spears."

"Cowards," von Abart said. "The king of beasts is a coward. He's frightened of a child's drum."

Stanton grinned at him. "Don't bet on it."

"Only their strength, Harry, only their strength," von Abart insisted. "When they are driven by their fear, they use their strength. And this is the only time they are dangerous. The only time."

"And we will still treat him with the greatest respect."

"By the time we get back to Munich, he will be eating out of my hand, because he will know that I have no fear of him. You will see. Animals...you must understand them. Like women. It only needs to understand them. Then, you can take whenever you want from them."

Stanton looked across to Anna. The close presence of the tiger, a savage bulk of contained virility, seemed to stir her strangely. It held a fascination for her, and as he watched he could see that under her seeming inertia there was a latent excitement that was quite ready to burst into violent eruption. Momentarily, it alarmed him, and when she turned to look at him her eyes were wide and solemn and inquiring, and he knew then that they shared a common stimulation. In spite of the efforts of the day and the exertion of the long march, he felt the heat rising in him as he looked at her, and knew that she was aware of it as her eyes held his for a long time. He saw her shudder, and her hand went to her breast to pull the white cloth of her shirt free, and she turned quickly away as though to hide the fact that her breath was coming faster, suddenly. Then she turned back to him again, her composure regained, as von Abart said smugly, "They've a great deal in common, you know. The woman is still closer to the animals than the man. That's what makes her so desirable, *nicht wahr?*"

Anna smiled and said nothing, and he marveled at her rapid assumption of control after that fleeting moment when, her nipples hard with desire, she had clutched at her throat and turned from him in sudden helplessness. Stanton thought, *You conceited idiot. For two pins I'd take her away from you, here and now, roll her in the earth in the shadow of that animal up there in front of the boys, too, let them see what I'd do to her. They at least understand these things.* He looked at her again, letting her see what he was thinking, and she bent down to take off a boot and shake the mud off it, holding on to his arm to steady herself as she did so.

Von Abart, watching them, said, "The boys did well. We should give them something tonight. Some beer, perhaps."

"And rice wine and some cigarettes?"

"Good. When they get him back to the camp." He thudded his fist into the struggling tiger, pounding it into the flank. "A fine specimen. Almost as good as my trophy."

"Only this one," Stanton said, "is alive. Let's get him back."

It took six men to carry him, three at each end of a long pole that they cut for the purpose, and as soon as the slow line of porters moved off, shouting and singing now that they had a captive, they walked up the steep slope of the hill to where the truck was parked beyond the red bluff, and drove slowly back to the camp.

That night there was a celebration. Some beer, some rice wine, some cigarettes. It did not take much.

There had been an incident, an excitement, that had seemed, somehow, to put a finishing touch to the day's labors. On the way into the camp, a huge king cobra had reared up on its coils, its hood open as it swung back to strike. Anna, stepping over a fallen tree, had stood for a moment as though petrified, staring at it and not moving, knowing that the blow was coming straight for her and knowing that she felt the sour fear of it. Talib, in sudden alarm, had raised his ancient rifle, but then Stanton stepped forward, swung his parang in a swift downward stroke, and neatly sliced off the grinning, evil head. It lay among the writhing coils, still part of them, and he looked at Anna's white face, and shrugged, and moved on.

They shot some game on the way back, some wild boar and a small buffalo, and soon, when the fires were brightly flickering, defining the camp area against the black impenetrable wall they had come from, the gongs and the nose-flutes and the bamboo harps were brought out, and someone began a song.

> The tiger roars at the end of the hunt.
> What does he want? He wants to eat.
> To eat wildfowl, to eat wild boar,
> To eat the deer and the old, old man,
> Do not forget this in the telling,
> The tiger has sworn, has sworn to kill us,
> He walks along the branch of the tree
> He rises up to walk to the forest.
> The tiger looks for beasts that live.
> Do not forget this in the telling.

Somebody unwrapped a rare bamboo harp from its carefully wound rags, a length of thick bamboo along which the skin had been gently raised, cut into long slithers between two nodes, and stretched with the aid of wooden "pillows".

Talib came over to them and told them how good the meat was, how excellent the beer was, how important he himself was as head-boy, and at last Stanton got the point and gave him some watered whisky in the bottom of a bottle so that he could stand among the lesser men and say he was drinking the strong stuff which his boss had given him, and so enhance his prestige among them.

The feast went on. They were close to savagery, these tribes, with the admixture of Besisi, Negrito, Semang, carelessly mixed with the native Senoi blood. They lived in the depths of the jungle, close to, but fearful of, the fringes of an encroaching civilization that seemed chary of bridging the tiny gap that kept them apart, and now, bloated with food and drink, their sweating bodies were once more close to the animals from which they believed they had sprung, part of the hot wet earth and of the stupefying, steaming vegetation.

At last, drunk and exhausted, the last of them fell asleep; it was Talib. He lay down where he had been clutching at one of the younger girls who had watched on the edge of the circle, his empty whisky bottle, symbol of his importance, clasped in a huge, damp hand. He groaned in his coma, and belched loudly, and then he was asleep.

Standing in the door of his tent, Stanton said, "Well, thank God for a little peace!"

Anna had joined him silently in the darkness, coming to him like a ghost out of the shadows and standing beside him with an absence of greeting that seemed to take their closeness for granted. Listening to the night sounds of the jungle that came alive only after the sun had gone down, when the sleeping animals would rise and stretch their taut limbs going out to seek their prey and to propagate their species after the long sleep of the hot moist day. It was rough, harsh country where all was at rest while the bright sun stood high and broiled the stewing morass that was the jungle, and only sprang, like an uncoiling spring, into dark and menacing activity in the stealthy secrecy of the night.

It was at night that the animals prowled, all of them, in

stealth and in treachery.

Looking at her now, he thought, *We're night-people, too, you and I, and only your lover is asleep in the darkness.*

She wore a long green bathrobe loosely tied at her waist, flapping about her with a carelessness to which he had not quite grown accustomed. He knew that she had just come from the shower because, watching secretly, he had seen the half-caste girl, Chep, carrying the cans of water to her tent and had heard the splashing as the water was poured over her naked body into the canvas tub. He could smell the sweet scent of the soap and of the cinnamon oil which, he guessed, had been rubbed into her smooth white body by the smooth yellow hands of the young girl, herself half naked in the darkness. The picture of them together in the soft cool light of a kerosene lamp was still vivid in his imagination, a slave girl and her mistress.

She stood beside him silently for a while, not speaking, not even waiting for him to speak, but just standing and looking at the darkness as though it was there that all the solutions could be found to all the problems that might be vexing her. This is my home, she had said, and now, watching her, he could feel the affinity she had with the jungle and with the darkness. He could feel, too, that the desire was on her, her skin still tingling from the touch of alien hands, and that she was looking for comfort in the closeness of him, the closeness of a male of the species.

She took hold of the front of her robe, at the shoulders, and fanned herself with it, letting the air play down the front of her body, treating his presence with a casual absence of modesty, because there were just the two of them, with her lover away, half a world apart from the confining restraints of a newer culture that had somehow surrounded itself with the ancient taboos that out here, in their origins, no longer existed.

It was not, he was sure, a deliberate attempt to show herself to him. Rather, it was an indication of her complete acceptance of him as part—whatever part he chose to take—of herself. He moved sideways a little so that he could observe her, seeing that she was naked underneath, looking at the smooth skin of her breast and wanting to touch it. He was facing von Abart's tent and trying to decide if a man could see them from there, had he the inclination to peer out into the darkness from his hidden position behind the flap.

She said, not looking at him, "I don't know how he can sleep through it. But he does."

"Are you tired?"

"No, not very."

"It's hot under the trees here. Why don't we stroll over to the edge of the bluff? There might be more of a breeze there."

"All right."

"Five minutes of fresh air." He took her arm gently and moved her into the shadow, trying to make it look natural and knowing, too, that she knew damn well what he was up to. As soon as they were clear of von Abart's tent, he slipped his hand round her waist, helping her to move over the broken ground that was blackly invisible under their feet, stumbling and holding on to her tightly. He was glad that she was slim enough to permit his arm to go right around her so that his hand was nearer the front of her body, so that he could feel the resilience of her ribs where the lower bone curled gently around, above the stomach. And when he moved it up a little to feel the side of her breast, she put her hand over his, not moving it away but stopping him, for the time being, from going any farther into a caress. He knew that this too, was part of the game, merely a token struggle so that he should not go too far too quickly. His heart was pounding hard and he knew that he would soon be making love to her and that she wanted him to and that it was only a matter of time now, perhaps of only a few days, perhaps this very night, if they could find a place where they would not be discovered.

Bantering, curbing his excitement, he said easily, "The old man seems to leave you pretty well alone, doesn't he?"

They had come to the edge of the bluff and the whole valley was spread out below them. Now, they could see that the moon, which had sunk below their specific horizon at the camp, was still above it out on the plain, glowing with an extraordinary whiteness out there; it seemed as if they were above it, and that it was just below their line of vision. She said, "It's strange to look down on a moon."

"It's the same one you look up at in Munich. In that musty old house." Remembering what she had said to him, *One day I'll get tired of being another trophy*, he added, "A musty old house full of stuffed animals."

"And of history."

"For what it's worth."

"Yes, I know, Harry. It's not worth very much really, is it?"

Pushing it hard, he said, "Are you happy that you came with us?"

"Yes. Yes, I am."

The next line, "Are you happy—period?"

She turned and looked up at him, more solemn than he had seen her before. "You mean with Otto? Yes, I'm happy, I suppose."

He said flippantly, "Well, it's nice to be so sure."

"He's very good to me, Harry. He's done a great deal for me."

"Oh? Like what, for instance? Three meals a day? He smiled so that it would not sound harsh, and she looked up at him with that secret smile again and said, "I'm not a whore, Harry, if that's what you're thinking."

The word grated on him and he tried hard not to be taken aback. Stumbling now, he said, "I didn't mean that at all. I'm just trying to make conversation. Was it the wrong thing to say?"

"No, not really. He's very kind to me, and...well, we've been together for a long time now."

113

"What's a long time among friends?"

"Ten years."

"Ten years! Good heavens, I...well, that *is* a long time."

"You've seen my passport, Harry, you know how old I am. I was fourteen then."

"Well..." His voice trailed off lamely. Recovering, he said, "Well, down in the deep south, back home..."

"Yes, yes, I know that, too."

"He's a good fellow, all right, in patches, but...Shall we sit down for a while?"

"If you like. No scorpions?"

He took off his bush-jacket and spread it on the ground, feeling the cool air on his naked chest. "No scorpions."

She sat down carefully in the middle of it, and he sank down beside her, twisting round so that he could half-face her, leaning on one elbow so as to leave one hand carefully free when he should need it. He said to himself, *Well, what the hell am I waiting for?*

The dry grass was sweet-smelling with wild basil, and he rubbed his hand into it and gave it to her to smell, and she said, laughing, "It reminds me of goulash."

He laughed with her then, and said, "That's a hell of a gambit to open a love-play with."

She turned and looked at him, and he thought he detected a masked hostility which he could not understand. "Is that what this is, Harry? A love-play?"

"I'd like it to be."

She looked away from him, not answering, and he put out his hand and slipped it under her robe, feeling the soft roughness of the terrycloth at the back of his hand and the smoothness of her breast under his fingertips. He felt her tremble, and sure now that the moment had come, he slid his hand on to the taut flesh of her stomach, pulling her close to him and kissing her, and when she did not struggle, he lay back with her on his side, letting her be beneath him and feeling with his lips the hot flesh of her shoulder. She began to struggle, and he said, very softly, "Anna, my darling, keep still" She said, "No - no, Harry," and her struggles became violent. He could not see her face, and knowing that this was all part of the rigmarole, the ancient show of a fight, he pulled the robe away from her breast and slipped it back under her shoulder, looking at the beauty of her and feeling the softness of her under his cheek. Her breathing was hard, and her struggling stopped, and then, in his moment of triumph, there was a sudden searing pain at the side of his neck, and when he twisted away in shock he saw her hand move away, one deliberate finger curled in a short sharp motion that had ripped the skin off his throat and brought the blood flowing. He rolled away from her in surprise, staring at her, not understanding. Her breast was exposed, and she lay there not moving, looking at him with venom in her eyes and he did not know why. Then she moved to cover herself and said quietly, "I said no, Harry."

He could feel the blood on his hand when he touched his throat, and the sudden anger began to mount in him. He climbed to his feet and she put out a hand for him to help her, and he lifted her up and stood there for a moment, bewildered, saying nothing while she straightened her robe and went quickly away from him. He watched her go towards her tent, waiting for her to look back and show that she would change her mind, but in a little while, when there was no sign from her, he went after her to where the tents were and saw that her light was out.

He could feel the sharp pain of the fury inside him. He stumbled over to where Talib lay and shook him, and said savagely, "The girl Chep, send her to me, now."

He went to his tent and undressed and lay on his cot and waited, and when she came, moving silently in the absolute darkness so that he had to grope for her and was not sure, at first, who it was, he pulled her down beside him and made long and violent love to her, a fifteen-year-old slave girl whose only

115

purpose in life was to serve those who were her betters in whatever way she was needed.

And when he had finished with her, he lay back exhausted, too spent to hear the soft rustle she made as she wound her silk sarong round her tiny waist and moved like a shadow out of the tent and into the darkness again. Sleep would not come to him, and he tossed and turned, waiting for the violent anger to go from him.

The light in the east was touching the sky before he fell asleep.

CHAPTER 8

When he came to breakfast the next morning, hesitant, the thin red scar on his throat covered with a strip of plaster, von Abart was already sitting, with Anna, at the folding canvas and hardwood table where they had their meals.

There had been a long moment of fear, when he was quite sure that she would have told her lover what had happened, and that there would be a stand-up row there and then, with all the cards on the table and no gambits barred. He had braced himself for trouble, for bad trouble, going so far as to convince himself that the only way out of it all would be to lie solidly and convincingly and say, with blatant and bewildered innocence, that Anna was simply not telling the truth. He had pursued the fancy through the next logical steps.

"Oh, and why not, Mr. Stanton?"

(A shrug.) "Well, you know her better than I do."

"I don't think she would lie for no reason."

"The heart has its reasons, etcetera, etcetera."

"You are a fool, Mr. Stanton, and a swine."

"Go to hell, Herr von Abart! Go to hell!"

And the next step? A farcical Teutonic duel, with honor and dignity looming large? A sabre-cut across the cheek and all is well? A secret stalking in the jungle with a quick bullet to put an end to it all? Was the German capable of so definite a solution to his problems? Was he himself capable of it? The thought was a sudden shock to him, and he shuddered and went out to face what was there for him.

Von Abart, his mouth full, looked at the plaster and said, "Cut yourself, Harry? Good morning."

He knew then that all his worrying was for nothing. He smiled easily and said, "A dull razor. How did we all sleep?"

Anna was pouring his coffee for him with a gesture that he found—what was the word? Domestic? She passed his cup and said, "I slept like a log. A really good night's rest." She looked at the reds and the greens of the trees and the earth, and said, "A day like this, it's good to be alive."

He knew then that for reasons of her own, she would keep the secret that was between them, and from this thought came another. *Oh? Then that means I must try again, and soon, too.* The secret was a bond between them, linking them together, and he knew, from long experience, that in the proper order of things there came first the mental intercourse and then the physical. It was part of a ritual as old as the swamps themselves, and he was happy to accept it as such. He looked at her and saw that she smiled back at him, and he tucked the awareness of her secret pleasure at the back of his mind, knowing now that the first and greatest danger was gone, and that now, however violent should be his attempts on her, the secret would always have to be kept because now it was too late for her to do anything about it at all. Now, he thought, it is only a matter of time.

He looked her over coolly, enjoying again, in retrospect, the close intimate touch of her body, of the hidden flesh, and knowing that the first step, already taken, had been a giant one. The night's abortive efforts had not been wasted. He ate with enjoyment, looking out over the brightness of the grass beyond the shades of the trees, seeing the sudden bright patches of red and yellow flowers, and thinking that the Malaya he loved had never been so beautiful as it was now, at this minute.

The excitement was on him. The hunting that he loved was under way, in both fields, he told himself, the wide green field that is the trapping ground, and the narrow red field that is the bed. And as an afterthought, he added to himself, *And en route, on the way there, there's always Chep.*

Von Abart looked at him and said, "The tiger, I moved him into a bigger cage this morning."

"Oh? That's what the noise was."

"Easy enough. He's already beginning to quieten down. He's a beauty, I think he knows he's the first captive, the head of the list. It gives him a sense of authority, a certain prestige. I think he knows this."

"And very proper, too."

"There's always the king," von Abart said, musing. "Nobility of birth, there's no substitute for it. The lesser animals, they always try to rob the king of his pride or sit in his shadow, but they'll never take away his nobility. It's here, Harry." He tapped at his chest. "Here, inside him. Sometimes he'll let the carrion-eaters feast on what he's finished with, but only when he has no further use for it. Ever notice that, Harry? Of course, you must have. Only when he's through with it."

The unease was there again. It was hard not to look across at Anna and see what she was thinking, He heard her say dryly, "It's not always easy to know, Otto, just when the tiger has finished his meal, is it? He likes to leave it tucked away some place and come back to it when his appetite returns."

It was getting altogether too apposite. He said heartily, forcing a smile, "A good beginning, a good specimen. Now it's a leopard we want, a big one."

"Another thing," von Abart said. "Talib tells me that some lemur were seen in the trees over there this morning. Black and white."

"Oh? The Indris?"

"Sounds like it, I thought I'd walk over and take a look. We may as well take a couple if they're coming to our front doorstep."

"Good. We'll need the light nets, some axes."

Von Abart pushed his plate away and brushed the back of his hand across his mouth. "What about the leopard? Today? Tomorrow?"

"I'm waiting for Baka to come in."

"Then I'll go and look at the lemur. If you want me, fire a couple of shots."

"All right."

As soon as he had gone, his bulk moving easily and lightly past the ferns and the bamboos, Stanton said softly, "I was afraid for a moment that there was an allegory in what he was saying."

He could not tell whether the almost imperceptible smile on her face was for him or for herself. She said calmly, "He is not so subtle."

He touched the plaster at his throat and said, forcing the game, "Your nails are sharp."

Her pale eyes examined him for a moment, and then she looked away. He said easily, pushing home the advantage, "I hope you don't feel too badly about last night. As badly as I do."

She would not be drawn into the fight. He went on, "A beautiful woman, a dark warm night. You're beginning to mean a lot to me. More than you should. You're important to me, you must know that."

"I'm important to him, too, Harry," It was a flat statement of fact, challenging him. He wanted to answer sharply, And is he important to you? But he did not like the finality of the implication this might make, so he said instead, knowing that he could bide his time and saying to himself again, *Well, there's always Chep...*

"Yes, I suppose you are. Though without wanting to pry

too much into your affairs..." A little hesitation, to be sure, and then, "I'm a light sleeper. Unless he moves very quietly in the night, he stays in his own tent. Doesn't he?"

She bit her lip and he chalked up a victory. She said, a faint edge to her voice, "It's not quite as simple as all that, Harry."

"No? He doesn't exactly present the picture of a jealous lover, does he? Or did you expect me not to notice? He seems quite happy that we're frequently alone together. Is he so sure of you, is that it? Or is he so sure of me? Hell, what a thought!"

The tension was gone again, so completely that he wondered if it had ever been there. She said (a little sadly, he thought), "He likes other men to admire me, Harry. As I told you before, I'm his best trophy. A showpiece that you can look at but mustn't touch. A stuffed head in a museum. Not quite under a glass case because it's not really as valuable as all that, but— well, a record catch. Evidence of past prowess rather than of present worth."

He knew that she was stumbling, trying to tell him something, hesitating not because she was afraid to come out and say it, but because she was not sure of his capacity to understand the motives that drove her. He wondered, too, if she was saying, *This far and no farther*, and he told himself that this just wasn't enough. He said, as lightly as he could manage, knowing that she was coming over to his side and if not yet giving way, at least knowing that his effort was a natural one, "That's a pretty unpleasant implication. And a pretty dangerous one, too, He must know that admiration can easily get out of hand."

Frowning, she said somberly, "I often wonder if he'd really mind. Inside him, I know...But don't you see, it would be beneath his dignity to let his feelings show, and to admit, openly, what he really felt. It's as though he wants me to be loved, I mean physically, and if he can't, if he doesn't have enough to offer me, then it's all right provided he doesn't openly know about it. Do you see what I mean?"

"Like hell?"

She stood up, and folded her arms tight across her body, walking slowly up and down as she talked, frowning, not quite being able to explain herself.

"There was a time once, Harry, when we had a young Czech writer staying with us, a good-looking boy not more than twenty-five, twenty-six years old. A ladies' man, very conscious of his good looks. He tried to court me, openly, embarrassingly, in front of Otto, not caring a damn. It so happens that I didn't like him, I even felt a strong distaste for him, you know how it is. I felt that if he wanted to - to cuckold Otto, then at least he could be courteous enough to hide it from him, but no, he couldn't be bothered, and it was this kind of contempt that I found unpleasant. I swear to you, there was never anything between us, even though once I had to fight him off, almost, physically, We were at the top of the stairs just outside my bedroom, and he was pushing me against the wall like a passionate schoolboy, just not understanding why I wouldn't go to bed with him, not believing that anyone could refuse him. You know the type. And then Otto came in unexpectedly, and although Franz, that's the Czech boy, had pulled away quickly and put on an air of innocence, Otto must have been able to tell that—well, at least that I'd been struggling, one way or another. He said nothing. Of course, he wouldn't. But later that night, just as I was going into my room, Otto stopped me and said, very carefully, 'Just never let me know, Anna.' That's all, right out of the blue. And nothing more was ever said about it. He couldn't have spoken to Franz either, because Franz was worse than ever, It was almost as if - as if he approved. And when Franz had gone back to Prague, a week later, when we were sitting together in the library looking over some old prints, Otto said casually, 'You didn't like our writer friend, did you?' I told him, then, that I didn't like people who tried to force themselves on me, and he said, 'Do you hate him?'

I knew exactly what he meant."

She stood in front of Stanton, looking down, using her hands to drive home the point. She said, "Otto will never come out and say what he really means. What he meant was, did I have *cause* to hate him? Had he made love to me before he went back to his ladies? So I said, 'No, I just don't like him, that's all.' He patted me affectionately, the way he does, and went back to concentrating on his prints. But I never quite knew what he was thinking. I didn't know whether or not he had made a deduction and nothing was going to change his mind, or whether he was just brushing the whole thing aside as of no consequence."

He could not make up his mind whether she was speaking kindly or harshly of von Abart. He said tartly, "Well, I'm damned if I'd want to share you with anyone else," and then said quickly, realizing that he could hardly support his argument, "Well, what I mean is...well, you know what I mean."

She said slowly, "You haven't understood a word of what I've been saying, Harry, have you?"

"Of course I have. You're telling me that he's a very liberal man, that's all. Only I don't know why you should feel badly about it."

Looking at him coldly, showing no love in her features, she said somberly, "Do I have to spell it out for you, Harry? I'm trying to tell you what's wrong with him. Don't you understand? He's impotent. Can you realize what that means to a man like Otto?"

Feeling like an imbecile, he sat and stared at her. He said at last, knowing that there were things here he would never understand, "But...I thought that..."

She waved her hand at him with an impatient gesture. "Not always, of course. But for the last two or three years. He used to be...well, quite different. He was strong and vigorous, all that a woman could want, but now it's two years or more since he...since he succeeded."

Putting himself in second place and not feeling the indignity of it, he said, "You're a hot-blooded woman, Anna, don't tell me you're not, I should have thought that, under the circumstances, you'd welcome a little emotional relief."

He could not have used a worse phrase. The coldness was there again. She stood up abruptly and said, "On my terms, Harry. On my terms."

She turned away and was gone to her tent before he could press her to tell him what those terms were.

Von Abart came back a couple of hours later, in a wonderful mood. He walked jauntily, his rifle slung upside-down over his shoulder. He said cheerfully, his voice loud, "The true Indris, Harry, three of them, black and white, splendid coats. They're high up in the trees there, and they look as though they're going to stay."

Stanton had been cleaning out the carburetor of one of the trucks that had become clogged with dirt. Now he was standing in the crude shelter that served as a shower-bath, while one of the Tamils, crouched in the branches of the tree above him, was pouring water out of an empty gasoline can over his body.

Anna came out of her tent and said excitedly, "It's too good to be true. Can we get them now?"

Von Abart found the brandy bottle and drank from its neck. The sweat was shining on his red face.

"Not a care in the world, sitting at the top of that clump of trees where the patch of scarlet is. Three of them, long, long coats, the best I've ever seen."

Anna turned and called to Stanton, "Did you hear, Harry? Let's get over there and bring them down."

Stanton wrapped a towel round his waist and came out of the shower. Standing there in the sunlight, with the water bright on the muscles of his chest, his feet wide-spread, he said, "Give me five minutes and I'm with you. Can we take a truck?"

"Why not? It's four miles, more or less, flat hard earth all the way."

"All right, round up some boys and the nets and I'll be right with you."

He went to his tent and slipped into his clothes, and in a few moments they all piled into one of the trucks with Talib and two of the Sakai. They crouched like animals, the Sakai, accepting now the wonder of the machine, smoking the cigarettes they had been given rather than the pipes they normally use because this lent them prestige. They sat on top of the leaky gas-cans, and smoked in cheerful innocence, and soon the truck was heading for the hills.

When they came to the tall clump of trees where the orchids were, they clambered down and stood looking up at the high, flimsy branches where the lemurs were squatting, and then one of the Sakai crushed out his cigarette (tucking the residue carefully into the band at his waist) and climbed quickly up the almost perpendicular trunk, moving with extraordinary rapidity because this was a thing he had been doing for a thousand years. But he wondered, with a kind of blank bewilderment, what the white men would want with this kind of monkey because it was not the kind that could be trained to fetch food for you and was, moreover, dangerous to tamper with. He disappeared into the branches high in the air, and they saw him re-emerge with an orchid that he had plucked, stuck into the hair behind his ear, and von Abart said impatiently, "For God's sake!"

Talib was standing by with a long wooden club, waiting. They heard the angry screech of the ape as the Sakai thrust his spear at it, prodding it, forcing it to fall, They saw it retreat higher to the topmost branches, the slender ones, too slender, it seemed to bear the weight of a man; too slender, perhaps, for a man, but not for a Sakai.

Soon, they could only hear the fight that was going on up

there, too deep in the foliage for them to see, and in a little while they heard the Sakai yell and Talib (a Malay, and therefore his old enemy, but the lords of the jungle had sent the white men to see that he would not be harmed) went running forward swinging his club. And then, with a swing and a jump, the lemur was on the ground, its long arms raised high above its head and scurrying for the shelter of the other trees from which it had so carelessly strayed. Talib, moving fast but not so fast as the ape, stopped and hurled his club. It hit squarely at the base of the skull and the animal went down, and then the Sakai came slipping down from the tree, staring in horror at the ape's limp body, and suddenly he was gone, gone from their sight back into the darkness of the jungle, and when Stanton, wondering, looked round for the other Sakai, he had disappeared too, and Talib, grinning and jeering, said, "They run, Tuan, they afraid."

Stanton nodded, knowing that for the Sakai, only witchcraft could cause an Indri to fall from a thrown stick because if you throw a spear at one of them he will catch it and throw it back with unerring accuracy, and never, in the long history of the Sakai and of the jungle, has an Indri failed to kill an assailant who was so thoughtless as to catch one in this manner. To them, it was frightening evidence of supernatural powers, and they had gone to mutter in their frightened hideouts, crouching in the darkness under the tree-roots until the awful danger should have passed them by.

He said, "Will they come back? To the camp?"

"They will come soon, Tuan, They will try and open cage, let monkey go free."

"Tell them...tell them that if they do that, I will send the devils to punish them."

Talib nodded gravely. "I tell them, Tuan. Also I put one man stay watching, all time, watching. Malay man, keep guard."

"Good. Now let's get him back to the camp."

Von Abart was peering up into the branches, his head

thrown back, squinting through the shadows of the leaves, "What about a female? There's a good one up there."

"Without the Sakai? Can you climb a tree like that?"

Von Abart, grinning, shook his head. "Talib?"

Talib was fastening a cord about the lemur's waist, its long black hair mingling with streaks of white so that its skin looked for all the world like an opera cloak from a past century. He nodded gravely, "I can climb, Tuan. With net, I catch."

"All right, get to work."

He took one of the nets from the truck, slipped a rope loosely round his ankles, and began the slow ascent, the net draped over his broad brown shoulders and his huge arms gripping the wide trunk. Soon, he was high in the upper branches, and the rustling of the struggle began as he edged slowly towards the ape which von Abart had pointed out to him. They stood below, watching, shouting encouragement, making a game of it because they were aware of Talib's faint shame that it should be harder for him than for a Sakai. Twice he threw the net and missed his mark, holding on to a corner of it and hauling it up to try again when it fell. Once he lost his balance and nearly dropped to the earth far below, but at last the net found its mark and the angry screeching told them the monkey was caught. They waited a long time now before it was secured, but then it came gently floating down, flurrying softly within the confines of the nylon mesh at the end of a long rope, grey and white and looking, in the shadows, like the ghost that had given it its name, Indri.

Soon, the pair of them, with cords around their waists, were bundled without ceremony, one of them unconscious and the other quickly resigned to her fate, into the back of the truck.

They drove slowly back to the camp, and soon a gentle, frightened whining told Stanton that both of them were recovering from the shock of the harsh treatment he had given them and were worried about their food. He climbed unsteadily into the rear and pulled some bananas off a hand that someone had procured. One of the lemurs took it from him with a worried look on its sad face, quite tame and mild-mannered, and began to eat it slowly, squatting there with its regal cape about its shoulders and looking like the ambassador to a foreign court. The other was lying on its back and scratching, quite unconcerned, at its belly, and when he examined it carefully, to make sure that Talib's club had done no harm, they looked at him and whimpered a little and then went back to their solemn musing. And at the compound, they allowed themselves to be led unprotesting into the cage that had been prepared for them. As they passed the tiger, stalking moodily close to the stakes that confined him, they scurried to the end of the rope in sudden fright, then walked into their cage holding hands like lovers on their way to a stroll in the fields.

Stanton wished his own life could be as simple and uncluttered as theirs.

CHAPTER 9

Now he began to look at von Abart as a rival to be dislodged from his secure position.

As a hunter, Stanton knew, the rivalry could no longer exist, because his own competence was as great as the German's and the fame, he knew, was coming to him surely as well, just as surely as, with age, it was leaving von Abart. Soon, Stanton would be the number one man in the field, the best hunter, the best trapper, an expert on his subject, a man who would write books about animals that would become major works of reference. It was important to him that this should be so, because the only lesson of his inheritance was the lesson of competition. They had drilled it into him even in school, and then in the Army the lesson had shown its value. Without that competitive edge of superiority he would not have survived, because the small, vicious, death-dealing Japanese had also learned both the terrors and the comforts of the jungle, and only by learning these things a little better himself had he been able to stay alive when the rest of his unit had slowly, one by one, died, leaving their crude graves to show that the competition had been lost.

The fight itself, like all fights in this philosophy, had become unimportant to him; it was the winning that counted. And now, looking at von Abart as a rival for Anna's acquiescence, he knew that he must make the effort and dislodge him, even temporarily, from a position that he did not have the stamina (and therefore the right) to hold any longer. A token victory would suffice; it need be no more than that.

At the back of his mind there was, on occasion, a faint distaste for what he was planning to do, because outright deceit was foreign to him - even though he had played this game many times before. But before, it had been a straight battle between man and woman with no one else on the sidelines; at least, not quite so close.

He remembered that there had once been a wild affair with a girl named Evelyn, who had a bad-tempered husband somewhere, but on that occasion he had carefully avoided meeting the husband, not because he feared him, but merely because he was able to persuade himself that it didn't really matter too much if the man he betrayed was a perfect stranger. He could always pretend that the unseen enemy was a lout who beat his wife up, and even though he didn't believe this, at least it was a salve to his conscience.

But von Abart was too damned close. He had accepted the position as second in command, the older man relegated to a Junior position, with no more than a passing comment on that one occasion, and after that he had been careful to make it clear that the major decisions would be left to him, to Stanton. His behavior, in this respect at least, had been impeccable. And there was always the sneaking regard for his damned reputation, an admiration which he could not successfully put behind him.

And so, not consciously looking for them, and not understanding the reason because he did not have the analytical habit, he began to find in von Abart little unpleasant quirks that he had not noticed before. They helped him to shoulder aside his feeling of trespass.

There was the way he always spoke with his mouth full, using his fork to gesture with (and even so, insisting always on his nobility of birth). There was the patronizing air he put on with the Malays and with the Tamils, treating them no better than the miserable, frightened Sakai, and therefore offending them mortally. And above all, there was the contemptuous ease with which he seemed willing to leave the two of them alone together, noticing but not caring that Anna's animal exuberance sometimes left her body casually displayed in doses that were rapidly becoming too much for Stanton. Justifying himself, he thought, *Can you look at so much beauty and not want to enjoy it move fully?*

They went deep into the jungle, on foot, leaving the camp far behind them.

In single file, Talib at their head, they marched through the tunnels which the elephant and the buffalo had made, feeling the splashes of water which dripped on them from the dark green roof above them, smelling the strong sour scent of rotting humus, plucking the leeches from their legs, the round fat leeches that were small enough to find their way through the eyeholes of their swamp boots and then swell up to disgusting and formidable balloons filled with blood. They splashed knee-deep through slimy water in which the crocodiles were sleeping, listening to the raucous sounds that came at them from the tree-tops, where somewhere up there in the thick green blanket the birds and the apes were watching them.

Once, they lost their way and found that the paths they were following had dwindled into a liana-covered morass of tightly woven vines that even their sharp parangs could not cut through, and they retraced their steps, knowing that here in the thorned tangle they could easily become, permanently, part of the slime that was building up there through the years. When darkness fell, they found a patch of drier land and slept there, finding relief from the merciless leeches that slept, like man, at night, but suffering the torments of the mosquitoes that clustered about their faces as they flung their nets about them. They rubbed themselves with cinnamon oil, uselessly, and drank heavily from the brandy bottles to stave off the coming malaria, and in the morning they woke to hear Talib, crouched on his haunches in the clearing, clutching two sticks and saying softly, "*Diam*, Tuan...quiet."

Stanton watched as he drummed softly on a spread banana leaf with his sticks, listening to the gentle rumbling and knowing that he was calling to someone. He climbed silently from his resting place, pushing aside the net, seeing the splashes of blood where, sleeping, he had struck at the biting mosquitoes. He moved quietly over to where Anna was waking up (glancing involuntarily at von Abart), and touched her on the arm. He whispered, "Have you seen this?"

She shook her head and watched, and von Abart slowly struggled out of his sleep and waited, and there was a great silence about them, broken only by Talib's faint, insistent drumming. They could hear the distant splash of water somewhere, faint, far away.

Soon, an answering drumming came to them, a faster, louder noise, and now, Stanton saw, one of the Sakai was creeping forward with a blowgun. He moved in absolute silence, crouched low, his agile limbs like roots of the trees about him, his scarred feet bare on the silent earth. The drumming stopped and Talib glanced at the Sakai and then began again, louder now, and in a moment a plandok, the small Malayan deer, poked its inquisitive nose into the clearing. They kept perfectly still, watching, and saw it look for a fallen leaf, find one, and start drumming with its hoofs, sending a message for its mate, answering the call of Talib's drum, deceived into its death. They heard the short sharp spit of the blowgun, and they saw the plandok leap into the air and fall struggling, and then it jumped to its feet again, stumbled once, and lay there, dead, and Talib went over and picked it up and cut its throat, and when he came back he said simply, "Breakfast, Tuan," and tossed it to the cook.

They ate their roast venison, drank their tea, and moved on, and by noon, not knowing that the sun was high, because they could not see beyond the jungles roof, they came to the salt lick they had been searching for. The Sakai who had come with them shouted their pleasure and ran to the muddy deposits, squatting down beside it, plunging their hands into it and licking their fingers ravenously. They sat there for an hour, ignoring Talib's anger, devouring the saline mud in astonishing gluttony, and when they had finished, they lay down and slept. Stanton, watching them said, "All right, let them sleep. There's plenty of work when they wake up." He called Talib over and said, "The white rhino? This is where he came?"

"Yes, Tuan." He pointed to the sharp scratches at the edge of the salt lick and said, "There, Tuan, like same animal. Rhino."

Anna looked down at it, then crouched on her haunches and examined it carefully, measuring the three-toed spoor, feeling the depth of it with the tips of her fingers. She nodded her agreement. "Sondaicus, Harry, I'm sure."

Von Abart, the perfect partner, was peering into the darkness of the jungle, pointing. "There," he said, "this is the way he comes. We'll dig a pit across the track. Just about here. Then, it's just a question of time."

Stanton looked at his watch, grimacing. "Six hours to darkness. The boys can start making a raft. We'll have to drag him over to the river and hope it's wide enough to float him down to the valley. Talib!"

Talib, calling the boys together, came back for his orders.

"A raft," Stanton said. "Get some bamboo cut, some rattan, make up a raft, a strong one. Send one of the men to find the nearest approach to the river, and you can cut a track through for four or five hours. No noise any later, in case he's close by. I want the raft on the river within two or three hours. One of the

Sakai can gather salt for the rest of them, make it up into banana-leaf pouches, and they can carry back as much as they want. But first, the raft. Then I want you to go with the Mem and she'll identify any other tracks you find for her, all right?" He turned to Anna and watched her rolling up the leg of her trousers.

He said cheerfully, "Leeches?" She nodded. He lit a cigarette and handed it to her and watched her burn the head of a sucker that was fastened tightly into the flesh of her calf, and said, grinning, "I should get a photograph of that for *Vogue*."

He turned back to Talib and said, "Four men with shovels to dig a pit, the Tuan will show you where. The length of a shovel deep, the length of two shovels broad, and right across the tunnel the rhino uses. I want it covered with liana, branches, leaves, anything you can find. But God help you if I can see it when you've finished with it, you understand?"

Talib nodded gravely. "You not see, Tuan, rhino not see. Even Sakai not see. No stakes in hole, Tuan, better we put net down there too?"

"Good. No stakes, we don't want to harm him. Spread a net across the bottom then, four ropes from the corners, and the rest is up to you. And I want a nice clear space to sleep on tonight, with some stakes for our mosquito nets. No fires after five o'clock, so tell Suleiman to get the evening meal cooked before then. No drinking for anybody until the animals have come to the lick and we've trapped our rhino, and if anybody makes a noise, well, you know what will happen to them."

"No noise, Tuan." Talib touched the parang he carried at his waist. "Parang sharp like kris, man make noise I cut bloody throat. No noise."

Von Abart, slapping at the insects that were feasting on him, went off along one of the trails, looking for spoor, and when he had gone, crouched low under the overhang, Stanton moved over to Anna, standing close beside her and helping her scrape the already caking mud off her clothes. It came off in flat chunks of clay, leaving dark marks on the khaki cloth at her flanks. He ran his hand along the smooth tautness of her thigh and said slowly, smiling his best smile, "The mortification of the flesh. Doesn't it seem a shame? The lice, the mosquitoes, the leeches, they're draining your blood."

"Woman into hunter, I think you said. The absence of elegance. Isn't that what you wanted, what you couldn't believe in?"

"I believe in it now. And I want you now. More than ever."

"I know that, Harry."

"On your terms, you said. Any terms will do, Anna." He said earnestly, showing her how sincere he was, "I need you badly, it's almost more than I can bear. I lie awake at night, thinking of you."

"You're supposed to be thinking of the hunt."

She began to laugh, then, knowing suddenly that this too was part of him, the hunt in both his fields, and to dull the edge of her malice, she said, "As long as you don't want to make me a trophy, too. Another skin to put under your feet."

"It's more than that, you must know it is."

"You mean a permanent arrangement? Is that what you want, Harry?"

He knew that he must not hesitate now, but he could not think up a reply quickly enough. He said lamely, again, "On any terms, Anna, anything you want."

"And yet you know nothing about me. Less than you knew about your Cora."

Now he was back in his stride again, He said quickly, "No, you're wrong there. It's important to me, the physical act. And it is to you, too, I know. Every time I touch you I can feel it, I know it." He wished that her English were not so fluent, so that he could take advantage of a tongue that was a little more foreign to her. "Do you know what I mean? You let me touch you, like this. There's only one end to the feeling I have for you, and sooner or later...Don't you think?"

"Sooner or later, Harry."

"Goddammit, don't be so goddam casual about it! You're not going to put me off by pretending it means so little to you, because I know better. Here, at least, I know you better than I knew Cora. Of this, I am sure. You want to tell me I'm wrong?"

"No, Harry, you're right."

Exasperated, he said, "Then for God's sake—I want to feel you in my arms, close to me, lovers, can't you understand that? Don't you know what I'm saying? I'm saying I love you, Anna."

His hand was on her breast, under her shirt, unheeded. She said coolly, "Here comes Otto, Harry." He thought she spoke a great deal louder than was necessary, and he hastily turned away, forcing himself not to turn red in the face, and then von Abart came into sight, moving backwards through the thick bushes, sweeping at the wet mud behind him with a branch to obliterate his trail. Stanton was surprised how quietly he moved; surprised, too, that she had heard him coming.

He said loudly, "Well, what did you find?"

Von Abart ran the back of his hand over his wet forehead. "The sooner we get out of this damned swamp the better I'll like it. But our sondaicus is out there. I found the tracks of a black rhino too, but a small one, no good to us."

"Oh? On the same trail as ours?"

"More or less. He's using the same tunnel, in parts. Let's hope he keeps out of our pit. I also picked up a water-snake."

He held out a stick at arm's length. A noose at the end was tight round the neck of a four-foot snake that writhed and twisted to get free. "Watch out for his teeth, he's poisonous. Have we got a canvas bag?"

Stanton opened one of the boxes that had been set down by the porters and pulled out a bag. Holding the neck wide, he said, "All right, in he goes."

"Look at the markings, like a moccasin. And you see the teeth? Three broken off and the successional teeth still not fully in place."

"Shove him in, for God's sake, we've got no serum with us."

Von Abart pushed the end of his stick deep into the bag, pulled the fastening cords tight, and pulled it out again. Stanton could feel the angry motion of its coils, and then it was still. He put the bag inside another, for added safety, and placed it carefully back in the box.

Deep in the forest they could hear the rhythmic chopping of the parangs on the stout bamboo stalks, and soon Talib came over and told him that the raft the men were making was ready. He nodded. "And a way to the river?"

"Very close, Tuan. Men cut track there now. Water wild, but not too much maybe."

"All right, let's take a look at the raft."

It was a little way down the trail that was being cut to the river, and one of the Semang Negritos, the expert, was standing by it waiting for the master's approbation. Twenty thick poles formed the bottom, their nodes making a natural buoyancy chamber, and a broad platform had been built across it from other poles that had been securely lashed into place with rattan. One end of the raft was pointed, and at the other a flat board of timber had been lashed to serve as a steering paddle, and two long stakes had been cut for the punters.

"Two men to punt, to push it along? That won't be enough."

"Enough, Tuan. The water very white, go down very fast."

"And where does it come out?"

"One man go down river, Tuan, find where best place we meet it, come back tonight. Like this, no trouble; take rhino through animal track, too heavy, water take him no cost, no trouble."

"Good. I want a good man on board. He'll have to watch out for the rocks. We lose the raft, we lose the rhino."

"No lose, Tuan. I tell Sakai man he get raft back to place we meet, he keep raft for him."

"Good. You're doing a good job, Talib."

"Best head-boy in business, Tuan."

"We get back to camp I'll find you that rifle I spoke about."

"Good, Tuan. Very pleased. Good gun, good head-boy."

Looking at his watch, he said, "Another hour it'll be dark. Tell Suleiman to serve dinner, and then I want absolute quiet for the rest of the night. If the rhino comes in the night, we'll leave him in the pit until morning and get him out in daylight."

They could hear the night birds all around them. The better to see what they could in the half-light where the moon filtered like a phantom through the trees on to the salt lick, they had taken up their positions high in the ironwood branches of a mangrove, its roots feeling at the caked mud of the salt lick like the elongated fingers of the Sakai who had so greedily scraped at its saline surfaces.

Throughout the long night the animals came to taste the salt. They could not hear their footfalls, but the sound of the gentle rasping came up to them as they sat there in the silence, as the coarse tongues of a dozen wild animals scraped at the hardened mud. There came, first, the small neat antelope that the Malays called Kanchil, and then a pack of wild dog which frightened the antelope away. A tapir wallowed deeper into the wet mud, splashing his great elephantine nose when he found the salt water, and then the dark grey bulk of a rhino. Stanton tensed, staring below and trying to make out its color, Anna put out her hand and touched his arm, and when he squeezed it surreptitiously she pulled it away and pointed to the bushes by their trap. As he watched, marveling at the acuteness of her senses, he saw the bright green eyes of a cat and saw that it was a panther, a black one. He made a motion with his hands, meaning too small, and the panther looked up at the mangrove and then was gone, moving as fast and as silently, almost, as a frightened Sakai. A wild buffalo, the seladang, came blundering noisily through the trees, contemptuous in its great size of any danger that might threaten, knowing that its massive shoulders could shrug it off unharmed. Stanton made a mental note to set up a pit for buffalo here, too, knowing that this could be left to the boys to handle.

They waited impatiently until the slight greying of the blackness told them that daylight, outside the dark confines of the jungle, was already making its appearance, and then they heard it. First, there was the sullen snorting that told them the rhino was close by, and this, at first, was all they learned.

But the Sakai, listening below in the cover they had chosen under the roots of the tree, could have told them more; that the scratching sound of sharp horn on timber meant its horn was a long one and that, therefore, it was a male, That the sound also meant there was only one horn instead of two, and therefore it was grey in color. That the faint muffled sound that accompanied its movement was the rubbing of its folds of skin over the fore shoulders and that therefore it was the kind they knew came many years ago from far to the south and that therefore the glue that held the hairs of its horn together would be an antidote to snake poison, as their ancestor, the python, had told them, many thousands of years ago, when the python had thrown his ancient venom away for the lesser snakes to pick up. His snorting told them, too, that he was angry, that he was suspicious, and that, although he could not see the pit they had so carefully hidden, he knew that something was not as it should be.

Crouching there among the wet roots, their naked bodies damp and cold, they listened and waited, knowing, too, from the direction of the sounds he made, that he was forcing a way past the trail where the pit was waiting, avoiding it, not knowing what was wrong but picking up a scent he did not like. They knew too, what the scent was—it was the stink of their ancient enemy the Malay, the big man, Talib his name, who would not harm them because the friendly white men who were his masters would not let him. But, they said to themselves wisely, you can't fool A-Gap the rhinoceros.

Now one of them, a frail old man named Ojag, his belly distended with the white man's rice, crept without sound out of his root-cover, moving over dry thorn and wet mud in the same absolute silence until he was standing at the edge of the clearing by the trail where the trap had been set. He stood up now, to his full proud height of five feet, and took off the bark-cloth that was tucked up under his loins, and waved it like a flag, dangling it on the ground and shaking it. And then the rhino looked at him, and at the rag, and began to worry the earth with the point of its horn, cutting deep angry furrows in the mud, snorting his bad temper at the disturbance. It kicked up the earth with its sharp hoofs, and then it charged, and Ojag, wise with the knowledge of his years, held his ground, and in a violent flurry of branches and leaves, the rhino went down, crashing into the pit and bellowing angrily, and then the white men came down from their trees, looking at the trapped animal and wondering at the size of him, and even the hated Malay, whose name was Talib, and who perhaps after all was a good man—but only while the white people would not let him kill them or drink their blood—was pleased with the action he had taken, pleased that he had known what to do and had, without orders, done it.

Talib, the good man, also knowing what to do, took hold of Ojag's hand and held it while he told the other Sakai, gravely, "This is a wise man, who knew that A-Gap the rhinoceros would not fall into the pit we had dug for him, and so went out in the night with courage to guide him to his capture, and for this he is a great man and I will tell my people that they must not enslave the people of Ojag the wise Sakai but must treat him with respect as a leader of his people. Moreover, when he goes back to his village, he will take bags of salt to the chief and maybe some cigarettes too and they will know of his great wisdom. And from this time, he shall no longer be called Ojag, but A-Gap."

When daylight came, they took hold of the ropes at the four corners of the sunken net, and they heaved and struggled, and soon the vicious, savage sondaicus, his ill-temper flaming in his tiny eyes, his grey hairs bristling, was being unceremoniously dragged to the edge of the river where the raft was waiting for him. And, as evidence of his new authority, A-Gap, who used to be known as Ojag, was put in charge of the journey downstream.

The shikar returned to its base.

The following day, they set out in the trucks from the camp, heading for the edge of the forest where the river, a raging torrent here, came out of the jungle and entered the wide cuneiform of the valley.

The clearing they were camped in—and where the building of the compound was going on apace - sloped gently down on one side until it reached the moist humus that lay below, and here the trees grew more densely, growing towards the jungle itself. The soft tones of the clearing turned to the harsher colors, and the hornbills sat sunning themselves there, never far from the cover they sometimes sought. In the river itself, the water snakes splashed and the crocodile rested like rotten logs while the tick-birds picked at the insects in their great yellow teeth, and the insects hummed about them. The water boiled fiercely here, bubbling angrily over the hidden edges of the granite bottom, and Stanton, not stopping the progress of the laboring vehicles, looked at it and worried, searching for an entry to the stream where the raft and the rhino would be appearing.

For a while, they drove along the water's edge, and when they came to a bluff that rose high above them, Stanton pointed and said, "If we can get up there we'll bypass the swamp and get the trucks farther up."

The trucks slowly ground to a halt, their radiators hissing and the oil smoking in the heat. Von Abart climbed down, looked at the bluff, and said, "Wait here, I'll find a way."

He jumped down and set off, his rifle slung over his shoulder, not looking back at them as they sat there and waited. When his figure was small against the hot skyline, Stanton took out his cigarettes. "You see? He likes to leave us alone together. I could have gone to find a route myself. I was just going to suggest it."

"A man of action, Harry. He'd rather keep moving than sit around."

"And he's anxious to show off his energy."

"Perhaps. That's the first true sign of old age."

"As long as you say it."

"It's what you were thinking, isn't it?"

"I was thinking how beautiful you are."

He climbed out of the truck and held cut his hand for her. Talib, his great round face expressionless, watched them move off slowly to the durian tree that stood close by. Looking up into the branches, Stanton said, musing, "You like them? We could knock a couple down."

She grimaced. "They taste like turpentine."

"I lived on them once, for more than a month. Before I learned how to catch meat without firing off a couple of noisy bullets."

"And still you like the jungle?"

"I love it, It's the one place in the world where you can live like a man, on the competence of your own two hands. I lived on durian until I learned to catch fish without a line, and I lived on fish until I could kill a boar with my dagger. Then the Sakai—they taught me how to find edible roots, how to listen to the noises of the jungle and interpret them, how to watch the mimosa for the approach of an animal."

"Mimosa?"

"Like that, over there, you see?"

He walked with her over to the bushes, touching her hand as he moved, and as he came close to the sensitive plant, it quickly folded its leaves one over the other and lay flat on the ground. "You see?" he said again. "When I was hiding from the Japanese, I used to watch the mimosa. The patrols make no sound, no sound at all, but the plant knew they were coming and gave me warning. A silent watchdog."

"Here, with the Sakai?"

"Farther south. Like these, but a little less—less distant. A poor people, dying out, caught up in what they think is civilization. It frightens them, and they die from it because they are not strong enough to fight it. Even here, one day..."

He sat in the long grass and brooded for a while, and said at last, "My home, Anna. This is where I belong. You, too."

She shook her head with a vehemence that surprised him. "Once in a while Harry, I desperately need to get away, just as you do. And then, when I go back to Munich..."

"To that musty old house."

"Yes, when I go back there it's a relief again."

"You feel homesick, already?"

"No, and Munich's not my home either. It's just that, before Otto, I had no defenses. And here, it's the same. If my competence should fail, I'd be on my own again. I don't want that. Ever."

He looked at her curiously. He said at last, "Tell me where you were born, Anna."

"In Silesia. There were twelve of us. My father was a

clerk in a Government office, too poor to feed us and too proud to ask for help. Our clothes went from one to the other. Until I was fourteen, I'd never had a new dress, a new pair of shoes."

"Till Otto came."

"After that, a house with a Cuvilliés staircase, pure silver and fine glasses on the table. I would have settled for two square meals a day. Sometimes, I think he knows that."

He leaned in to her and kissed her on the mouth. When she did not resist him, he said, smiling, "I'm getting to know you better, aren't I?"

He lay back in the grass with his hands at the back of his head, feeling the closeness of her and congratulating himself, a little complacently, that he was doing the right thing, the smart thing, in letting her see that he would not press his advantage. He watched the smoke of his cigarette spiraling up and listened to the sound of the parrots.

When von Abart came back to tell them he'd found a way up to the top, they took a load of boys aboard and went to look over the route. It was steep and sandy, and the soil was thickly studded with clumps of bushes, but as they climbed higher they came to fields of long grass where herds of sambur galloped away from them.

Farther off, they could see a long line of seladang strung out on the skyline, the big male looking down at them and waiting to give the alarm if it should seem necessary. A pair of elephants, shepherding a week-old baby, trumpeted angrily at them and herded their charge carefully back into the forest.

The foliage thickened, and then thinned out again, and suddenly the ground seemed to rise up ahead of them almost like a cliff, and the driver swung the wheel over hard to take it on the angle, and von Abart shouted, "Everybody out. Push hard."

They all jumped from the still-moving truck, feeling the

drunken twisting of its body, leaning heavily into the hot timbers of its sides, smelling the burning rubber as the wheels spun round to send out long spurts of biting grit.

Someone ran with his parang flailing and cut a branch of a durian tree, ramming it under the back wheels as they spun, but slowly the big lorry groaned to a halt. They stood for a while leaning against it, panting, feeling the sweat drip down their faces, feeling the burning of the sun, and then they left it and walked up to the top of the rise.

As far as they could see now, the wide sweep of the land stretched out before them, overpowering in the very size of it, dazzling in the brilliance of its colors. For ten or twenty miles the unbroken grass was long and bright and moist, and then the forest lay where the land began its upward slope once more, and beyond that, a hundred miles away perhaps, a long line of mountains thrust their snubbed points up to a sky so blue that it was almost too bright to look at.

The air here was thin, and Stanton wondered how high they had climbed in the last few hours. In the valley behind them, using their binoculars, they could see the pinpoints of their camp that lay like a child's top on a sand table, with thin columns of smoke rising where the boys were doing their cooking.

"The edge of the forest," von Abart said. "Over at the edge of the forest, that's where we should be." He turned his binoculars to the trees and said, "Take a look, see how broken up the ground is there. We should send some of the trackers over to take a look."

Stanton nodded and went to the edge where he could see the truck below. Cupping his hands to his mouth, he called for Talib, and when the Malay came panting up the steep sandstone sides, he said, "The river's down there somewhere. Send a man down to find it and signal us, and tell the driver to come up here." He turned to von Abart and said, "If we can get the truck over this last rise, we've got it made. The river's down there ahead of us somewhere, and somewhere, too, there's a rhino waiting for us, netted and roped and angry."

They all sat there for a while, their legs spread wide, letting the cool air freshen their lungs, chatting and smoking and feeling at peace, and when Talib came back with the driver, sweating up the steep slope of the hill, Stanton said carefully, "Tell him what he has to do, Talib. Take a box-spanner and remove the plugs, you know? The plugs. Put the truck in bottom gear, let him sit on the front bumper with the starting handle in its place, and then start winding, you understand? Wind the starting handle, the crank, with the truck in gear and the plugs out of the motor. Every time he turns the handle, the truck will come up an inch or two, no more than that, but if he keeps at it he'll get the truck up to the top and over the hill. After that, it's a straight run down the other side. You understand what he has to do?"

Wondering, Talib explained to the driver, gesturing broadly. There was a great deal of head-scratching, and at last von Abart got up and said, "These monkeys will never understand. I'll go and show them."

He went off with the two Malays and left them alone together. Stanton put a hand on her knee and looked at her, but she stood up, pointing, and said, "Isn't that sambur over there?"

A long way off, four hundred yards or more, a group of antelope were grazing, and when he looked through the binoculars he could see the long thin necks and the angled horns. He said, "Your eyesight's good. They're sambur."

"We need meat, don't we?"

"But you'll never get near them."

"They're good eating."

"You'll stalk them all day and never get any closer."

He did not mean it as a challenge, because he had come to regard her, once more, as a woman rather than as a hunter. Suddenly aware of this he put down his glasses and smiled at her, saying, "You know, a while back I'd have made a wager that you couldn't get near them."

"Oh?"

"To impress on you my opinion of your ability in the field. But now...now, I'm not so sure. I believe that perhaps you could. And I won't ask you to try because now that you've...well, how shall I put it? Now that I know you're one of the boys, I'm more concerned than ever with your femininity. Does that make sense?"

"No. No sense at all." She was laughing at him, and he suddenly felt very close to her. He said lightly, "I'm getting too damn fond of you, Anna, even when you fend me off."

"Fond of me? I thought you said you loved me."

"I do. But I've gone a step farther. I've grown fond of you, too."

"Well, that's a fine distinction."

She looked at him for a moment, smiling, knowing what was at the back of his mind, and then she looked back at the antelopes and raised her rifle. He said quickly, "You're too far, Anna." But she paid no attention and stood there, levelling her rifle carefully, and he said again, "Not at this range." When she paid him no heed but steadied her rifle by forcing it into the slender flesh of her shoulder, he said irritably, "Well, at least lie down for it. It's more than four hundred yards."

But she stood there quite still, and he saw that her rifle was quite steady and that the sights were set at four hundred and fifty, and he raised his glasses again, knowing that she'd miss by a dozen yards but feeling a sudden distaste that she should be so careless about the risk of wounding an animal rather than making a quick kill, and then, as he watched, he heard the shot and saw one of the animals drop, a male that was standing a little to one side of the rest of the herd, and he put down the glasses in surprise and said, "But I don't believe it. That looked like a very clean shot."

"Oh? And why shouldn't it be a clean shot?"

He was aware of a trace of impatience in her voice, of anger almost. He said awkwardly, "Well, at that distance..." and when he broke off, she looked him full in the face and he knew that she was going to tell him something very important, and the flash of irritation he felt was because he knew that she was treating him like a child who does not understand things very well.

She said deliberately, "One day, Harry, I'll tell you how many of those trophies are really Otto's."

Startled now, he said, "How many are Otto's?"

But she had gone, her rifle tucked under her arm, walking through the rich grass towards her kill, and he followed her, saying urgently, "Anna, what's that supposed to mean?"

She turned on him then, and he was well aware now of her exasperation. "Forget about it, Harry, it's not important."

He knew when to withdraw. Forcing a grin, he said, "Well that really was a damn good shot."

The rest of the herd ran off as they approached, moving fast, their thin necks working back and forth to give them speed and their tails doing the same thing in reverse, arching up and whipping back again as the neck swung forward. Watching them, he said, "The tail-raisers."

As he had suspected, it was a clean shot; her bullet had broken the spine at the base of the head. He put his rifle down and turned the animal over, admiring the angled shiny horns, and then stood up and took her by the shoulders. He said slowly, making a joke of it, "All right, answer me one question and I'll say no more about it. Was that shot a fluke, or wasn't it?"

"A fluke?"

"A flash in the pan. Or could you do it again?"

"I could do it again, Harry. I told you, I'm good shot."

"But dammit, without the glasses, I couldn't even see which were the males."

"I could."

His admiration was tinged with the sharp touch of jealousy, but he thrust the thought away with a certain anger at his own ungallantry, knowing that the qualities he liked most were all to be found here, knowing that he ought to be worrying about it because of the ancient fears that he had lumped together under the one generic term involvement. And knowing too that things would be different when they got back to Germany because it was only out here that the detachment and the isolation were great enough to leave them balanced, as it were, precariously at the lip of restriction where the restraints could easily be broken.

He put his arm round her and kissed her, looking back over her shoulder to where the plateau fell away to the valley below them, making sure that they were still out of sight. She put her arm round his neck and pressed herself close to him, forcing her body tight against his, making him want her. She held him tight for a moment, and then, as soon as he slipped his hand down to her groin, she pushed him away violently, a sudden anger fierce in her eyes. It was not, he was sure, a lawful anger, but something she was contriving for purposes of her own, and he fought against it. He clutched her to him, and when she struggled harder, he looked down briefly at the animal she had shot, understanding its helplessness, and then dropped easily to the ground, pulling her down beside him, using his brute strength on her and not caring whether she fought him or not, knowing only that he could not resist the hot pounding of the blood that she had sent, deliberately, he was sure, pounding so heatedly through his body.

She twisted under him, fighting silently, savagely, and he took an arm and wrenched it behind her back, then pulled at her shirt and at the tight belt at her waist.

Suddenly, she was limp, unresisting, and sure that he had won her, that this was the way she wanted to be taken, in battle, an animal being hunted, and marveling at how simple it all was, he looked at her eyes and began a careful smile. He was shocked by the absolute hatred he saw there, and as he hesitated she said quietly, coldly, dispassionately, "If you take me like this, Harry, I will kill you."

It was a plain statement of fact rather than the threat of an angry moment. Unsure of himself, he touched her and she did not move. He swore at her and stood up, and left her lying there, then turned on his heel and stalked angrily back to the truck, not looking over his shoulder, not caring whether she were following him or not, not caring what happened to her or what she was doing.

The anger inside him reached a pitch of intensity that he could not control, and he said aloud, over and over again, venting the hatred that was in him, "The bitch, the bitch, the bloody-minded German bitch!"

CHAPTER 10

He was still sulking when, towards evening, they finally found the point at which the river came out of the jungle.

A-Gap, who was once called Ojag, was there with the raft and the rhino and a group of admiring Sakai from the village who had gathered round him to inspect, not the captive animal that lay on its flank in hopeless anger, but the wide raft itself, which, the old man assured them, was his own personal property, a present from the white men.

The villagers scurried deep into the jungle at the first sound of the truck, and for a while they peered unseen at it from deep under cover, and then they decided that this monster could only have come to harm them and so they fled deeper in among the trees, there to cower in fright until their gods should tell them that it was safe to come out again. Only the Sakai from the camp stayed where they were, secure in their superiority over their more savage cousins, but, if the truth were known, a little scared also lest their confidence should lead them astray.

The raft had been hauled up on the bank, away from the turmoil of the water, which at this point bubbled whitely over the sharp sunken spikes that were the granite rocks; some of the bamboo nodes had been split wide open with the pounding of them. But on it, the rhino was secure in the nylon net, its porcine eyes alert with hatred and with impotent fury, its shoulder-folds

151

rustling as it moved, its grey hairs bristling.

They dragged it slowly, a dozen men straining at the ropes, closer to the big trees of the forest, and one of them shinned up to a high branch and flung a block and tackle over, and the driver backed up the steaming truck. Soon the rhino was lashed firmly into place, and the party was once more struggling back to the compounds.

For a long time, Stanton had not spoken. Von Abart, if he was aware of it, affected not to notice the mood that was on him, Anna, smiling a little too easily, looked at him as though examining in detail the depth of the wound she had caused and touching, with probing sadistic fingers, the edges of his humiliation. When she spoke, it was with an air of amusement, and he could not decide whether she was jeering at him or seeking to soften his pain. Looking at the rhino, she said, "If they only knew in Munich how easy it all is!"

The same sentiment, he thought, that her lover had expressed in the Zoo. *The team, von Abart and Kruger, Kruger and von Abart, Otto-Annaliese.*

He grunted and said sourly, "Animals are always easy. They're less complicated than people. It makes them easier to subdue."

On the way back, down where the steep bluff had nearly stopped their passage, they found Baka waiting for them. With no signal from them, the driver, drawing a little of Talib's competence from him, had slewed over to the side as soon as he saw the old Sakai standing alone, out in the open, not hiding because now he was part of the shikar and a man of competence. He stood there in the hot sunlight, waiting for them, his thin arms draped over the blowgun that was lying across his shoulders, so that his fingers pointed loosely down to the earth, probing, as though seeking the nourishment there that the poor Sakai could never find in adequate quantities for their survival. He crouched down when he was sure that they had seen him, and stood up again respectfully when the truck drew close, being ready, too, to run should it make up its mechanical mind and decide to charge him. They all jumped out to stretch their legs and have a conference, anything to break the monotony of the truck's hard bumping over the uneven plain and the steep hills, and for a while Talib and Baka stood close together talking, gesticulating, pointing, arguing.

At last, Talib turned to Stanton and said, "The leopard, Tuan. A big one, black, Baka see him, there, on mountain,"

"Good! When he says big, what does he mean?"

There was an argument again, and then Baka leaned down and drew the outline of a leopard's pug in the red earth, and von Abart, looking at it carefully, said, "A very big one, unless the stupid bastard is lying. Which he probably is."

Stanton brushed aside the irritation. "And whereabouts on the mountain?"

"There, Tuan, Where small top to mountain, blue trees, below this, one day march we get there."

"All right." He turned to the others. "Well, either we go back to the camp, dump the rhino, and set off again tomorrow morning, or we send what's his name, A-Gap, with the rhino on the truck and go straight there now. Anybody have any strong views?"

Von Abart was already pulling his rifle out of its holder on the truck. "By tomorrow, he may have gone. Let's get close now so that he'll know we're there, and start the hunt at sunup."

Stanton looked across at Anna, forcing himself to seek her advice. He thought she understood why he was asking her. She said slowly, "Yes, I think we should too, there's nothing we need in the camp. You think A-Gap can get the rhino into his compound?"

Stanton shrugged. "Why not? Drag him in, cut the net loose. Talib?"

"Boys in camp do this, Tuan, no worry for us, A-Gap

153

good man, even if Sakai, all right."

"Good! So we'll need you and Baka, all the porters we have with us now, with their loads, the nets, and the personal servants. The driver will take the truck with A-Gap back to camp, and the head-boy there can off-load. We'll be gone—who knows? A day, a week? Until we find Baka's leopard. Let's go."

The Sakai porters tumbled untidily out of the back of the truck, dragging their loads after them. A-Gap climbed proudly in, beside the driver, sitting on a proper seat and proud of his position, glancing sideways at the driver to make sure that there would be no sudden, violent, bloody objection from him, and then realizing that his security was assured because of what Talib the good man had told him about the enslavement of the A-Gap Sakai.

Soon the truck was a speck that wound its way through the trees below them as the long line of marching men climbed towards the mountain. Baka was in the lead, with Talib close behind him, then Stanton, Anna, von Abart, and the porters.

They pushed the pace hard, trying to get to the mountain before dark, and soon von Abart dropped behind, thrusting aside the foliage, growling, "I'll take the rear and keep those lazy savages moving. I should have a whip." He stood still as the long line went past him, his face red and sweaty in the heat, his pale eyes paler than ever.

At the bottom of the valley they splashed through dark and muddy swamp water, slashing at the crocodiles with long bamboo poles and waiting until they had angrily disappeared into their lairs, like frightened Sakai. Once they had to use a rifle to scare off a big male that turned on them, refusing to move from their path, waiting for them in vicious anticipation. Talib said, "Careful, Tuan, is bad one." He raised his rifle and fired two shots quickly at the long, ugly nose. It whipped its tail around then and fled thrashing into the jungle.

They stopped at midday to eat a hurried meal and to

scrape the leeches off their legs, and soon they were deep in the thick forest where the land was dry under their feet and the sunlight filtered through the broad leaves above. Great round boulders of yellow rock stood around them, and soon they turned into a canyon where the scrub was sparser.

Stanton, looking back at the long line of the shikar, said, "Leopard country, Anna." He pointed to the spoor of an antelope. "Kanchil. The leopard's favorite food."

Baka and Talib had stopped, squatting on their haunches together, examining the ground, and when they went up to them Talib stood up, pointed at the ground, and said, "There, Tuan, leopard. You see?"

"You know damn well I don't see, Talib. But I'll take your word for it."

Talib said earnestly, "Big mark, Tuan, very deep."

They peered at the ground together, then Stanton turned to Anna. "See anything?"

She shook her head. "Not a sign. But that doesn't mean there's nothing there."

"Uh-huh."

Baka, wondering why the whites, who were so clever in so many ways, could not see the obvious tracks in the earth that to him were as clear as a footprint in wet cement, moved forward, step by step, his finger outstretched to the ground, marking the pad marks one by one, speaking to Talib in short, guttural grunts. Talib, nodding wisely, said, "He is right, Tuan, leopard very close now."

"Oh? How old is the spoor?"

"Two, three hours. He come this way, go round, wait in bushes little while, kill mias, monkey, over here, then go back same way, hide some more, little while back move over there, in rocks."

"What's he hiding from?"

Von Abart, hurrying forward, said excitedly, "Farther

back there, on the flank, a spoor as big as your hand."

"Here, too. He's been hiding up under the bushes there."

"Yes? That can only mean one thing. He's doubled back on his tracks because he knows we're after him. Good, good!"

Stanton said, frowning, "Dark in an hour, and by morning he'll be twenty miles away."

Von Abart shook his head. "Don't you believe it. This is the best thing, Harry, the best thing that could happen." Peering at the high cliffs above them, he said, "He's up there watching us, and he'll stay there for a long time, to see what we're going to do."

"I hope you're right."

"Damn true I'm right! You want to know what he's doing? He's sitting up there on top of those rocks, watching us, and that's where he'll stay all night, to make sure he knows what we're up to. And at daylight he'll see the trackers move off and he'll watch them like a hawk and keep just outside their circle of movement. And when they're well out of his way, he'll come down here right in the middle of us to see if we're worth hunting. He'll find we're all together, too strong for him, and so he'll head for his lair."

"Yes, perhaps you're right."

"I'm damn right! This is a leopard, Harry, not a jackass. He'll keep close to us just in case he can make a kill. It's the only other animal that kills for the fun of it, and a little group like this will be too much for him to resist."

Stanton raised his eyebrows. "The only other animal?"

Von Abart lifted a didactic finger, the professor lecturing the pupil. He said, "The tiger will only kill when he's hungry, and the rhino only when he's disturbed. The elephant won't harm you unless you're fool enough to get between him and his females, and even the crocodile will let you swim in peace if his larder is full. But the leopard—for the sheer enjoyment of killing, just for the pleasure in it. He kills because he likes it. There's only one other animal that does that, Harry. And that's man."

"Well, we'll get him one way or another. They're a lot easier to kill than to capture, and even that isn't a pushover, I wonder if we should bait a trap and hope he'll walk into it?"

"Not a hope in hell."

"No, I'm afraid not. You know what that means, don't you? We've got to drive him to his lair, find where that is, and then get him out of it and into the nets. Well, let's get set up."

He called Talib over and had the nets laid out for his inspection. One of them had torn on the thorn-trees and he told Talib to get it patched. They found a small clearing surrounded with tall mimosa trees, and set up camp for the night. When they had eaten the venison steaks that Suleiman had prepared for them, they sat in their canvas chairs, drinking and chatting and watching the bright landscape under the white moon, listening to the night sounds around them, grateful for the dry air that kept the mosquitoes away from them, looking forward to the excitement that the morrow would bring. And when the moon went down and left them in absolute darkness, Anna got up and left them, going to the shelter where the boys had poured the water into the canvas wash-basin, and watching her go, von Abart said quietly, "You're getting to be good friends, you two. I fancied you'd been quarrelling this morning." His voice was slurred.

"Quarrelling?" Stanton forced a short laugh. "No, of course not. I must admit my temper was all fouled up today. Got out of bed the wrong side."

"You like her, don't you?"

He said easily, knowing that sooner or later this would come, "Yes, I like her very much. She's damn good company. I'm glad we brought her along. And a hell of a good shot. Remember that sambur she got the other day? She shot it at four hundred and fifty yards, through the neck, a clean shot."

For a moment, von Abart said nothing. Watching him,

Stanton was conscious that he had adroitly, though quite unintentionally, put a new suspicion into his mind. It was a reflex, he thought, coming to his rescue. He called for drinks, and for a while they said nothing, sipping their brandy in silence.

The remark she had made about von Abart's trophies had both puzzled and worried him. She had meant, clearly enough, that some of them had not fallen to his gun, but to hers. And now his unthinking reference to her marksmanship had evoked no approving response from von Abart, but only, instead, the trace of a suspicion, as though he were thinking, *Oh, what has she been telling you?*

Conscious that chance had come to his rescue, turning the suspicion into safer channels, he said at last, smiling, "I still think it was a fluke."

Von Abart quickly recovered his good humor. He said casually, "Oh, she's a good enough shot, for a woman."

The matter of the friendship, of the rivalry, had been forgotten and by the time it was remembered again it was too late to pursue the subject. Anna came back to them, her hair brushed and hanging down to her shoulders, her body smelling sweetly of perfume, her green housecoat loose about her. He poured her a glass of brandy and handed it to her, and von Abart looked at her and said abruptly, "Well, it's all right for you young people, but I'm going to bed."

Stanton said quickly, "Yes, I won't be up long either. We must be under way by dawn."

"I know. G'night."

He went unsteadily to the sleeping-bag which had been laid out for him under the overhang of an outcrop, and they saw the flicker of light as he lit a cigarette, and then the faint glow of its spark in the darkness, and then it was out and they heard his drunken snoring coming gently to them across the intervening space.

For or a while they sat there, not talking, smoking in

158

silence and feeling the coldness of the air closing in on them. Speaking very quietly, Stanton said, "Aren't you cold?"

"No, not very."

"A big day tomorrow. A big leopard."

"It's important to you, isn't it?"

Surprised, he said, "But of course it is. That's the reason we're here. Kind of luck I'm having lately, it'll turn out to be a white one."

"There were some black hairs on the thorns by the track back there."

"Oh? I didn't see them." He thought she might have pointed them out to him, and said, "They could be from a tapir, a jungle cat."

Smiling at his efforts, she said, "From a leopard, a black leopard."

"I sometimes think you go out of your way to exasperate me."

He was trying his best not to sulk.

"Because I can identify an animal? That's my trade, Harry."

"Because you take a kind of pleasure in making me feel small."

"No. I don't."

"I wish I could believe that."

For a moment she said nothing, and then she got up from her chair and went over to him, and standing above him, she leaned forward and kissed him on the lips. He made no move, no move at all, and then she took his head between her hands and kissed him again, slowly, letting him feel the moistness of her mouth. He slipped his hands, both of them, under her housecoat, and put them on her breasts, not moving any more, just keeping them there, knowing with precise exactitude what she was doing, knowing that she was assuring herself that when she whistled he would come running. He held himself carefully in check to make sure that she understood that, even if he would come, he would come of his own free will and not because she called him, like a slave, like an animal. He felt that he was trembling, and knew that she could feel this, too, and as soon as his hands began to move, in spite of himself, she stood up, smiling, knowing how the game was going, and he smiled back at her and said, "Your skin burns me."

She said quietly, "You should be thinking about leopards, Harry."

"I am."

"It's not going to be easy. Tomorrow."

"No. You can't drive a leopard the way you drive a tiger."

"And you can't trick them either."

"No? We'll see."

"They know all the tricks in the book."

"Just like a woman."

Assured that he had understood what she was doing to him, and that he was prepared to accept it, she kissed him quickly and turned away. "Good night, Harry. Sleep well."

"See you in the morning. A very early start."

"Good night."

She walked quietly away in the darkness, and for a little while he thought about leopards, saying to himself, *You never quite know what they're up to*. Then, with the fires spotting the darkness and the sounds of the crickets discordant in his ears, he went to his sack and lay down, turning on his stomach to think of the hunt, of the leopard, and of Anna. His last thought, before he fell asleep, was. And now, at least, I know what her terms are.

The first grey had not even reached the eastern horizon when Stanton, with the old knowledge and awareness of the jungle, was awake and brushing the sleep from his eyes. Talib, he saw, was already up, and there was the sweet-sour smell of coffee on the cold air.

Soon the whole camp was awake and moving, shivering in the early cold, getting the nets folded tightly and slung over the bent backs of the porters, getting the axes out, moving in single file after Baka the tracker. They saw their first clear spoor as the sun hit the slope of the mountain, and crouching beside it, Stanton whistled, "Look at it. The size of it!"

Von Abart, tingling with the anticipation of the challenge, nodded. "Let's get hard behind him. He knows we're coming."

Stanton turned to Talib. "All right, from this point onwards, no sound. No talking, no coughing, nothing, you understand? If we lose the spoor, have Baka cast about to find it again and we'll wait. And while we're waiting, I want absolute silence. And no smoking."

"No noise, Tuan. Nothing."

"He knows we're after him, but I don't want him to know how close we are, not until he holes up, understand?"

"Understand, Tuan."

"Good. Single file, and keep the Sakai quiet." He knew that nothing would be quieter than a quiet Sakai, The tension in him was mounting. To the others, he said, "Well, this is it. We don't stop now until we've got him."

He could see the light of the excitement in their eyes and thought, *All over again. However often you hunt, there's always the climax. By tonight, it will all be over, but for the present, this is the moment.*

In single file, the shikar moved slowly, carefully, silently forward.

CHAPTER 11

The hunt was the turning point.

All day long the trackers had been following the spoor. It had carried them to a wide outlandish valley of freakish formations beyond the crevice in the cliff where their quarry had first been sighted, and thence to a broken cluster of rocks where there were petrified wood and striated limestone in which were fossils from a great, untouched age. It was almost as if they were on another planet. The silence was frightening, because it seemed to them all as though the orchestra of the jungle sounds had been silenced so that all could watch the drama that was about to be played out there.

They had seen spoor in plenty, and von Abart had been proved right. The tracks had led, at first, to the top of the cliff where there was a cluster of bright-green bushes that carried yellow, poisonous-locking berries, and there the leopard had stayed for several hours, looking down on the camp below, just as von Abart had said he would. They could even see the faint mark in the sand where his jaw had rested while he lay crouched and watching them with tireless and angry interest.

Again, they had marveled at the size of it, and when the tracks had taken them, next, to a broad flat surface of red lava that was hard and brittle as marble, von Abart had scratched his chin and said, "An old one, this, and wise. He's been hunted

162

before."

The trackers had circled round in a wide arc, and the others had rested while they waited for the spoor to be picked up again, And an hour later one of the Sakai came running back with news that they had found it. Now they were moving along a ledge, quite narrow in parts, where the rock fell away a thousand feet below them to the flat green tops of the trees that looked like toys so far below. Above them, the rocks went higher still, fifty, a hundred, five hundred feet above them in red glaring brilliance that was painful to look at in the brightness of the hot sun. The sweat poured off their bodies as the heat came up to them in almost overpowering waves. There was no sound to break the silence, and even the ubiquitous rats had scuttled back into the dark recesses of their tiny caves, leaving nothing out there in the sun but a long thin Indian file of hunters, like ants creeping along the dangerous confines of a broken rocky shelf above the vast expanse of the plateau.

They were close to him now. They could sense it. It was as though a shadowy form that was the essence of terror lurked close behind them so that they dared not look over their shoulders. There had been a patch of grass on the ledge, and when they had passed it Talib had knelt down quickly, pointing to it and whispering, "Just now, little while ago, he come here. Look." They could see nothing, but when Baka came up he laid his thin, gnarled hand on the clump and pushed the blades of grass down, letting them slowly come back to their natural position, and then nodded wisely, meaning, "Here—just now. A short while ago."

When Talib had spoken, his voice had been slighter than the sound of the grass itself, the merest zephyr of a whisper. Now he beckoned urgently to Baka and the two of them went back the way they had come for a hundred paces, and there was a whispered consultation. When Talib returned he put his mouth close to Stanton's ear and said, "Just a little way, sir, very close now."

They moved on in utter silence, their rifles at the ready, and in a little while they came to an opening in the rocks beside them and Talib put his fingers to the sandstone and sniffed them, and then looked at the ground carefully, crouching down in the sun like a statue. Behind him, the slanting fissures in the rock were painted slashes on a demented canvas, and they pressed themselves close into the overhang to get away from the burning heat of the mocking sun.

Then they froze. It was Talib who heard it first, and his eyes grew wide with fright. He did not move. There was a cough in the silence, a slight, ineffective sound that could easily have been lost to them had they not been so tensed for the slightest variation in the burning stillness, It was the warning cough of an angry leopard. Von Abart's rifle was pointed down to where Talib crouched, and there, close beside their ankles, Stanton saw that there was a slit in the rock that lay a foot from the floor of the ledge they were on, a long horizontal cut that was a crack in the ancient lava.

Frowning, he shook his head, meaning, "No, it's too small." But von Abart nodded, his hand to his lips, and then Talib stood up slowly, holding his spear in the jabbing position, ready to protect himself against the sudden onrush.

Von Abart made a silent gesture, and Talib, with the hunter's good sense, nodded once and went climbing up the face of the cliff. Stanton knew that he was looking for an exit to the cave, and with the knowledge there came a moment of irritation that von Abart was trying to take command from him. But knowing also that this was the right thing to do he said nothing, nodding his approval.

They stood there for a while, watching the Malay giant climb slowly and surely up the cliff face, the sun glinting on the dark sheen of his muscled back until he became no more than a toy black figure clinging precariously to the fissures of the hot red sandstone. When he reached the top, he stood there for a while looking around him, and then disappeared from their view. They waited, and when at last he reappeared he cupped his hands to his mouth and shouted in Sakai, and von Abart whispered angrily, "You yellow bastard, you want to scare him away?"

Stanton was jubilant. He said, "He knows what he's doing. He wouldn't be shouting unless he'd found the back entrance. That means the leopard is holed up there."

Below them, farther back along the ledge, the Sakai porters were hurrying forward, climbing lithely up the cliff face in blissful contempt of the deadly drop below them, scurrying up like so many baboons, finding handholds where none existed, dragging their nets with them, knowing that no leopard would ever take refuge in a cave that had no back way out of it, knowing that even this one which the Tuan, in his wisdom, had described as old and wise, could still be trapped because there were great men pitted against him, men who had hunted much before and knew the ways of the animals. They knew that all they had to do now was to cover up the two entrances to the cave with their nets and then...then what?

They knew that they could leave the answer to this vexing problem in the hands of the white people, but some of them, the older ones, were wondering just how you could catch an angry, oversized leopard that could rip a man to pieces in seconds. They knew how he could be killed, but no amount of head-scratching could tell them how he could be trapped.

Von Abart said brusquely, "Stay here. I'm going up to the top. Better keep this end well covered. If he guesses what we're up to, he'll come out in a rush."

Stanton nodded. Asserting his authority, he said, "Make sure the nets are well tied down. We'll try and drive him out from this end - it'll give us more room to maneuver. It's not going to be easy, at that."

Von Abart said contemptuously, "We'll have him trussed

like a hog before dark."

"Are you sure you can get up there? The valley's a thousand feet below us."

Von Abart did not answer. He was scowling at the face of the cliff, searching for footholds, looking to see where Talib had passed, and then he slung his rifle over his shoulder and went up, easily, moving the bulk of his body without over-much effort, pausing once in a while to get his breath and to rub the sweat off his hands against the soiled khaki of his trousers. They watched him, staring up with the sun beating down on their backs, forgetting the immediate danger that lurked in the fissure at their feet.

There was one frightening instant when he nearly fell. There were a scuffle and a small slide of rock, and they saw him cling hard to the root of a thorn that had worked its way out of the soil, and Anna put out a hand on Stanton's arm. Looking at her quickly, he saw no alarm in her face, but only excitement, as though the spectacle of her lover's danger made her pulse beat faster, but not with fear. For a moment it disturbed him, and then, searching her face closely, he was aware of a calculating alertness in her eyes as though she were carefully planning what she would do if he should fall.

He said, "He's all right, just a slip."

"Another one like that and he'll go down." She said bitterly, "He's getting too old to climb, but not too old to feel he must prove his competence."

His exasperation put an edge of asperity to his voice. He said sourly, "Your loyalty touches me. One day you must tell me about fidelity, about its finer points. When I try to get close to you, it seems to stand between us. And now...Is it that you're not sure, is that it?"

"No, Harry." She refused to be goaded. "It's a great deal simpler than that. Last night, he deliberately left us alone. Deliberately, a forcing gambit. He wanted to find out. I could feel the workings of his brain. I grew up with Otto, Harry, I know every thought he has, better than he knows it himself."

"You mean he was—he was waiting for us to...He wanted to know?"

"He's the one who wanted to be sure, Harry. Now he is. He knows that he's safe, from you. He was lying awake there in the darkness, snoring away and watching us."

The knowledge of the danger that had passed him by so easily scared him. "And, knowing this, you still tried... Goddammit, I damn nearly threw you on the ground and took you, there and then, by force!" He said, growling at her, "And I don't know why I don't do that now, in front of all the boys. They at least understand these things."

"Last night, I thought for a moment you would. But now, don't you see? He's sure. So it's reflecting on him today. He's been second in command all the time, knowing that he's the better man, Harry. Up to last night he was afraid that he'd been losing out. But he lay awake and watched us, and now he knows that everything is just the way it should be."

The deviousness of her mind intrigued and disturbed him, and the more he thought about it the less he liked it. He said angrily, "And if I hadn't behaved precisely like the boor you take me for, we'd have had a load of trouble on our hands. We damn nearly did."

She said, very calmly, "Yes, we nearly did."

"It's sometimes a damn fool thing to do, to force an issue like that."

"Not if the issue needs forcing."

"Maybe."

She said lightly, "But at least it's shown you one little facet of his character. You've been in command of this operation all along, and he's put up with that uncomplainingly, though God alone knows what it cost him. Now, look at him."

Was she goading him, he wondered? And to what end?

He let her talk, hoping she would give herself away, turning her own tactics back on her. She said patiently, "He thought he might be losing me, and now he's sure that he's not. It's pretty simple, really. He's developed a kind of scorn for you, because he thinks you're behaving properly. In his world, you fight for what you want, you fight all the way. It's not just a question of brief attacks, of skirmishes, of half-hearted probes; you go all the way, Harry. Up to last night there was—how shall I put it? An imbalance. Now, it's back to normal again. So he's in good form, and that means he wants to be in command, too. I don't know why you put up with it."

With forced fairness, he said, "Why shouldn't I put up with it? He's a good man. I wish I knew half as much as he does. I wish I enjoyed the respect that he has."

She turned on him then and said quite coldly, "He has nothing, Harry, that you can't take from him. You understand? Nothing."

"I don't want to take anything from him." It was said before he had time to realize what, exactly, she was thinking. He said quickly, "You know what I mean. I don't want to rob him of—of anything. Well..." Knowing that he was getting deeper and deeper into it, he said with exasperation, "And this is hardly the time for a discussion like this. That damned cat's liable to come out of there in a minute. I think we'd better move away a little, get a bit of room to move fast if we have to."

It was only a tiny victory, but it brought her good spirits back again. She said, smiling, "All right, what do we do if he comes out with a rush? We should have netted here, too, you realize that?"

"Yes, we should have, shouldn't we?"

"I told you that you were losing control of this operation."

She was laughing at him now, and he felt good again. He said, "They got the nets up there, but in any case..."

He called one of the Sakai over and said, "Fire. Make fire."

The Sakai shook his head, puzzled, and Stanton went through the motions of building a fire, blowing on it, wishing he had picked up some words of Sakai. "Fire," he repeated. "Make fire."

The Sakai nodded, not understanding, but knowing that he could make an impression by assuming an intelligence he did not have, and went off to find what fire meant, and in what language. And in a moment, after he had conferred with one of the Malays who knew a little English, he came back grinning and carrying an armful of twigs and saying happily, "Fiah...fiah...fiah."

Stanton said cheerfully, "He's got it. Why the hell don't they have a civilized language?"

"Sakai, Malay, Tamil, Chinese—even a little English. They understand them all. It's not hard to manage, really."

The Sakai had crouched down near the fissure where the leopard was, glancing inside to the dark shadows fearfully, striking his flint and iron together and applying it to a bundle of dried grass and sighing happily when it flared because now, he knew, he was safe against attack from the monstrous animal that the whites had so thoughtlessly put him dangerously close to. He waited until the twigs were burning, and then stood up and said again: "Fiah...fiah," meaning, "Well, there's the fire. Now what am I supposed to do with it?"

Stanton waited until it was burning fiercely, and then pushed it gently with his boot right into the mouth of the cave. He said, "That'll keep him in there. Where's Suleiman?" He looked at the Sakai again and said, "*Suleiman menong?*"

Not understanding Malay, but knowing that Suleiman was the cook and that the white people were always eating, he put his hand to his mouth and then pointed, meaning, "Suleiman's over there, cooking a meal. What else would he be

ALAN CAILLOU

doing?"

Stanton saw that this was the old tribesman who had come to their camp on the day of the affair of the rifles. He wondered at Talib's diplomacy, knowing that to give the more intractable Sakai some paid work to do would help to keep the rest of them friendly. Following up the gesture, he pointed to the knife at the Sakai's waistcloth, so that the old man, showing his yellow teeth, red-stained by betel nut, pulled it out of the scabbard and handed it over, using both hands to show that there would be no treachery. When Stanton tested it on the black hairs at his wrist, seeing the blade cut easily and smoothly, he nodded his approval, and the old man nodded gravely and even went so far as to laugh, showing that now they were the best of friends.

He looked at Anna and said, "A gesture, it's all that's needed. If you know what a man needs, it's easy to get close to him, isn't it? A woman too, maybe."

She would not fight. She looked at him, smiling, and said, "Maybe."

Von Abart had disappeared from their sight, and now the fire at their feet was burning brightly. Staring into its flames, Anna said, "Have you decided how we're going to get him out?"

"Well—normally, I'd say we should kill a goat."

"He'll never come out. He knows what we're up to."

"Dammit, we haven't even seen him yet!"

"But he's seen us. He can stay in there for a week. There'll be kijang for him to live on. He'll try to get out the back way, he'll smell the nets, and he'll sneak back in and wait for us to go."

"The question is, who has the more patience? Sooner or later, he's got to come out."

"He could stay there for a week, for a month. He'll die there of starvation rather than come out now that he's seen the fire."

He thought, *Goddammit, that's exactly what he'll do!*

170

Aloud, he said, "Why do women always understand animals better than men?"

"Do they?"

"You do."

Mocking, she said, "I've a lot in common with the leopard."

"Yes. Yes, you have."

"Is that why you love me?" She was still laughing at him, but subconsciously she had lowered her voice.

"There are more important things for me than animals."

"Yes?"

Irritably, he said, "All right, how do we get him out?"

"We drive him out with flares."

"Yes? You want to go in there with a firebrand in your tiny little hand?"

"If you send me in there, I will go in there."

"Goddammit, I believe you would!"

"Let's see what Otto says."

Otto was working his way down the cliff, slithering down and sending showers of stones down ahead of him. When he reached the ledge, he said excitedly, "He's in there. I can smell him and I can hear him. It's a tunnel, a long, sloping tunnel that leads up from here to the top of the cliff. He chose a good spot to hide in. If we hadn't looked for his way out, he could have slipped out up there while we weren't looking. While we waited here like a bunch of idiots he'd have been twenty miles away. We've got him, Harry. I told you. By dark, he'll be trussed like a hog."

"Good! What about the nets?"

"Pegged down over the exit and covered with grass. He'll smell them, of course, but he'll like the smell of the nets better than our smell, because only the Sakai have been handling them, so that's the way he'll try to get out. We've got the nets well covered, so he'll try to force a way through them, and then, by

God, he's ours!"

"Good! Only one thing: how do we force him out? I thought we might fire a couple of rounds in there and see if it will scare him enough to make him run for the exit. Only ricocheting around in there we're liable to wound him."

"There's nothing easier, Harry. We go in with flares."

It was exactly what she had said, he thought angrily. Are they a team, these two? Am I the interloper? Is this the way they've accumulated all those trophies? Together? A team? An impotent old man and an expert and beautiful young huntress who can bring an antelope down at four hundred yards with a clean and precise neck shot?

"You think we can get in there? It looks very tight."

Von Abart crouched down on his haunches and peered inside. He said slowly, "From up there it looks like a crack, like a fissure, straight down to this point here. If we can get through the opening...I believe we can."

"With a leopard hiding out there?"

"A good flare, that's all that's needed. He'll back away from it. And if he backs far enough away...He's got to decide whether to charge the flares, or charge the nets. And take my word for it, he'll choose to run."

"It's a terrible risk. I wish there were some other way. If only we could sit it out."

Von Abart stood up and looked at him. Stanton fancied that there was the trace of a sneer on his face. An infinitely aristocratic sneer, but a sneer none the less. Smiling very faintly, he said, "You'd better let me go in."

This was the moment. The fear of it that had been building up in him passed him by quickly, and he knew what he had to do. He looked at Anna and saw that she was tensed, waiting for him to say, "No, I'll do it, you wait here," waiting for him to assert his superiority, his authority, and his manliness, waiting for him to throw von Abart to one side carelessly, and knowing that he would do this because he had every right, as the leader, to take the most dangerous course for himself and at the same time to stake his claim to her. She was too cool, too carefully restrained, and it showed on her.

He said casually, "All right. Better get some dry bamboo."

He was conscious that Anna had turned away from him, angry and contemptuous, and then she turned back and looked at him questioningly, puzzled, not sure that he had done what he had done for the reasons which were most apparent. It seemed to him that she had come to a different deduction, and he knew that in making von Abart the guinea-pig for his own emotional experiments he was treating him with a great deal of disrespect. He knew, too, that von Abart could easily be killed in there, but he would not pursue the thought any farther, saying to himself, *Well, he asked for it, and maybe now I'm forcing the issue, just as she says; sometimes it has to be done, and if he gets killed in there...It's dangerous, frighteningly dangerous, but this is what he wants, to show that he's the better man. All right, now let him prove it.*

He heard von Abart say to Talib, "Well, don't stand there, you idiot. You heard what the Tuan said, go and get me a bamboo flare."

Talib stood there stolidly, and said, "He kill you, Tuan. You go in there, leopard kill you." There was no expression on his face.

Von Abart turned his cold, triumphant eyes on him. "He wouldn't dare, Talib. He wouldn't dare. Now do as you're bloody well told."

For an instant, Talib's white eyes flickered at Anna and then over to Stanton, and Stanton knew he was thinking, *This man no good, Memsahib, better you take other man, you know he look at you with hot blood, better you go sleep with him.* He turned and shouted an order, and in a little while the flares had

173

been prepared. Talib, saying nothing, thrust the flares into the fire and handed one of them to von Abart.

Now is the moment, Stanton thought.

Now is the time to let us see whether he's the man he really thinks he is or not. He was thinking, *I wouldn't go in there for a million dollars.* He knew that he should hate von Abart for what he was doing. Looking at Anna, sensing her scorn, he thought, *Well, say what you like, he's got guts.* He was even sorry that he was treating him so badly, but then he thought, *Well, as long as he doesn't find out. What he doesn't know can't harm him. And I wish I had his confidence.*

Von Abart took the flare, inspected it to see that there was a sufficiency of the flimsy split canes to keep it burning long and vigorously, and then lay flat on his stomach and wormed his way into the cave.

Outside, in the safety of the broad hot daylight, Stanton and Anna settled down to wait. Watching her, he was conscious of a strange, detached air that was reflected in the somber grey of her eyes. She looked across at him once, not smiling, then turned her head away, and he knew that she was unaccountably frightened, feeling again the danger that was always there, knowing how frail was the protective barrier of their weapons and their competence. It was as though, suddenly, she had become aware of the need for protection, as though all her self-mastery were now clearly no more than a superficial veneer that was quite insufficient to comfort her.

As von Abart lay there in the darkness, a fire in one hand and a rifle in the other, the first thing he was conscious of was the overpowering stench.

It was the stench of animal droppings, of darkness, and of antiquity. As the daylight was blacked out by the bulk of his own body in the narrow aperture, he became aware of another, secret world, where the bats were hidden out and the muskrats were gripping the edges of the age-old rock with their tiny frightened claws, watching him with apprehensive black eyes and wondering what strange apparition this was that was invading the recesses that had been theirs for a million years.

He could hear them scuttling away from the danger of the unaccustomed fire, scurrying back into the darkness, their tiny ears twitching in fright. And he knew that theirs were not the only eyes that were watching him.

He thrust the flare ahead of him, lying flat and worming his way forward, stopping to look carefully into every dark recess, knowing the danger of passing a crevice and finding his prey behind him.

He was not frightened. Instead of the fear which he knew he should be feeling, there was only the sensation of mastery. He had seen the fear in Stanton's face when he had said, "It's a terrible risk. I wish there were some other way," and he knew that there was no substitute for the heritage of his breeding, with which came the cold proud courage that had always been his, and the knowledge of his own rightful supremacy over the upstarts that came across five thousand miles of time and distance to flaunt their unpolished competence under his aristocratic nose. He was alone now, alone in the darkness and in danger, and they were outside together, waiting...waiting for what?

He had seen the way Stanton had looked at her, right from the beginning, trying to hide his lust under the veneer of his bourgeois Americanism, and for a while it had looked as though she might have been impressed, in spite of all that he had taught her, by his easy youthful graces. There was a moment of unease when he forced himself to realize that a woman needs love, too, the physical kind, that he had not been able to give her for—how long was it? A year? Was it more than that? And then he thought, *She wouldn't dare, and besides, if there's one thing I've taught her, it is an appreciation of quality, and this American oaf will mean no more to her than a passing infatuation to be brushed aside easily because I have taught her to ignore all those things which do not matter.*

The dismay came back again when he thought of the look he had seen on her face, just before the decision was made. She had been waiting, watching, looking for the proof of his superiority, as though it would not need much to make her change her allegiance. And then, more happily now, he thought of the hesitation in Stanton's decision, and he said to himself, *A flicker of fear, of simple, unadulterated fear.*

It made him the king again, and his confidence came swirling back to him, and he thought, *The upstart, the amateur, the impertinent, arrogant upstart.*

The stench was overpowering. He pushed himself forward again, wishing that there was more headroom and knowing that, like a woman, the leopard had chosen to fight him on grounds that would favor him the most, and he thought, *We don't even know if it's a male or female.* A male, Talib had said, but when he had looked for the signs himself, he had been unable to see a thing, and he had known that the Malay was merely asserting his own expertise, taking a fifty-fifty chance of being proved right and trusting to his own particular god to back him up.

The tunnel was narrowing now, and there was a moment of alarm, of frustration, when he thought that perhaps he would not be able to find his way to the end of it. Holding the flare ahead of him, shaking it from time to time to make it burn more brightly, he slithered forward, feeling the oppression of the rocks above his head, wondering how long it had been since man had moved in here, A thousand years! A hundred thousand? A million?

And then he saw it. There was an evil glimmer of light, two pinpricks of fire that glared at him out of the darkness above him, two wicked eyes catching the reflected light of his flare.

There was a snarl, an angry, vicious sound that seemed to spit itself out at him, and momentarily he was frightened. He thrust his flare forward and when the tiny lights went out he knew that the leopard had retreated and there was a triumphant spasm of contempt as he pushed forward again, worming his way deeper into the darkness.

He could not see the entrance he had used now, and the rock was as tight-fitting as an overcoat. He fought the claustrophobic effect of it, knowing that even here, in the primeval depths of the ancient earth, he was still the master. Again, he heard the snarl, and he knew that there was only a little farther to go.

And then, suddenly, there was nothing but fear and pain and terror replacing the smug complacency. There was a heated rush of venom, so fast and furious that he closed his eyes in instinctive fright, feeling the blood pouring out of his face, feeling the pain that struck across his chest, feeling that he was blinded and slashed and terrified, fumbling for his throat to see if it was from the jugular vein that the blood was pouring. And then, sensing the closeness of death, he screamed. And in the tight confine of the tunnel his screams were a madman's cry in his own ears and all was darkness and then there was a numb pain in his ankles, too, and the earth was tearing at him, pulling his clothes off him, ripping savagely into his stomach, and then it was light again and Stanton was bending over him saying grimly, "So he's there all right."

Anna was crouched beside him, her face white, and he was surprised that he could see, and he said weakly, "What happened?"

"He slashed you. When you yelled, I pulled you out."

"Slashed me? I don't remember."

"I think you must have fainted. Keep still, it's not too bad. We'll have to watch for infection."

"Fainted?" The shame of it.

"Don't talk, you've lost a lot of blood."

He struggled to a sitting position, locking aghast at the blood that had soaked into his clothes, feeling gingerly at the cut that ran from his face down to his chest, a savage incision an inch or more deep, in four precisely parallel lines that still gushed blood when he moved. He said angrily, "Nonsense, I'll be all right. A little iodine."

With the shame and the anguish came the fear of the poison, the deadly poison of decayed flesh that lies in the hollows of the leopard's claws.

Talib had come running up with the first-aid kit, and Stanton tore open a packet of sulfanilamide and scattered it over the wounds, then tore off some strips of adhesive plaster and pressed them over the gashes, saying, "You're lucky he missed the throat. That's what he was aiming for."

Von Abart said nothing. There was an overpowering weakness on him, and he wondered if he were dying. He looked at Anna and saw that she was smoothing the plaster across his chest. He had not even felt the touch of her fingers. Angrily, he struggled to his feet, pushing her aside when she sought to restrain him. He stood there for a moment, swaying slightly and looking at Stanton's face, thinking, *All right, I fainted. The exhaustion, the stifling air. You think it was fear, you oaf?*

Admiringly, Stanton said, "Well, I take my hat off to you. A rip like that would have killed a lesser man."

Von Abart nodded stupidly, feeling the nausea sweep over him. He heard Anna say, "Look out, he's falling." And then the blackness swept over him and the last thing he knew was that she was looking at him without emotion, and then the earth came up and hit him and the world was gone from his cognizance.

He came to a short while later, a few minutes at the most, and Stanton had already had the boys bring up branches from the tree that stood out starkly like an accusing finger from the rocks, placing them over his body to shield him from the glare of the sun. He shook his head, forcing awareness back to his mind, and said again, "I'm all right, I'm all right."

The cut across his face was painful and he knew that on his chest it was dangerous. He said, "Give me a few minutes. I'll be all right."

"You're lucky to get away with it. If he'd caught your throat..."

"I was flat on my stomach."

"Lucky. Well, at least we know he's scared."

"He's still in there?"

"Of course. There's no way out."

"We'll have to starve him out. It's the only way. I should have listened to you in the first place."

"No, you were right. We haven't the time. And now that you've thoroughly scared him for me, I'm going in after him."

Well, there it was, for better or worse. He was conscious that Anna was looking at him, conscious, too, that von Abart was studiously not answering him.

Her eyes gleaming, Anna said, "He'll be more angry than ever now."

"And more scared. More liable to run."

Von Abart said, "He's a bad one, Stanton. A bad one."

"It's now or never."

"He'll get you. Tell him, Anna. Tell him. He'll listen to you. Tell him to wait."

They were conscious, all of them, of a sudden tension. Anna looked at von Abart very briefly, a casual, dismissing glance that said clearly, *You've lost your chance, Otto.* She said slowly, "I think he'll run, too. I agree with Harry."

Knowing that with that remark, a casual, nonchalant agreement with him, she had openly shown von Abart that she was ready to change her attachment, Stanton felt a sudden depression settling over him. He bent down and picked up a flare, twisting it round in his hands and carefully not looking at von Abart. He said slowly, "You've softened him up, and now we'll have to finish him off. I'm only sorry that he made such a mess of your face just when the job was almost completed."

He could not look at Anna.

He lay down on the ground and wormed his way into the cave.

Ten minutes later the boys at the top gave an excited shout and ran forward to the struggling mass of violent, savage, black and vicious temper that was the leopard. He was inextricably entangled in Talib's nets. And, a moment later, Stanton himself emerged from the cave, his flare still burning, his face begrimed and wet with sweat, his clothes torn and his flesh bruised.

Panting, he flopped to the ground, not caring to look at their captive. When Baka came running over, grinning delightedly, he said, lying on his back, panting, and looking up at the hot white sky, "Tie his legs. Be careful. Get the others."

Baka went running off to call down the slope of the cliff, and he lay there, breathing in great gulps of the clean fresh air, glad that the stifling oppression of the cave was behind him but not liking the triumph that was undoubtedly his, wishing that he too had failed and could honestly say, *It's too much for me, you'll have to try again when you feel stronger*. The wish came to him naturally, without forcing, and there was an immense sadness in him, because he knew that all von Abart's world had collapsed about him; knew, too, that the consolation of his mistress would henceforth be denied him forever.

CHAPTER 12

They struggled laboriously back to the place where the trucks were, shouting angrily at the Malayans as they man-handled the flimsy temporary cage they had built for the leopard, wondering if the bindings were strong enough to contain its furious rushes, knowing the hatred that was in its wicked heart for them.

It had been an uncomfortable journey. Von Abart was sullen and angry because he had failed, and to make matters worse he insisted on walking down the steep slope of the mountain instead of being carried.

Stanton had said to him, "But dammit, you've lost a hell of a lot of blood!"

"Only enough to cleanse the wound. I can walk."

Stanton was fearful, too, of the complications that could set in, knowing the danger of blood poisoning. And so, slowly, they had walked, matching the pace of the shikar to his, and knowing that he was struggling to keep up through sheer obstinacy and nothing else.

With Anna, von Abart had been short and angry, almost brutal, but she had paid no more than token attention to him before dismissing him almost completely, and now, for the first time, Stanton saw that the German was an old, lonely, unloved man, struggling to maintain his position and not quite succeeding.

It was an unbalanced shikar. Out in front, with Stanton leading, and Anna and von Abart close behind him, there was a sullen silence. Behind them, the long line of porters and trackers was turning the march into a dance of jubilation, stomping their feet and clapping their hands and chanting their songs. Sometimes, one of the men would run forward and spit at the leopard, and once Talib had to stop one of them forcibly from hurling his spear at it to show his contempt now that it was a helpless captive.

Its cage was slung on the shoulders of four of the porters, balanced precariously on their sweating backs, and inside the confined space the animal snarled and spat and hissed at them, its evil eyes gleaming. When they put it down to rest it paced up and down in unrelenting anger, letting them see that, though imprisoned, it was not resigned to its fate.

It was large, the largest they had ever seen, and there was not a mark on its sleek flank. As it moved in the sunlight, the skin was black, jet-black, until the sun caught it at just the right angle, and then it was a rich red-brown in which the jet-black spots stood out vividly. Then it would move again and the spots would be gone to melt into the overall sheen of the soft skin.

And when they reached the camp, with the white stars bright in the dark blue-black of the cold sky, it was transferred to the stronger cage that was waiting for it, with the Malayans prodding at it with their spears in the darkness, forcing it to slink in vicious anger through the bars that led from one confinement to another, It seemed to know that they were all there waiting for it, ready to kill should it burst out, and in its smoldering eyes there was a hatred that seemed to show an impatient waiting for a better opportunity.

Von Abart, pale and haggard, went to his tent in silence, and Anna called for water and stripped off her dusty clothes in the privacy of the screened shower-bath, letting them drop around her ankles as the water poured down cold over her heated skin from the can in the tree above her.

The boys were making up their beds, and Talib was making his final rounds of the compound, checking the fires and knowing that other animals, dangerous ones, could be drawn by the scents of the camp.

In the flickering light of the flames, Stanton stood and watched the leopard. He thought he had never seen anything so beautiful. It moved in utter silence, feline, long-bodied and graceful, with a rhythm to its motion that was hypnotic, He could not believe that anything so beautiful could be so dangerous, but looking at the white teeth, whiter by far than usual, he knew that the hatred there was a wicked, deadly thing. Its fascination for him increased as he stood there staring at it, and he marveled than in so short a time the struggle between them could have become so personal. He was saddened that the shikar was drawing to an end, knowing that much had happened that had been quite beyond his control, knowing that the climax of it was yet to come. He feared it, although he trembled with a kind of fervent excitation when he thought of it.

He knew now exactly what Anna had meant. Her terms, she had said, and it was as clear to him now as she had expected it to be then, It was clear, too, why she had gone out of her way to goad him into touching her, to hold him at the edge of her ability, to keep him at all times within reach so that when she wanted him—or in case she wanted him—he would be there. He knew now that she was only waiting for the moment, and that it would be soon.

And he knew just how she would stalk him; carefully at first, to assure herself that he would not get away from her once she had decided to trap him. It would be slow, and careful, and seemingly casual.

He turned at a slight sound, knowing that she was beside him, and for a moment he half-decided to fight against her, not wanting to give way under her conditions, knowing that to betray her lover when he would expect it was a great deal worse than doing it at any other time. At any other time the secret could be kept, and if this was the fine edge of decency, at least it made a certain amount of sense.

He turned and looked at her, and all his half-hearted determination was gone, just as he knew it must go. Her hair, long and fair and polished, hung down to her shoulders, and the sheen on her face, devoid of makeup, gave her a clean and healthy look which he knew was deliberate, a sop to the great American god of wholesomeness. She wore the same green housecoat that seemed to have become so essential a part of her, and it was tighter than usual about her waist as though she were making some sort of effort, a token effort at least, to pass the initiative over to him.

For a little while she stood beside him, smoking, and then she took a cigarette from the case in her pocket and lit it for him, passing it over to him as though to show him that her hand was quite steady. Saying nothing, he took it from her, knowing that even this was part of the stalk, part of the intimacy.

She said at last, moving her head towards the leopard, "A beauty, Harry. The best I've ever seen."

"A dangerous beauty."

"I suppose so. You always see the danger first, Harry, don't you?"

"No, not really. It's a good thing to know that it's there."

"And be ready to run from it?"

"If necessary. But sometimes, the beauty is—it's hypnotic, you can't run from it even if you want to, even if it's the wiser course."

Did that tell her what she wanted to know? He wondered. He said carefully, in spite of himself, not looking at her, "Shall we walk over to the bluff?"

"If you like."

They walked without speaking through the tall ferns that splayed their delicate foliage above them, hearing their faint rustle in the breeze, and for a while they stood close together, so close that he could smell her perfume, just looking out at the darkness of the hot, moist carpet that was the jungle, silent at this distance but full of living things that were stalking each other, living and dying and giving birth and adding to the sum of creation.

He sat down in the long grass, and then lay back and looked at the sky, seeing her tall and slim beside him, and soon she sat down and looked at him and said, very quietly, "Sometimes, the only thing to do with unhappiness, Harry, is to put it behind you, out of sight."

"Maybe. But it's still there. The struthionine approach— it's fine for an ostrich. For us, it's not quite so easy."

"Otto?"

"Otto."

"Worrying about it won't help him, or you. Or me."

"It's sad to see a man come to the end of his little path."

"He'll get over it. Tomorrow, he'll be his usual, jovial self. He can take defeat like an overdose of brandy; he just sleeps it off. Only underneath it all, he's learned something he must really have known, deep down inside him, right from the start. Something that even I wasn't sure of."

"Yes? What's that?"

"That you're a better man than he is."

He said rudely, trying to find succor in rudeness, "Oh, baloney?"

She said again, "A better man, Harry. He's known for a long time that he's not the man he was once, but it was never overtly shown. Nobody else knew it but me, and I could be relied upon to keep quiet because I was just a chattel, a trophy myself, a peasant he'd picked up and trained. He'd trained me to stand there admiringly while he showed off all the other trophies, even though for years now he hasn't been able to hit a haystack at a hundred yards. All those heads on the wall, those skins on the floor...don't you realize it, Harry? They're mine. He boasts about them and shows them off, the great white hunter, and I stand there and say nothing because he's the best man there is and no one can argue with him, and who am I to stand up against him? I'll tell you who I am. I'm a fourteen-year-old girl, a fine specimen, worth taking, and I finished up in his house to be shown off with the rest of them. That's who I am."

There was a muted fury in her voice. Uncomfortably, he said, "He must know that you could always leave him if you wanted to." The specter she was painting of an old man living again his vicarious triumphs saddened him.

Her anger had quickly gone. "It was a slow decline, Harry, a slow one. There was never a neatly defined breaking-point. Perhaps it would have been easier if there had been. Perhaps it's come now."

He did not answer her, and knowing what he was thinking, she said slowly, "Do you want to change the whole world, Harry?"

"No. Not even this little part of it."

"Perhaps that's all the jungle will ever teach us, that we're just a part of it. A very small part."

"You don't have to convince me."

"No? I thought perhaps that you weren't sure." She leaned down in to him and kissed him on the lips, just as she had done that night, when Otto had been watching them, listening, waiting. He knew that if he did not get up and go, now, at this minute, it would be too late, that he would be inextricably entangled forever. He thought, *Goddammit, that's what I've been trying to do for more than a month, what am I thinking of, it's only a question of getting myself out of it, later, some other time, not now*. He put his hands on her shoulders and pulled her down beside him, and then he drew away from her and knelt at her side, and she lay quite still, slim and straight and beautiful while he looked at her, saying nothing, for a long time while he savored the thought of her body.

At last he leaned forward and very gently undid the sash that was round her waist and pulled back the green robe, opening it carefully and folding it back from her with meticulous precision and laying it on the darker green of the grass, even going so far as to smooth it out with hands before he touched her. She did not move. Her pale eyes were wide and solemn and even, he thought, a little sad with the sadness that comes at the end of an era, not at its beginning, as though what he was about to do would not give her a kind of rebirth, but rather would kill her; as though all she had ever loved was behind her now and the future might bring anything—trouble or happiness, but most probably trouble. There was pathos in her motionless, quiet body, stretched out in the moonlight, naked under his probing hands, faintly brown like ivory, smooth and supple and infinitely tender, and for an incongruous moment he thought of the half-caste girl, Chep, wondering where she was at this moment, grateful to her and knowing that she had forgotten him as he had forgotten her, thinking nothing of it any more.

He looked at her until he could endure the pain of it no longer, feeling the alabaster touch of her flesh and letting the fire build up inside him for the recondite pleasure of containing it until it would no longer be contained, not caring what happened to her in the process, not caring for von Abart, not caring for himself, caring for nothing except the coming explosion. And when at last she moved, she put up her arms and he felt the fierce, ecstatic pain of her finger-nails biting into his skin, just as he had felt it once before. But now, she was pulling him down tight to her, saying over and over again, "Love me, Harry, love me..." and he rolled over on top of her and made violent love with her, feeling the smooth oiliness of the perspiration that came to her, and then nothing mattered any more except that all he had ever wanted or loved or fought for was here, now close to him, tight in his arms, There was nothing in the world except that which was in his embrace.

When she left him a little later, she was smiling secretly, and she touched him on the cheek with her fingers, and looked back at him as she walked away, and he smoked a cigarette in the darkness, wondering if the cards were on the table now or if he were still playing a secret hand, wondering if their secret would be kept and fearing that she might choose otherwise.

He walked slowly back to the compound, and when he passed her tent she was standing there waiting for him, calling him inside with a finger to her lips and a quick look at Otto's tent. He slipped in with her and stripped off his clothes, and when he sat on the edge of the bed she said, whispering so quietly that he could hardly hear her, "Not on the cot—it makes too much noise. On the floor."

He knew then that for the time being, at least, the hand could still be played, and when he had loved her again he began to plan and to devise and to hope, while the crickets were sounding off in the trees around them and the night animals were prowling, and the noise of the jungle came floating on the still air across the broad plateau. He lay awake for a long time, his hand on her breast, feeling the patriarchal essence of his touch, knowing that in spite of the frightening dangers, in spite of the urgent need for a detached and skillful caution, he had never been so happy in his life.

Beside him, her naked body warm and soft and leopard-like, Anna was sleeping like a child.

Gently, he slipped from her embrace and went quietly back to his tent. And in the morning, when the three of them were sitting at their prosaic breakfast, there was nothing to show that the world, during the night, had been changed.

The camp had grown in the month they had been there. Where once there had been a wild profusion of trees, there was now almost a village.

The hastily built huts of kajang had been tightened and trimmed, and even the low-roofed Sakai shelter had a homey appearance. Graceful Malay women winnowed rice, their slim brown arms moving in a dancing, swaying rhythm. The men, with their sarongs rolled up, moved their muscled bodies as they split the tough rattan cane with sharp knives to bind together the stout branches of the cages. Behind their ears they wore cream-colored temple flowers that gave off a thick, sweet odor.

Rain had fallen, but the sun had dried up the earth, missing only the minute pools of water that gathered in the huge leaves of the red-flared cannas.

More Sakai had come into the camp, too; they squatted on their haunches, sharpening their knives, cutting out the jiggers from their broad, strong toenails, while their women, naked except for a bunch of leaves, skinned the pangolin, the scaly anteater. Some of the men cut strips from the leaf rib of a palm to make darts for their blowpipes, and others made carefully intricate patterns on their quivers. A mother painted her child's face with red and white stripes, because life was good, and why shouldn't you show it?

Another compound had been built for the animals. There were two tigers now, a pair of sambur, a rhinoceros, a peacock and peahen with their brood, a pair of young orangutan males for breeding, a seladang, three barking deer, some smaller apes and the leopard. And every day more were coming in. The pits had been dug and the traps set out in forest and plain, and under Talib's skilled direction the team of trackers and porters had been out every morning to bring in the catch. At the compound the poor specimens had been released and the good ones kept. A score of Malays had been put to the task of making portable cages for them, and all day long there was the sound of chipping wood as their axes and their parangs cut at the hard ironwood.

As they took their meals, relaxing now that the greater part of their work was finished, Stanton noticed that von Abart was making good use of the brandy bottle. He remembered that Anna had told him, on their first night out, that he had been drunk, and now, watching, he wondered that he had not noticed before the flush that came over his face when he was drinking.

The final days went slowly by. They sent a runner, their fastest Sakai, carrying a message to bring Hadjian out to arrange for the loading and the freighting, but it was nearly a week later before he appeared, in the heat of the afternoon, in answer to their summons. He was riding a small jungle pony, panting and sweating and looking extremely uncomfortable as he balanced his plumpness precariously atop it. A Malay was leading the horse to make sure that it should not stumble. He waved at them and shouted, and when he drew near he tumbled down untidily and looked about him, beaming at what he saw.

He said cheerfully, "Very good camp, I think, no? You are pleased with Talib? He has been good?"

Stanton took his hand and shook it, feeling the hot, sweaty pudginess of it. "Very good. You got here quickly."

"I took my truck, Mr. Stanton, as far as I could, and then I came on with this unhappy animal. Really, its back is most uncomfortable. I see we have a great deal of work to do. There are many animals. May I take a look?"

"Of course. What's the best way to get them to the coast? I thought we'd carry them to the railway line and ship them through Pehang. Can we get enough flatcars?"

"Of course, Mr. Stanton, it is simple. I will see how many we need and make the necessary arrangements." Looking at von Abart's face, he said, "I see we have had a little trouble. The tigers? One of the monkeys?"

"A leopard. The black one."

"A leopard! You are very lucky, Mr. von Abart. Perhaps I

should send for some herbs. If we crush some garlic?"

"We have sulfanilamide."

"Oh yes, of course, that's always a good second best, isn't it, if you can't find garlic. Are you sure it will be all right?"

"It's all right."

"It is very poisonous, you know."

"I know that, too."

"Yes. Yes, of course."

In the sudden awkward silence, Stanton said heartily, "Well, I guess you must be hungry, are you? We have some kijang, some partridge, pheasant...And there's some fairly cold beer, too."

"Ah, splendid. I must confess that I am a little hungry. And I took the liberty of bringing you a bottle of wine. As a token of my esteem."

"Well, that's very kind of you."

Hadjian shouted to the Malay, who ran back to the pack horse and produced a bottle of liquor. The servant polished it quickly on his loincloth and ran forward with it and held it out with both hands, and when Stanton took it he bowed and nodded his head with a courtly, old-fashioned gesture. Then they all gathered round the table, and while Suleiman prepared a meal they took out their maps and studied the best route home.

They went over to look at the long line of cages, neatly laid out now in the order in which they would be carried, while the porters stood by twisting their ropes and binding pads on their shoulders, tugging at the wooden bars to see that they were tight and firm, and when the darkness began to show itself in the cooling of the hot air, they sat down for their final meal at the green canvas table, feeling a nostalgic regret for the sounds and the silences of the bush that would soon be so far behind them, no more than another memory among a thousand memories.

They went late to bed that night, sitting up and chatting with the Armenian, listening to his inconsequential chatter, and then, when the camp was quiet again and all the fires were down to the last red embers, Stanton rose and walked over to the bluff where their first frenzied love had been, standing and looking down at the soft red earth that had cradled her body, and when he walked back to the camp in the silence, he stood for a while and watched the tents, seeing that the light was still burning in Anna's and wondering if she were waiting for him. And then Chep came out, a small half-caste girl carrying towels and a basin of water, and she threw the water on to the ground and walked into the shadows and waited, looking at him. He shook his head slowly, and she turned away and went slowly over to the fire where the other women were.

He stood there in the darkness until the small light of the kerosene lamp went out, and then he went to Anna's tent and slipped inside.

And at daybreak, the shikar was on its long and tortuous way to the railway line.

It took them seven slow and laborious days to reach it.

They marched from sunup to sundown, sweating through the steaming jungle, slashing at the lianas that seemed to be conscious of an effort to delay them, to hold them, as though deliberately, within the stinking confines of their dark green humus. The leeches sucked at them in the swamps, and the mosquitoes ravaged their faces and their arms, and everywhere was the sour-sweat smell of decaying vegetation.

They dropped from the high plateau to the dark wet forest of the plain, and every morning one of them shot a sambur or a pig for the day's food supply, and every night they slept by the light of the bamboo flares. Once even the competent Talib lost his way and the stolid Sakai waited patiently with a blind trust in the whites who would somehow, one day, lead them back to the territory they knew. One of the Malays climbed a tall palm that thrust its top out into the bright sky, then clambered down and mutely signaled the direction they should take.

Hadjian had left them as soon as they had passed down from the high plateau and reached the edges of the forest, and had gone on with his bearers to find the truck that he had left by the side of the track, stumbling along on his wiry little mount, wobbling from side to side and wishing he were back in his house, but calculating that he was making a lot of money out of all this. And when he had found the truck parked under the shade of a bamboo clump with the driver fast asleep, and a little drunk as well, lying in the cool earth under its shadow, he drove off at high speed to the little village he called his home, and telephoned to the Railway Company at Pehang to ensure that the flatcars would be ready as promised.

Then he went back to his friendly house to add a little more to his account and to sleep off the exhaustion of his long and tiring journey.

Then there was the angry, hurried, impatient loading of the animals at the port, with Talib still standing sadly there, knowing that his work had come to an end, knowing that there was a big bonus in the Tuan's pocket for him, and knowing too that no amount of money could repay him for the loss of the new friends he had made. He stood there, a giant among his fellows, taller than they, far darker too, and somber in his loneliness. And when the work was done, and the boys had all gone back to continue the lives they had known before, when the freighter was steaming slowly away from the hot shoreline, Stanton could remember only the lone sight of Talib, standing in solitary dignity in his finest sarong, a small red cap on his head, a bright blue sash at his waist, clutching the fine rifle that the Tuan had given him, had given to the best head-boy in the business, standing huge and proud and waiting until the ship was far out to

193

sea and to the Tuan on board he had become only a symbol, a cipher, and a reminder that now they were headed for the cold, graceless rush of civilization and away from the jungle where the earth had been born.

CHAPTER 13

It was not until they had been five days in the Indian Ocean, steaming west towards Colombo, with the flying fish thudding on the deck, that the first warning came of serious trouble.

Von Abart had long since, it seemed, recovered from the attack of depression that had settled over him after the incident in the leopard's cave. There was a joviality about him which, though it was patently forced, at least seemed to indicate that he was doing his best not to let the indignity take too strong a hold on him.

But he was not a man to let an affront to his arrogance be forgotten. There were times when Stanton caught him looking across the narrow table at him with a great deal of distaste in his eyes, and then he would look away quickly as though ashamed, not of relishing what he was thinking, but of being caught at it. Sometimes in the middle of a harmless conversation he would suddenly fall silent and moody, seeming not to hear what was said to him, and then Stanton would look across at Anna and she would turn away, saying nothing, too, and there would be a harsh and unpleasant atmosphere settling over them that could not be dispelled.

ALAN CAILLOU

They began snapping at each other, all three of them, and there were moments of bitter anger over trivial matters of no importance. On one such occasion, Stanton had said mildly, "We ought to have proper cages made for the transportation across Italy, you know. I don't like the idea of keeping them in these wooden things." He had been about to add, "They're strong enough, really, but steel cages would be better," But von Abart had interrupted him rudely.

"Sticks tied together with string. If anything goes wrong we'll be in trouble. You should have done something about it."

"We still can. We can order some as soon as we get to Colombo. Send a cable to one of the German firms."

"And then sit on the docks for a month while we wait for them."

Saying no more, von Abart got up and stalked out. He went to the stern of the little freighter and watched the water swirling in its wake, and alone inside the cabin they could see his outline against the bright patch of hot sky that came to them down the long corridor and into the lounge. It was almost as if he had purposely placed himself where they could see him in the distance and could retain his position as the menace that was threatening them.

Stanton said irritably, "I'll be glad to get off this goddam ship."

"And then, Harry, what will you do then?"

There it was again, the eternal problem. It was a question which, from the very beginning, he had not been able to answer. He said lamely, "I don't know. So many things can happen."

"You mean it's a problem you'll face when you come to it."

It was a flat statement, meaning, *You'll sleep with me as long as I'm around, but once we're home you're on your own.* She looked at him with a sort of amused tolerance, as though, knowing what he was thinking, she were able to assure herself that he would not be able to get away from her quite so easily. Seeking to impress herself on him, she moved a little closer, knowing that the cold detachment with which he tried to view their affair was only possible while he did not feel the physical need for her. She smiled and said, "I've only got to touch you, Harry, you know that."

She was telling him, quite openly, of the hold she had on him, telling him that she knew they were together now, for keeps, and that sooner or later von Abart would get his marching orders and then it would be just the two of them, Stanton and Kruger, Kruger and Stanton, partners, lovers. She knew, too, that in his cold detachment this was the last thing he wanted. He wanted an end to the affair, sooner or later, before it became a thing of permanence. And yet the love in him for her, a purely physical love perhaps, was so overpowering that the vaccine of his dead love for Cora could not serve to inoculate him against a second dose of the disease he so greatly dreaded. He said to himself, *You think you've got me over a barrel, you bitch, and maybe you have, but I don't think so.* He was trying desperately to convince himself of his ability to take her when he wanted her and to leave her when he was ready to.

It was the old pattern, the game he had learned a long time ago, in school even, when it was matter of prestige to play the field and let those who would find themselves embroiled in too deep affection. All through his life, he had made it a cardinal rule. And always he had succeeded, except in that one disastrous affair with Cora, the woman who, at first, would not come to him without the bourgeois touch of sanctity, so that in a rash determination to take her at all costs, even the cost of sacrificing his liberty, he had married her, feeling a triumph, feeling that there was always a way even if it was a desperate one; and on this unfortunate premise the marriage had immediately begun to break up.

She had remained a frigid, beautiful animal that had made

197

him sick at heart because he could not bear the thought of such great beauty going to what he had come to look upon as waste. She had the skin and the breasts and the feline grace of a great courtesan, and yet, for her, the act of love was a slightly degrading necessity, like going to the bathroom, a thing that had to be got over with as quickly and as discreetly as possible.

Thinking of her now and looking at Anna, he was well aware of the difference between the two of them. She had all of Cora's grace and most of her beauty, but more than that she had an excess of rank, outright desire that matched his own - and the competence to give that desire the full rein it deserved. Drawing on his cigarette, saying nothing, he thought. *If I had to marry again, that's the kind of woman I would want, Let the lusts be satisfied and the other little troubles are of no significance. There's no argument that can't be settled in bed.*

Taking his silence for acquiescence, gathering herself for a fight, she said insistently, "Is that what you mean, Harry? There's no time like the future?"

He said suddenly, "He knows about us, Anna, doesn't he?"

"No, Harry. He doesn't."

"I'm damn sure he does. Ever since the matter of the leopard. It seems a hundred years ago."

"You underestimate his pride."

"It's more than an assault on his ego that's worrying him."

"It's exactly that. No more, no less."

"Two weeks now, he's been looking at me like...as though he'd like to get me in the sights of his rifle. You think I can't tell what's on his mind?"

"The downhill process is a slow one, Harry, you must know that. He lost the leopard, and at the same time he made a bad showing in front of me, a worse showing than you did. It's this which has built up his hate."

"Build up is right. You can see the bricks going up, one on top of the other. Sooner or later the whole thing's going to come tumbling down in a cloud of dust."

"Maybe."

"You take it pretty calmly."

"I can if I have to."

He knew that this was the time to say it, that this was the time to make it clear to her. But, looking at her now, the great surge of his love for her swept over him and he knew that he could not survive without her; knew, too, that the moment she was gone he would kick himself for not having made the break. He was on the edge of that void that lies between the two great loves, the love that is in the mind and the love that is in the loins, and there was a great struggle going on inside him, a struggle to keep it confined to his lusts, to a force that he could understand and satisfy. Ever since that fierce and strangely empty night when he had taken her out there on the hot red earth, the fight between them had been going on. He told himself time and time again that a woman does not love what she already has; but he omitted to tell himself, too, that she will not easily let what she holds get away from her either. This was the problem between them, and this was the way they had fought each other.

He said again, "It's all building up inside him."

"It's the natural result of the life he chose for himself."

"A good man, and we're slowly killing him. I suppose you know that?"

He was telling her, stay with him, Anna, and I'll be around somewhere, from time to time, once a year or so if I can afford it, and you'll have to sneak out of the house somehow and I'll be there, in Munich, in some grubby little hotel and nobody need know about it. Impermanence. In case she didn't understand, he said, "He must never know, Anna. Never."

She did not answer, not accepting the showdown. He scowled and said, "He's a better man than I am in every possible way."

"Is he?"

"Of course he is."

"He's on the way down, Harry. You're on the way up."

"And that means that you want to switch your affections? Isn't that a little callous?"

"No more callous than your calculating love-making, Harry."

Had it then been so clear to her? Had his self-control been so obvious even in the heat of his fury with her? Perhaps it had. You cannot hide a lifetime of habit, and he knew that after the act he had always been most careful to make a joke of these endearing phrases so that she would not think he had abandoned the cold intelligence he had always tried to apply, had not lost it to the heated emotions of the moment. He had always made this clear to her; that his relationship with her was to be a thing of physical satisfaction, mutual, perhaps, but no more than that.

He had said to himself, *She's von Abart's mistress, not his wife, she's fair game for anyone passing by, and if this makes her a whore what right has she to consider herself anything better?* What right indeed.

And so, when he had loved her, he had said, many times, "I love you," not expecting, and not wanting, that she should believe it. It was merely part of the game you played, a polite way of saying thank you and I hope you liked it, too.

That's all she gets, he said to himself, *that's her ration, whether she likes it or not.* But looking at her now, feeling the need for her creeping over him again, because she was merely talking about their love and showing him, quite clearly, that she wanted him, he was not at all sure that he could still regard her with the cool dispassion he had always so carefully exercised.

The dark brown flush of her flesh made her hair, bleached by the sun, lighter than ever, and the heat of her seemed close to the surface of her skin as though the sun had raised the temperature of her blood; as though in the stifling heat the need for bodily contact had been artificially heightened. She wore a white dress made up of a short skirt and a halter that left so much of her exposed that even now, knowing the danger of what she had in mind, knowing that a false move now would embroil him with her irrevocably, he could not resist the temptation to put out his hand and touch her leg.

Stroking her thigh, cocking an eye towards the patch of bright outside light where von Abart was, he said gently, "My love-making's not calculating, you know that. On the contrary. When I get close to you there's not a vestige of control."

The heat of her transfused itself through the tips of his fingers, and looking across the tiny cabin to the bar he saw that the solitary steward on the freighter, a tall thin Arab, had discreetly gone to his quarters to leave them alone.

She said suddenly, "I'm going to tell him, Harry."

His hand stopped moving. He said slowly, "He already knows. I'm sure of it."

"He doesn't."

"How can you be so sure?"

"I know him well, Harry. Ten years is a long time."

"But he must."

"He only knows the half of it."

He was sure that it was coming now, that the cards were going to be laid neatly out for his scrutiny. He wished that he could find a way to make a joke of it, to change the subject abruptly. There was a look in her pale eyes, a look of intense, defiant concentration, as though she were challenging him to withdraw. He thought graphically of the leopard, letting his mind wander because any escape, however brief, would do, and he could see it standing there on the bluff, ready to seize the bait, taking it with almost contemptuous assurance, seeming to know that the one weapon he feared, their guns, would not be used on him and that without this weapon there was nothing to stop him from taking what he wanted to take.

He said sourly, "The half of it? What's that supposed to mean?"

She got up and went to the bar and reached for the bottle of brandy that the steward had left on the counter, and when she came back to the table, giving von Abart no more than a brief glance as she passed the doorway, she poured out two glasses as though to say, sit down and be comfortable, and let's have a nice long chat. As she passed the glass to him, leaning over him and sitting closer than she had been before, he could smell the blood-quickening scent of her.

She said very quietly, "He suspects, Harry, that you've made love to me. Once, twice, half a dozen times. He suspected it even before it happened. Long before it happened."

He took a deep breath. "Then I was right."

"No, Harry. You were wrong."

Not understanding, he stared at her. She said patiently, "Only the half of it. A passing affair, a brief interlude, why should it worry him too much? He'd accept the pain of it in the same way that he'd accept the scratch of an animal, something which is annoying, painful perhaps, but will heal. He must have been sure, always, over these last few years, that I was being unfaithful to him, even though..." She turned to him and said, "I wasn't, Harry. I promise you that I wasn't. And so, right from the beginning, he's suspected you."

"And he never said a goddam word, not till right at the end."

"Why should he?"

"For God's sake! He could have put a bullet through my head any time out there. Any time at all."

"There was no reason to until the leopard."

He sat and stared at her, then took a drink to break the rigidity of the moment, feeling that any movement would cause a semblance of an ease he did not really feel.

He said, "Don't you think you'd better start talking? Maybe you understand all this Gothic gobbledygook, but I'm damned if I do."

"It's very simple, really. I told you, I told you a long time ago, that he's grown to depend on me in the house, in the bush...especially in the bush. He could always get another woman to look decorative around his library, to entertain his guests, to bolster the front he puts on, to show him off as the man of taste and quality. He could even find someone who'd sleep with him without feeling disgusted by his hopeless attempts. And it is hopeless, believe me. But he'd never find someone who would go with him out into the bush and bring back trophies he could say were his, and this is the most important thing in his life, don't you see that? He's the great von Abart, and no one knows that he's lost his greatness except me. Hell, he can't even shoot straight any more, and when there's a good specimen to be picked up, I'm the one who does the shooting. Don't you realize what that means to a man whose whole life has been built around that one premise—that there's no one in the trade better than he is? That he's the top man, the acknowledged leader? Can't you realize what it meant to him when Mendel, back in Munich, told him that you, an American, had been chosen for this assignment? Can't you realize that? Did you know that there was a time when they contemplated sending you by yourself and leaving him out of it altogether? And do you know why they changed their minds and let him go along as your number two? Well, I'll tell you. It was because I pointed out the need for a face-saving. Not for Otto but for Bavaria, for Germany even. I told them what the Society would think if we had to go abroad for our hunters, particularly if we had to go to America, because, take my word for it, the Americans are held in a great deal of contempt in Germany today, in spite of all you've done for us and in spite of all you want to do. Does that make it clear to you? Indignity is the one thing Otto cannot tolerate, and they had to choose an

American to replace him. An American! He was a prisoner during the war, did you know that? And all he knows of Americans is that they were people who put him behind barbed wire, like an animal, He swallowed his hatred and he swallowed it well, but its deep inside him still and its turning his stomach over. And all the time you've been in complete ignorance of it. Why don't you grow up, Harry?"

He felt that he was trembling. He said, muttering, knowing the inadequacy of it, "We've been getting along fine."

She said scornfully, "If only you knew! He saw all this coming even before I did, and he pushed it aside as something too unpleasant to contemplate. He's a once-great man who still lives in a mythical world of his memories, a man who won't let go. He's a cripple who's been shouldered aside to make way for a new leader, and in the process he's lost his crutch. And only since the leopard has he realized that he's lost it."

He took a deep breath. "And yet, if he knew before...He doesn't seem to mind the fact that..." He wondered how he could put it without too great indelicacy. "The fact that I've been, shall I say, misusing his crutch?"

She smoothed her brief skirt over her thighs, fanning it to let the breeze get at her legs. Not looking at him, she said, "To you, it's only a question of biology, isn't it? The great American preoccupation with the purity of the body. Can't you understand that to us there are more important things than flesh and blood? The body can be used, misused, it doesn't really matter. But it's here, inside you—that's the thing that really matters."

She leaned forward and put her hand to her breast, saying, "Here, deep inside, that's where the important things are. Bodily infidelity doesn't mean too much to us because the body is not as important as all that. It's what's underneath it that counts. Believe me, Harry, I can love you in bed without being unfaithful to Otto, and he understands that. He understands it clearly. And he understands too that my infidelity starts the moment I can love you without physical contact, because that's when the important things inside of me are being brought into use - the things that have always been Otto's. For the rest...you'll never understand it, Harry, will you?" She took a drink of her brandy and said steadily, "What does it matter to Otto or anyone else if I go to bed with you? As long as I'm not unfaithful to him."

"Well, that's putting a fine Germanic edge on it."

"You think so? The body's a pretty lousy piece of mechanism, Harry. You should know that. It doesn't matter a great deal what you do with it. But inside you, in the heart, the mind...The soul, if you like."

"I wish to hell I knew what you are driving at."

"At this, Harry. Otto has long been resigned to the fact that his showpiece needs a little attention, biologically, once in a while. I told you as much out there in the bush. He accepts it, because he knows he must."

"The complaisant lover."

"Don't mock him for it. He's prepared to hide from a fact that would be unpleasant to him if it showed itself out in the open. So he runs from it. And to a man like Otto it's not easy to run from anything. It takes a great deal of courage for a brave man to be a coward."

"All right. And now?"

"Now he knows that. He knows that inside me, too, that bond between us has been broken, after all this time. That's the thing he won't accept."

When he stared at her, saying nothing, she smiled at the look on his face and said gently, "My body went off to someone else's bed, Harry, and in a little while my mind followed it, too. That's where Otto's trouble is. He knows it. But don't worry, Harry. I know what I have to do. It's not going to be easy either for Otto or for me. But I'm going to do it. My mind's made up."

The little pang of alarm was in him again, twisting itself

into his consciousness, forcing upon him an awareness of the irrevocability of the step he had taken out there in the bush when he had so casually, without thought of the latent complications that might arise, pulled her down beside him in the cool long grass where the moon had seemed to be floating along below them, making him feel, in the delicately prolonged ecstasy of her embrace, that he was a god. But he was not; he was just a nice guy out for a good time, and now the credit card had come home in the mail.

He said, "Go on, I'm listening."

"I'm going to leave him, Harry. After all this time, I'm going to leave him. I want a man who can love me. For keeps."

There it was, neatly laid out on the table at last. For keeps.

How do you tell a woman who has proposed to you that you want her only as an occasional mistress? Particularly, how do you tell it to this woman? And how do you say to a man, I'm sorry, pal, I've always admired you, looked up to you, hell, I've even read your books, and I've taken your woman away from you and here she is back on a platter, a little soiled, perhaps, but still usable.

This was his cue, he told himself, to get up quietly and go, tiptoeing out into the night and catching the first train out of there, as, indeed, he had done on occasions before. He listened to the gentle slap of the Red Sea waves and felt the rocking of the boat that was his prison and said to himself, *Yeah, get the first train out.*

He passed her a cigarette, saying nothing, and lit one himself, looking at her obliquely and trying to figure out how callous he could be about it, trying, too, to muster his courage. But looking at the long slim ivory softness of her leg, the memory of her body came back to him, and he was kneeling there again in the darkness with his hands at her waist, gently undoing her sash and watching the reflection of the moon that drenched her long white torso that was faintly touched with brown; he remembered the great sadness in her eyes.

At last he sighed, and smiled at her, and leaned in to her and said, earnestly, "Wait a little while, Anna, please. To please me."

Momentarily, there was a brief light of anger on her face, and then she smiled with that superior, tolerant smile she had, and said slowly, putting out a hand and touching him, "All right, if that's what you want."

"It's what I want, Anna. It's a question of—of timing."

"Yes, yes, I suppose so."

She was still watching him carefully, watching his struggles. She said, "But meanwhile, be nice to him, won't you?"

Be nice to him. He had done just that. With a forced cheerfulness, he had gone on deck, slapped Otto heartily on the back, and had said, "Well, come inside and have a drink before we finish the bottle."

Ten minutes later, they were chatting together as though nothing had happened. The tension and the fear and the apprehension were gone; they were just below the surface of their emotions, lying dormant and waiting to be sparked into violent, angry passion.

The watery world was spraying up under their bows as the ship steamed slowly home.

CHAPTER 14

All through the long weary journey they had maintained at least a semblance, a superficial varnish, of an adequate relationship.

Von Abart had retired into the protective shell of his introspective silence, sitting for hours at a time without a word, smoking innumerable cigarettes and drinking innumerable glasses of brandy, regardless of the time of the day or night.

Once, late at night, when he had retired to his room, and Anna had gone to hers, Stanton was alone on the deck looking out to sea and feeling the cold night-time breeze of the Mediterranean, when von Abart came and stood silently beside him, saying nothing at first but just standing there as though to show his presence and to ask, silently, for something that he was not prepared openly to beg for. It was as though, like a dog that is too well trained to bark for its food but will nonetheless stand patiently by its owner to wait, he were placing himself into the picture of Stanton's awareness and thus demanding his quota of attention. And what form that attention was supposed to take, Stanton could only guess.

He looked at his watch and saw that it was nearly one o'clock. Putting his back to the rail, feeling the cold hard presence of it in the small of his back, he said, "Late for you, isn't it? It's a nice night."

Von Abart looked at him with a great deal of distaste and leaned his bulk against it, staring down at the water. For a long time he said nothing, and Stanton, looking sideways at the hard set of his mouth, knew that he was struggling to put into simple speech some unpleasant thoughts that he did not really want to share. At last, looking down into the water, he said, "You'll never get her, Stanton."

So, it was out at last. Ready for it, knowing exactly what he had to say, he answered, "You'll have to explain that, Otto. I'm not trying to get anything that belongs to you. In spite of what you think."

"No?"

"No."

"A little innocent hand-holding in the moonlight, is that all it is? I've seen the way you look at her. But take my word for it, Stanton, you'll never get more than the inessentials from her. She'll take what she can from you, and then she'll come back to me because I'm the man who made her what she is. She was nothing when I found her, nothing at all. Everything she is today, I made. And she knows it. She'll never give you more than her fur to stroke."

"There's no reason why she should. Why I should want her to."

"In other words, you're going to deny everything."

"There's nothing to deny, Otto. Nothing at all."

"Yes, that's your best approach. But I know exactly what goes on in that petty bourgeois mind of yours, Stanton. There's a pretty girl with a much older man, and it's hot and dark and uncivilized. All right, I'll agree with you on one thing: I'm at a disadvantage on the surface. Your good looks, your youth, your boyish naiveté - I suppose they mean something to an impressionable woman. But Anna's not as impressionable as all that, Stanton, take my word for it. You're wasting your time."

A liner passed them by in the darkness, far off in the

distance, too far to be more than a silent, eerie thing of light gliding over the water. Playing for time, trying to find out more, knowing that this was all part of the game too, he said, "She's a beautiful woman, Otto, of course I'm attracted to her. But I'm attracted to a dozen lovely women, and that doesn't mean...It doesn't mean a damn thing. I have no intention of trying to cause trouble with Anna or with anyone else."

"It would be a waste of your time."

"Then why do you bother to come and warn me off?"

That's the crux of the matter, he was thinking. *He's not sure of himself any more, but one thing is getting clearer every minute—he knows a damn sight less than Anna believed he knew, up to this minute, Now it's a matter of holding on tight, keeping things just as they are. An unsteady course but a safe one. Thank God I started out with a denial, just a matter of routine and it always pays off.*

Von Abart looked at him with a great deal of distaste and said clearly, "Because there is a turning point in any man's career, Stanton. And if Anna should succumb to the boyish charm you've been waving in her face so blatantly, that would be my turning point. I'm not ready for it yet. Oh. I don't mind a little innocent flirtation. But she belongs to me, Stanton, and don't you forget it. Everything she is, I made her. She's mine."

"And yet you're scared she'll leave you."

"Leave me?" Von Abart was genuinely surprised. "Leave me? She'd never do that, never. I'm only scared, if that's the word, that she may begin to doubt me, to wish that I had...that had more to offer her. I don't want her to stay with me wishing every minute that you were there, too."

"And you think that's likely?"

Slowly, he was gaining the upper hand. His position was strengthening with every revelation of von Abart's ignorance, and he began to wonder if Anna had magnified his knowledge for her own distorted purpose. When von Abart did not answer, he said blandly, "I've a great deal of respect for you, Otto; you must know that. I don't want to make enemies among men of your caliber."

"No, I don't believe you would." He turned away from the water and looked Stanton straight in the eye. "I believe that this, at least, is one of your democratic virtues, It hasn't been easy for me to say this, Harry. It's not pleasant to distrust a man you like, even if it's only a grudging affection. Yes, I'll be frank with you—I have no reason to like your kind, and if you weren't one of the clan things might be very different between us. And it's harder still to tax a man with your distrust. Can you understand that?"

"Yes, I think I can." The cloak of virtue was warm on his shoulders. "I'm sorry if I've...well, if I've almost stepped out of line. But I haven't quite, you know. Only almost."

He was smiling in the friendliest possible manner, an open-faced, good-natured smile, proclaiming his absolute innocence. And then, suddenly, an awareness came over him that von Abart was about to strike him. He knew instantly that his denial was exactly what had been expected of him, that von Abart was merely sounding him out, also playing the game but playing it better because he'd been at it longer and the process of deception came to him more easily. There was a cold hatred, an overwhelming loathing, as clearly marked on von Abart's face as though he had already raised a horsewhip and was about to bring it down. Stanton was shocked. There was sudden physical fear in him, not fear for himself but fear of what he might have to do, and he was thinking, *By God, he's going to hit me, he'll try and throw me overboard.* The consciousness of the cold water behind and below him was sharp in his mind, and he thought, *If he does that, if he starts a fight...In spite of his size, in spite of his strength, I can lick him, I can lick him easily, and what then? To fight with a man old enough to be my father? To beat up an elderly man who's only trying to hold on to the woman he loves and with whom I've been amusing myself? Is this what I've started, is this what I've come to?*

He was trembling suddenly, and then von Abart turned on his heel and stalked away into the darkness of the cabin, and left him there, more scared than ever and still knowing absolutely nothing. He said to himself, *So he does know, after all. She was right. And he wants to know what I propose to do about it. And how the hell can you tell a man that you propose to crawl like an insect back to the slime you came from?*

And yet, he thought, *can I do that? Can I forget her quite so easily? The long supple warmth and the love of her, the uncontrolled, animal passion of her? Can I so easily kiss her good-bye and find someone else to take her place? Will someone else do? Just anyone else?*

He knew that the time had come to make his decision. And he knew also that intention was no substitute for action.

They reached Naples four days later.

There had been no more trouble. It was as though von Abart had lost completely all the doubts that had been troubling him and was once more in complete control of his reasoning. Stanton, watching him closely, knew that the clear knowledge that had come after their talk had replaced those doubts and left him calmer, more composed and sure in his own mind of what he had to do. Uneasily, Stanton wished he knew what that was.

But he noticed that Anna had become more wary. She, too, had sensed that something had radically changed her lover's thinking. Just before they had docked, when von Abart had been below supervising the readying of the cages, she had come to him with an unaccustomed uncertainty in her manner, talking quietly as though she were now, at last, in fear of being discovered.

She said, "What's happened to him, Harry?"

He said, troubled, "I thought you knew all about him."

"I do. I know enough to realize that I've lost my understanding of him, if only for the moment. Something's happened between you, hasn't it?"

He hesitated before telling her, then decided that it might clear the way for him. He said slowly, "He came to me one night and asked me to leave you alone."

Astonished, she said, "I don't believe it"

"No, neither do I, not now. But that's what I believed, at first, He seemed to think that...well, that I had been trying to get closer to you than I should, and I said I hadn't. It's as simple as that. Only I think I should have admitted, even if only tacitly, a little more than I did. He didn't believe me. He was just clarifying a point or two in that mind of his, wanting to see how I'd react. He must have taken me for a bloody idiot. What's more, he was right."

"I see."

"Have you told him?"

"No. No, I haven't."

"Why not?"

"You didn't want me to, did you?"

"I don't think this is the right time."

Stall her again, it's going well, keep stalling. He said earnestly, "Let's get this job finished, Anna. Let's get these animals back safely first. Then we can decide what we have to do."

He could feel the impact of her mind boring a neat hole through the facade of his bluff, as though all the attempts he might make at dissimulation were quite worthless. She said, "Is that a decision you still have to make, Harry?"

"That's not what I mean. Sure, we've got to tell him, sooner or later. But since he knows already..."

"He only knows what we've done. Not what we're going to do."

213

ALAN CAILLOU

"He sure as hell knows what *he's* going to do."

"And what's that?"

He shook his head. He said glumly, "Your guess is as good as mine."

She said nothing; but he knew, looking at her now, that her guess was a great deal better than his. Von Abart came up the companionway (in the nick of time, Stanton thought) and called out to them that the cages were all secured and ready for the slings. They all went to the rail and watched the freighter easing itself gently into the dock, and then they heard a shout from the shore and there was Mendel, beaming and waving at them, waving a sheaf of papers delightedly, almost jumping up and down in his excitement.

A moment later, the ship was secured.

There was no time, once they were ashore, to worry about von Abart. He had the animals to fuss over.

The cages, looking sadly insecure in their Malayan lashings, were carefully slung ashore and on to the boxcars that Mendel had waiting for them. He was delighted. He stood and stared at the leopard with open mouth, stuttering his astonishment. "But - but it's enormous. And not a blemish on the skin, not a blemish..."

He turned to Stanton and said, "You've done a fine job, Mr. Stanton, a fine job." Von Abart, nearby, turned away, and Anna watched him as he went over to busy himself with the loading, hiding his anger by not letting himself be seen. "A good team," Mendel said, "an excellent team." He too watched von Abart's disappearance, and peering at Stanton anxiously, said, "No—no difficulties in the field, I hope? No trouble?"

Stanton said smoothly, "Of course not. Why should there be?"

"No, no, of course not." He was still watching von

Abart's broad back, hesitating to speak his mind. He looked at Anna and back to Stanton, and then said cheerfully, "Well, that's all right then, I've reserved a coach for you on the train with the animals. A special, six wagons for them and one for you, I thought I'd fly back to Munich to get there ahead of you, make sure that everything is in order at the other end. We can't be too careful, can we? You'll be glad to know that the new buildings in the Zoo are ready, just waiting for the new arrivals. I can't tell you how pleased everyone will be. I've arranged a dinner for tomorrow night at the Bayerischer Hotel. Everybody's going to be there, just about everybody. You'll be the guest of honor, of course—the guests of honor." There was just enough accent on the plural to make up for the oversight before. Compounding the apology, he said, "Perhaps you will both make speeches. I'm sure you will have a lot to tell us."

"Yes, of course. Though perhaps that had better be left to von Abart. My German, you know. I think he can speak for both of us."

"Good, that's delightful."

Everything was well again, and the moment of anxiety had passed, Stanton was thinking, *You don't miss much, do you?*

Now, looking back on that moment, realizing that even Mendel had sensed the tension that was there, he could not believe that he had been prepared to treat it so lightly.

The train was swaying angrily from side to side as he crouched down in the corner of one of the wagons, filling the water bowl for the tapirs, wedging it firmly into an angle of their cage. They grunted at him in fright, fearing the noise and the motion and the unaccustomed cold of the mountain air. He put a small hand of bananas in with the Indri monkeys, and watched them for a moment, amused at the patient sadness of their faces, admiring the fine long hair of their black and white skins that seemed to trail like cloaks behind them.

He moved on to the next wagon, passing out into the open and crossing carefully over the iron coupling, clutching at the smoky iron handgrips and feeling the onrush of cold air that hit him like a tornado. For a moment he clung there, watching the track speed by beneath him, locking down and not liking the danger, and then he had the second door open and had pulled himself to safety again. The young elephant was here, and two monitor lizards, with the rhino lying down and sleeping passively on his bed of dry straw. He checked the lashings of the cages, and then, satisfied that they were still holding well, moved on to the next wagon, the last, wondering why he hadn't thought to put the leopard farther forward on the train where the whipping of the wagons would disturb him less. The tigers were here, too, and they snarled at him savagely as he threw open the door, letting in a sudden burst of wind, then pulled himself aboard and slammed it shut behind him.

In a moment, all was in uproar. The two tigers snarled at him, roaring their discomfort, striking at the bars of their cage until he feared they would break. He stood there close by the doorway, ready to leap out again, mentally figuring out the exact placement of the heavy iron coupling he would have to stand on, watching them and waiting, knowing that if they broke loose there would be a moment of danger and then no more, because the wagon was shut fast and there was no way out.

But the strong wooden bars held firm, and he thought with nostalgic pleasure of Talib's placid efficiency and his slow, careful binding of the rattan ropes that held the cages together. They calmed down then, the tigers, as soon as they saw that he had not come to harm them, and first the female and then the male lay down in their straw with only an occasional snarl to assert their displeasure.

He went down to the other end of the wagon to look at the leopard, and it ceased its restless pacing for a moment and looked at him and then snarled once and sank low on its haunches, not taking its eyes off him, its green, evil eyes that seemed as if there were a fire behind them, eyes that picked up every wandering ray of light and hurled it, concentrated with venom, back at him, He saw that one of the stout ironwood poles had been chewed nearly halfway through, and wondered how long it had taken him to do that.

They watched each other for a moment. The spots on its black flank were blacker still where the light caught them, shining like smooth black broken ovals. It lay at rest, still and quiet and infinitely menacing. He could smell the venom on its breath, and when he turned away he heard, with a sudden shock of alarm, the violent onrush as the leopard threw itself against the wooden bars, instantly seizing the moment of attack. He turned back quickly, seeing that the bars held firm, seeing that the lashings were still secure, and he said aloud, "I'll be glad when we can get you out of that and into something a little stronger."

He went back to it, standing close to the cage, feeling that he was home among the lower animals whom he loved the most and holding his authority by forcing the animal into an awareness of its helplessness. And then he saw, by no more than a flicker of its eyes, that something had attracted its attention, and when he looked over his shoulder he could see that Anna was standing outside the wagon, looking in through the pane of glass in the iron door, and he ran quickly and opened it, bracing himself against the wind and pulling her body into safety.

She was panting with the effort. Touching a hand to her hair, she said, "It's quite a job to cross in the open like that."

"You shouldn't be here. I can see to all this."

"I know. I came to see how they were."

"They're fine, all of them. The seladang looks a little sick back there."

"Yes, I noticed. It's colic, nothing to worry about. As soon as we get to Munich he'll be taken care of. The apes look good."

"They always travel well. Even the orangutan."

"And how's our friend the leopard?"

"Come and look."

He wanted to see them face to face, the two of them. And when they had reached the cage, he watched them both, almost surreptitiously, wondering at the similarities they showed. They both had that calm, deceptive stillness that seemed only to indicate the more that they were both ready for instant action, ready to seize at once on any apparent weakness that they could turn to their own advantage. There was the same deceptive elegance, too, a softness of texture that was dangerous because it was misleading, an infinite grace that left him awed and thinking only that he must not be hypnotized by it.

The leopard sensed it, too. He drew back and snarled as if one of his own kind were approaching, and when Anna put out her hand and touched the cage, before she could pull her hand away the leopard had spat once and struck forward with a vicious paw. She pulled her hand back quickly and he saw her shudder, marveling that anything at all would frighten her.

As if knowing what he was thinking, she said slowly, "You know, I've never felt frightened by an animal in my life."

"But this one?"

"I don't think I've ever seen such a...such a capacity for evil!"

"Evil? There's no evil there. Just an honest, straight-forward danger that both of us can understand."

"Maybe." She shuddered again. "Out there in the bush, I watched him a dozen times. I fed him, and watered him. And I was only aware of the need for normal caution. But now, in here, there is something Asmodean about him."

He struggled for a moment with his recollections of the demons, and said slowly, "The god of covetousness, of infidelity."

"And of hatred. He doesn't belong to us here. He belongs in a world that is all his own. And we are the intruders. Can't you feel it?"

"I can see only his beauty. It's almost a narcotic."

"There's a danger in beauty, too, if you can see nothing else beyond it, I tell you he's frightening."

Could he tell her that her fear gave him pleasure? He did not understand, himself, the reason for it. He pulled her close and put his arm round her waist as though he were loving her and held her there, close to the cage, making her feel the danger of it, making her face her fear and hoping that she would not be able to conquer it. He said again, "Just a straightforward danger. No evil at all."

Feeling the strength of him, she let herself go, not straining against it, knowing what he was trying to do to her and trying to control the fear, knowing that this was the one thing that could undo all the work that she had done. She stood quite still trembling slightly, saying nothing, waiting for him to move.

He said, "You can feel it, can't you? You're both of a kind. Asmodean is the right word, for both of you."

The pattern fell quickly into place for her. She said, "Yes. We're one and the same. Asmodean. We're both dangerous and destructive, is that what you mean?"

The pleasure had gone as soon as he had known her awareness of it. He let go of her waist and muttered, "Let's get back to Otto."

She did not move. She said slowly, "He's drunk again, Harry."

"What do you mean, drunk? He was all right a few minutes ago."

"A few minutes? You've been down here more than an hour. I imagined that you were trying to find some sort of consolation among them."

"I was feeding them and checking the cages."

ALAN CAILLOU

"Yes, I know."

"We're nearly in Munich, We'd better get back and sober him up."

"It won't be easy, Harry."

"A pot of hot coffee will work wonders."

She still did not move. Nervously, he said, "There's something wrong, isn't there?"

She turned and faced him, leaning back against the cold iron wall of the wagon, listening to the roar of the wheels underneath. She said, looking at him, "I told him, Harry."

He knew that it was coming. He had known it for a long time. He felt a grip of despair on him, and then it was gone because he knew that now the damage was done and that it was not so bad after all. The apprehension, he knew, is always worse than the fact itself. He took a deep breath and said, "So you told him. It was a damn fool thing to do."

"I told him that I was going to leave him."

"But why, in God's name? Why? Why now?"

"He forced it on me, Harry. He sat there and told me that he knew, just as I said he knew, that I'd been sleeping with you. He'd made up his mind to tell me that all was forgiven and that this was the end of the road. He said...You know what he said to me, Harry?"

"Go on."

"He said, 'He's back there with the animals. Go back and lie there in the straw with him, where you both belong, and then come back to me. And that will be the last time.' That's exactly what he said, Harry."

"Go on."

"So I told him, quite calmly, that this time it was...it was for keeps. I said that I'd never go back to his house, never. He just sat there and looked at me for a long time, without saying a word, and then he raised his hand and hit me, just once, hard, across the face, here." She touched a hand to her cheek. "Then he reached for the bottle and took a long drink straight out of it and said, 'Get out of here, you whore!' It's the end, Harry. The end."

He saw now, for the first time, the deep red flush on one side of her face. He took a long deep breath and said, feeling with relief that he could be flippant about it, "Well, that puts the baby squarely in my lap, doesn't it?"

"You can do whatever you like with it, Harry. Whatever you like."

He put his arm round her again and touched the cheek where von Abart had hit her, and said, "You want to come back to the States with me?"

"To the States, to Malaya—anywhere. I don't care where it is, Harry."

"I don't have a house like von Abart's. No kings ever slept there and the stairway was just built by the guy in the next block."

"I don't care."

"And I don't have any trophies, either. But there's a good garbage disposal."

He wondered how he could so easily make light of it when the scent of her was enveloping him, when the closeness of her was more than he could bear. His hand that had been on her cheek moved down to her shoulder and to her breast, and then he kissed her and felt all the passion that was in her mounting into a violence that seemed, somehow, cleaner than it had ever been before. It was as though a great danger had passed them by, and when he pulled her down into the deep straw, he could see the leopard glaring down at them, crouching still and taut and defiant in the corner of its cage; and now, he felt its evil, too.

But he fought against it, pushing it to the back of his mind where it became only an awareness that he was meeting his destruction at the hands of a woman, and it seemed for a moment that he was rolling over and over in the straw with the leopard, clutching at its throat, forcing himself to master its evil and to make it acknowledge his supremacy. And then, when he lay back exhausted, he saw that there was a look almost of fright in her eyes and he wondered if he had hurt her.

He put out a hand and said unsteadily, "For a moment..." But she shook her head and clambered to her feet, brushing at the straw on her dress, and then she went to the door of the wagon and came back quickly and said in a whisper, "Harry, we're on our own."

"Yes. We're on our own now."

"I don't mean that. Look!"

Feeling the contagion of the alarm in her voice, he jumped up and ran to the door and stared out at the blue sky through the glass, pressing his face to it and wondering why it was so bright and clear. He threw open the door and then he saw the rest of the train was far away in the distance and that they were slowing down behind it, the distance between them lengthening as he watched.

Straining his eyes, squinting against the wind, he could see that on the body of the train von Abart was clutching at the ironwork, standing on the coupling, a small, insignificant figure in the distance. He fancied that he could even see the iron pin that he held in his hand, the pin he had pulled from the coupling.

As he watched, the wagon slowed to a halt and then began to run down the hill. There was a moment of surprise that the slope was so steep, and then, as it gathered momentum and swung wildly round the bend, he yelled, "Come on, let's jump for it?"

She ran forward to him and he pushed her out and leaped after her, and as they rolled over and over down the steep bank, feeling the earth thudding into their bodies and the cinders ripping at their flesh, they saw the solitary wagon hurtling down the hill, a wild, uncontrolled thing moving fast to destruction, and carrying with it two angry tigers and an Asmodean leopard.

CHAPTER 15

Working on the line, a laborer looked up as the unscheduled interruption broke the pattern of his concentration.

First, he shouted the alarm. Then he sprinted fast, dropping his shovel, to the telephone that stood close by, and with Germanic calm he rang twice for the signal-box. But the signalman had already seen what had happened and had thrown the switch, and the wagon swung fast round a bend, teetering dangerously as it passed the points, and then screeched on to the rusted line that lay, long unused, between the Munich Main Station and the old freight yards.

It was a matter for rapid and precise calculation, and the signalman had seen (quickly computing its speed) that it would miss the oncoming Special that was now, at this exact moment, leaving the yard. A buffer was waiting to receive it, to deaden the shock on its heavy springs, and had his calculations gone unhampered, the crash, perhaps, would not have been so serious a matter.

But the Special had not quite reached the switch when its driver, peering with narrowed eyes along the grass-bordered track, saw the wagon careening along towards him. There was only a split second for the decision, and in that second he pushed forward the throttle and speeded up, racing for the points before he should be cut off, the iron wheels sparking the rails as the clumsy freighter leaped along the line.

It was far in the distance when he had first seen it, and he saw a moment later that the red band of the signal was squarely across his path, but it was too late to stop and he pushed more steam, holding his breath and willing more speed out of the ancient engine. The head of the train swung over the switch, and the second, third, fourth, and fifth wagons followed it to safety. But then, at the sixth, the two behemoths met with a violent crash as the runaway struck, angled-on and swinging wildly. There was the bitter, grinding, angry sound of metal being torn, and the engineer was flung bodily out of his cab, not knowing that his arm had been torn off in the wreckage, and when he looked up from the hard ground on which he was lying, he saw a small round barrel perched crazily on top of a broken mass of twisted framework, and as he watched it came tumbling down in what seemed to him to be slow motion. He heard, far off, a siren sound, and then he saw a small wisp of smoke spiraling up out of the wreckage and could smell the sweet scent of burning straw.

Some men came running, and he was thinking, *Get me away from here before the whole lot bursts into flame*, and worrying too much because he did not yet know what the dull pain in his side meant, nor did he understand that the shock of the collision had toppled his engine over. And then he looked at the bloody stub of his arm and went white, wondering why he could not feel the pain of it. Then a new horror came over him and be blinked his disbelief as a tiger came slowly out of the wrecked wagon and walked quite slowly over to him, smelling the blood and fearing the fire behind him.

He forced himself to his feet and clutched his bleeding side, feeling the blood gushing out of his arteries, and then he stumbled and the tiger stalked majestically over to him and hit him with one paw, knocking him to the ground, and as he began to scream, it sunk its molars quite delicately into the sides of his temples, killing him at once. And then it dragged him away, leaping over a low fence with him with no apparent effort at all.

A woman who had come running up, a waitress from the restaurant, started to scream hysterically, and then two people came running fast at her, an American and a blonde woman, both of them panting and covered with grime, and the man took her by the shoulders and shook her, saying in halting German, "Where did it go? Which way?"

When she could not stop her screaming, the woman slapped her face, calming her, and she pointed her shaking hand and said, "Over there. Over the fence. It was carrying a man."

Stanton dropped her arm, and then the smashed wagon burst into violent flame behind him, and he spun around and went running towards it, shouting, "A rifle, for God's sake get a rifle" And as Anna went running towards the station he tore at the hot timbers, scorching his hands and burning his clothes, but the fierce heat of it drove him back, and when a crew of men came hurrying along with a hose line, he tried to stop them, saying, "No. Let it burn. There's a dangerous animal in there somewhere. If it gets out..."

But they did not understand what he was trying to say to them, and they turned their hoses full on the burning wagon and when he struggled with them they pushed him away until someone who spoke English heard him and repeated stupidly, "A leopard? Is that what you said?"

"There's a leopard in there. If it gets out there'll be trouble. There's a tiger loose already. He's killed one of your men - did you see it?" He pointed to the sobbing woman, and the man went over and talked with her, and then came running back and called the firemen away, and they joined the crowd that had gathered, watching the fire and waiting for it to burn out, not knowing what was happening, knowing only that a mad American had told them that the wagon was full of wild animals and that they'd better be careful.

And then, as it always will, word spread round the crowd

that someone had been killed, and when a police car came screeching up to the yard, bumping its way down the track itself to get there quickly, they all knew exactly what to say, what to tell them. For a moment a young police officer, very calm and blond and efficient, listened with a semblance of patience and then went over to Stanton and said, in English:

"Are you this American hunter? My name is Auer. I'm told that an animal—a tiger—is loose. Is this true?"

"It's true enough. I'm afraid he's already killed a man. I saw it as I was running up."

"I see." There was no alarm. Auer un-holstered his pistol. "These, no doubt, are the animals that the Zoo is expecting?"

"Yes."

"And the others?"

"The last wagon only—it came adrift and crashed. I suppose the others are still out there on the line somewhere."

"And in this wagon..."

"That's exactly it. There's another tiger, and a leopard. A black one. Let me have your pistol."

Auer smiled quickly, "If you will forgive me. I know who you are, of course, but please understand, it is not permitted. But these animals must be shot, of course, you realize that?"

"I suppose there's nothing else we can do. If they'd been in captivity for another month or two, perhaps we could still trap them, but...We'd better take a look at that wagon. And for God's sake keep your gun ready. We need a rifle."

They went over to the smoldering wagon, and in answer to Auer's abrupt orders a workman, not too happily, levered at the long timbers with an iron bar, calling for help when he could not move them. When a crew came up and threw their weight into the job, they forced a passage through into the smoldering interior, and as Stanton stepped forward Auer gently put a hand on his arm and said courteously, "If you will permit me." With his Luger ready, a cartridge in the breech and ready to fire, he eased his way into the smoking mass of hot, wet, steaming wreckage. Stanton, watching, muttered, "A rifle. Wait for a rifle for God's sake!" As the timbers fell apart, they stooped and smelled the sour scent of death.

In a moment they found the other tiger. It was dead, its head crushed between two thick steel beams and wedged there, as though for a long time it had tried to pull itself free and had succeeded in freeing only the long yellow muscular body. The skin was burned and seared, and the odor of burned flesh clung to it.

Of the leopard, there was no sign at all.

They found its cage, smashed in two and smoldering still, and Stanton looked at the fiber lashings and found them torn apart, those that had not been burned, and he knew that the cage had broken at the first fast impact, twisting itself out of shape until the wood could no longer be confined by its ropes and then bursting open. They poked over the wreckage, looking under every steaming timber, under each still-hot girder, and at last Stanton muttered, "But he can't have got away. Someone must have seen it."

"One would think so." Auer stood frowning, coughing the smoke out of his lungs. "I think we should get into the fresh air. There is nothing here."

They pushed their way out into the watching crowd, and then Mendel came hurrying down the line from the station, his face white. Behind him, Anna was hurrying to catch up, seeming to hold him by the arm to restrain him. He said, "Is it true? They have escaped?"

"I'm afraid so. One of the tigers, and the leopard. The tiger's already made a kill. He didn't waste much time."

"But—but what happened? How did the wagon come adrift like that? I could not understand what they said on the phone."

Before Stanton could answer, Anna said, "We don't

know. Mr. Stanton and I were feeding the animals in the last wagon, on the slope, and I suppose the coupling slipped. We just don't know."

Stanton looked at her and said nothing, knowing that this was the only thing they could do now. His face was drawn and there was a terrible sickness in his heart. He looked at the sobbing woman and went over to her and said, "I'm sorry. Is there something I can do?"

When she did not reply, he said gently, "It was your husband?"

Her face was streaked with tears and grime. "My father."

"I'm sorry. If there's anything I can do."

He knew there was nothing. He knew that in Malaya this was one of the risks you took, that when you were dead it didn't matter whether you were eaten by worms and maggots or by leopards and tigers; it was all the same, the feeding of one species upon another, But here, in the stone and concrete cities, it was better if you were killed by a street car, or died of pleurisy in bed, because then there was less consciousness of the physical disgust at the eating. And how could he tell her that the gentle penetration of the two long molars would do the killing and that afterwards he would know nothing of the dreadful thing that was happening to him? It was a question of geography, as simple as that, and there was nothing he could do to make her understand.

Mendel stood wondering what to do, and Auer, the young police officer with the Luger, said, "Well, the railway police will take care of everything here. You and I, Mr. Stanton, will have to hunt those animals down. And quickly."

"Yes, yes, of course."

"It shouldn't take long. A few hours."

"That's all we have until dark. After that..."

"Yes, we shall have to hurry." He turned away and Stanton saw that the "We shall have to hunt them" was no more than a courtesy. He said angrily, "I don't think you realize how

228

difficult this is going to be. A tiger in the city, that's bad enough, but a leopard..."

Auer turned back to him. "I understand fully, Mr. Stanton. I take it the tiger will do no more hunting tonight, am I right?"

How could you say, "No, he's had his meal," when the woman was sobbing so close to him? He said instead, "It's the leopard we have to worry about. If we could get some men to watch out—at the street corners, on the roofs. They'd have to be armed. And for God's sake get rid of that pistol. It's worse than useless."

Auer pointed to the big BMW that was pulling up close by the station. He said, "There's my car. Perhaps they will have brought my rifle. A great deal has already been done."

"But not enough," Mendel said urgently. His face was white, and he used his arms violently in unaccustomed gestures. "I agree with you, Mr. Stanton, this is not going to be easy. But the police. They will do what they can, of course, but will it be enough? You and I both know...What can they do?"

An officer came running from the car, and there was a whispered conference, and then Auer said, quite calmly, "It's all under control, Herr Mendel, the area is being cordoned off. And I'm happy to tell you that your leopard has been seen. A woman saw it, it walked right past her, over in Kaufingerstrasse. Within ten minutes there will be a hundred men round the area. He will not get through, I promise you."

He could hear the shrill whistles of the police, and when they reached the car he could hear a loudspeaker blaring from the top of a patrolling Volkswagen, telling the people to get indoors and stay there. He looked at his watch and wondered how they had managed to get the patrols out so quickly, and then a group of six men went running past, carrying rifles, scattering to their guard positions, taking up their posts as an officer directed them. One of them was clambering up the side of the building, his gun slung over his shoulder, and when he reached the top he stumbled and turned quickly and yelled, and immediately someone else shouted, and, not knowing what was happening, he said to Auer, "A rifle, give me a rifle."

A woman picked up a child and ran, and a man dashed out of a building and helped her in, slamming the door shut behind her, and he heard a radio somewhere with an excited announcer's voice, and he said, "What's happened, for God's sake? Has he seen something?"

Auer was talking urgently into the microphone of his radio and Stanton flung up his hands in disgust and said to Anna, "For God's sake, do they know what they're doing?"

She was looking up at the guard on the roof. He was pointing now to the other side of the building, shouting still, and Anna said, "He says he's seen the tiger, it's in a courtyard over there. He said he seems to be eating a man."

As he watched, the sentry threw up his rifle and fired, and again it seemed as though the panic increased its velocity. Someone screamed, and there were people running, some going into the buildings and some going out. He saw that some of them were laughing, as though this were a small piece of excitement to change the routine of their drab and uninteresting lives. Auer turned from his set and shouted, "Get those people back into the buildings. I don't want anyone on the streets."

Mendel was talking to one of the Security Officers from the railroad, and he pulled Anna away and said, "Let's find out what the hell they're up to."

He said to Mendel, "Are we doing any good here? Why don't we just go home and leave it to these idiots? If they'd only let me have a rifle."

Mendel made a quick introduction to the Security Officer and said, "There are forty men covering the area, Mr. Stanton, and two more squads are on their way here. They've been ordered to shoot on sight. Perhaps...I do not know. A lot of men...The rest of the wagons have been shunted into a siding, but Herr von Abart is not on the train, I do not understand it. He should be there with them. They tell me that all his baggage is there, but Herr von Abart...It's quite inexplicable."

Anna said quickly, "He must know what's happened. He's probably hunting the animals himself. Were his rifles there, did they say?"

Mendel spread his arms wide. "I do not know how many he had."

"Four."

Mendel spoke to the Security man and said, "There are only three...Then you are right, he is out hunting, too. Your own guns?"

"On the train."

"Good. I will send a man for them. Perhaps you would like to rest, or...I" He was peering at the scratches down the side of Stanton's face where the gravel of the track had ripped him.

Stanton shook his head. "The best thing would be to tell the police to lay off, let us handle it. Let them keep the area surrounded and try and keep the animals inside their cordon. But if they start shooting, then someone's going to be hurt. This isn't like hunting rabbits, and if they wound them instead of killing, then we're going to have double trouble on our hands. We've only a few hours left. Once it's dark, God knows where they'll be by morning!"

"Yes, I think you are right. If the police can keep the people off the streets, if they can give you a clear field...I will see about the rifles. Where will you be?"

Auer came hurrying over, his young face flushed. He said apologetically, "I have just been told, Mr. Stanton, to give you every possible assistance. Forgive me if I did not realize."

"Of course. Someone's gone for our rifles."

"Then I suggest that you come with me in my car. We will be in touch with the others all the time. And I will show you what we have done.

Mendel went hurrying off to see about the guns, and they went over to the car and sat in the back, and Auer produced a street map and marked it with a silver pencil, saying, "This is where we are now, and over this way we have two squads of twenty men each, another ten men covering this side here, and there are thirty more waiting for instructions. The leopard was seen here, at this point, that's the Kaufingerstrasse."

Worrying about it, Stanton said angrily, "The center of the town. He couldn't have chosen a better place. How the hell did he get so far before he was seen? I hope the men have been told what a dangerous animal this is."

"They know, Mr. Stanton. They know."

"It's not like hunting rabbits. He'll outsmart them at every move they make."

"The tiger?"

"The leopard. The tiger won't give us too much trouble as long as no one tries to approach him, or gets in a bad shot. It's the leopard we have to worry about. And worry plenty."

The radio was crackling, and Auer leaned forward and pushed the button and spoke into it, and when he had finished, he said, "Good. We must go over and see that the patrols are in position."

"They should be off the ground. Somewhere an animal can't get at them too easily."

"Yes, of course." Auer spoke into the radio again, and the car moved off silently into the town.

It was not until more than an hour later that they found the first of the animals. It was the tiger.

Stanton was looking at his watch anxiously, looking up at the sky and worrying about how much more daylight there was. There was an uncanny silence all around them, mute evidence of the efficiency with which the police had cleared the area, more than ten city blocks square. The streets were empty and silent, quite deserted, and only an occasional opening of a shutter showed that there was life within the buildings themselves. The shutters had gone over the expensive plate-glass windows of the fashionable shops, and their lights were out.

They were standing by the car, waiting for the reports to come in, and when a shot sounded suddenly close by, Stanton turned as though to run towards it and Auer put out a hand to hold him, saying, "No, wait." And in a moment the word came over the radio, and Auer said, "It's over on Krentz Strasse, let's go." The car swept forward with a burst of sudden speed and in a moment they drew up by a group of police who ran towards them, and Anna, listening, said, "They've seen it—the tiger. One of them fired and hit it. He's gone to follow up..."

"Follow up? What the hell does that mean?"

She shook her head, listening to their conversation, and then said, "Two of them. They went off to chase it. They're sure it was wounded." As she spoke, she was slipping a cartridge into the bolt of her rifle, and Stanton nodded. "We're in trouble now."

He worked the breech of his rifle and ran with her to the corner where one of the police was pointing, and as they ran there was a scream, and when they rounded the corner into the tiny courtyard, a policeman was standing there, staring stupidly at the bloody body of another man who lay screaming on the pavement. His shoulder had been ripped open and his arm was gone, and the policeman turned to them blankly, shaking his head and stuttering. Auer came running up, and the policeman pointed and said, "He went there. We were just coming to kill him. He was waiting for us. He jumped, and I could not shoot again, I was too much afraid to hit—to hit..."

Auer bent over the wounded man and as the car came around the corner he shouted an order to the driver to get the ambulance. Then he turned to Stanton and said, "I may be wrong but if he has gone where this man said he has gone..."

"Yes?"

"There is a dead-end street. He must be in there somewhere. There is no way out. If the man is right."

"Well, well soon find out."

He turned to Anna and said, "Well, you feel up to it? You take one end and I'll take the other. There must be a way into it over the building. Where's that street map?"

Auer brought it out quickly and unfolded it, and Stanton noted with alarm that he had automatically switched on his flashlight; the sky was darkening rapidly. They looked at the plan for a moment, just the two of them, while Anna stood guard with her rifle ready, watching the corner unblinkingly.

When he was quite sure he knew the layout, Stanton said, "All right, this is how we go in. There's a matter of eighty yards of street, closed at the other end by a ten-foot brick wall that's the back of a garage. There's a small alleyway off it on the right, from this end, that doesn't lead anywhere, and there are two enclosed yards with fences he could jump, one halfway down on the left, and the other a little farther on. Now, if you can get round to the back of the garage and get up on to the roof, I'll take this end. I want a man up on the roof just above us and another on the opposite roof. If they see him, let them shout, good and loud and at once. It'll scare the tiger, but it won't be able to get up to them, so they'll be quite safe. And no one is to fire except one of us, all right?"

There was no question of his authority. Auer nodded, sent two men to climb up the buildings by the stairs inside, and said, "If the Fräulein wishes, I will help her over the garage." Stanton was aware of his curiosity, and to ease his mind he said, "The Fräulein is a first-rate hunter. A crack shot, an expert."

Auer nodded, smiling slightly, and held open the door of the car. As she went in, Stanton said, "Show yourself as soon as you're in position. And keep up on the roof there. It's just a low one, but...well, don't come down."

He was conscious of the flush on her face and the excitement in her eyes, and he was wondering if she was thinking that at last she was openly proving what she had always been, clandestinely: that she was no longer hiding her expertise under the cloak of a passé hunter's incompetence. As the car swung round out of sight, he looked around him and signaled for the others to take cover, and then walked into the center of the narrow cul-de-sac.

The lights had come on, sending their yellow beams across the wet cobblestones, and casting shadows where he did not want them, and for a while he stood there, his rifle held loosely in both hands, looking towards the blank wall at the other end, wondering where the tiger would be lurking, waiting for Anna to appear on the roof at the end. The gargoyles up there seemed to grimace down on him in the reflected beams of the searchlights. There was a slight drizzle beginning to fall now, and the evening was turning colder. He looked carefully for the two fences that hid the yards, and worried when he realized how low they were, and he stared at the little obstructions of the street—a barrel here, a projection there - trying to force into his cognizance an awareness of what would be the best possible cover.

Then Anna appeared at the end of the street, high on the wall that was the back of the garage, and at the same moment he heard Auer's calm voice on the loudspeaker of the patrol car, the sound blaring out at him in the stillness and momentarily shocking him.

"Herr Stanton," the cold, disembodied voice said, "there is a woman on the fourth floor of the building on your left. She has seen the tiger in the street below you, just a moment ago." The message was repeated, and he looked up to his left and saw the woman at the shutters of her window, dim against the grey sky. She was pointing down below her where some garbage cans were standing on the pavement, and he began a slow and watchful walk down the street towards them, his rifle ready, moving very slowly. He was conscious that, as he began to move, even up there the impact of the tiger could be felt. He heard the shutters slam fast as the woman retreated and he thought angrily for a moment, *You damned fool, you think he can get up there?*

He walked slowly, in the center of the street, watching carefully as he went, peering into every obscure corner, knowing that if he walked past it then things would be far worse than they had been before, and knowing, too, that this was what the tiger would be hoping for and trying to force him into doing.

He reached the garbage cans and stood close by them for a moment, wondering if the bulk of them were enough to shelter a full-grown tiger, knowing that they were not, and knowing that his quarry had gone. Quickly, he backed off to the end of the street again and stood there for a while, and then he shouted, raising his voice and shouting loudly, "Anna! Can you see anything?"

Her voice came back at him from the distance and the darkness. "Nothing."

He shouted again, "He's not at this end. I don't want to go too far down in case I miss him."

He heard her call, "Walk towards me, I'll drive him."

Before he could shout back at her, before he could tell her to stay where she was, she had slipped down the side of the wall, her rifle dangerously over her shoulders, and was gripping the top of the wall with both hands, exposing her back and hanging there. Then she dropped lightly to the ground and had her rifle at the ready again, and for a few moments they both stood there, facing each other at eighty yards distance, both knowing that they were in a narrow concrete pit with a wounded tiger.

She began moving forward then, and as he watched, with the fear for her mounting in him, she raised the barrel of her rifle and fired once, then quickly worked the breech and fired again, then again and again, moving slowly forward as she fired into the air. And when she had gone ten paces and fired ten shots he knew that she was stopping to reload, that only one round was left in the rifle, and the fear was aggravated by her calmness, He raised his gun and pointed it towards her, feeling somehow sure that the tiger was waiting for just this instant to charge her and wanting to be ready with an accurate, fast shot, not daring to breathe but waiting for the sudden onrush.

Then she had loaded her rifle, and as she began firing again and moving towards him, driving the tiger into the open, he saw it. It came from the garbage cans that he had already inspected so carefully without seeing a thing, and there was just time to see the flicker of its tail that meant it was going to charge, and he shouted, "Down!" just once. In the split second that he saw her drop to the ground, he fired, knowing that his bullet would find its mark and continue on its way within a few inches of her body. He had already pumped another round into the breech before he ran forward, and the first thing he saw was that the tiger was dead, its spine shattered at the base of the neck. Then he saw that Anna, too, was lying quite still and there was a surge of terrifying fright that perhaps he had killed her. And then as she heard his footsteps she raised her head and he saw that she was all right.

She pushed herself slowly to her feet and went over to the dead tiger and said, looking down at it, "The neck shot—the expert."

He could not control his trembling. He put a hand on her arm and said, "You don't know how close that was. You were right in my line of fire."

"I know." She looked at him quite calmly, knowing that what they had done they had done together. "I heard the bullet go over my head."

"Thank God you dropped quickly!"

"I would have, even if you hadn't shouted. The moment I saw you raise your rifle."

"You must have a lot of confidence in my marksmanship."

"I knew that only one of us could fire. We were all in line, all three of us. One of us had to fire, one had to clear, and one had to die."

For a horrible moment, there was an analogy in what she was saying. The fear of it brought von Abart sharply back into focus, and he looked over his shoulder apprehensively, half expecting to find him there behind him in the darkness with his rifle raised, yet knowing still that this figment was more of his guilt than of his imaginings. There was only the emptiness of the street there, and as he watched, the others came rushing round the corner, knowing with the sure knowledge of admiration that the first enemy was dead, but standing there until they could be sure.

He turned back to her and put a hand on her arm. His voice was shaky. "Thank God you're all right! Thank God!"

"Now, the leopard."

"Yes, the leopard."

Slowly, they walked back to the corner where the others were waiting.

CHAPTER 16

Somehow, the leopard had found its way into one of the buildings.

While the streets were empty and silent, while the fear was in the open and the only seeming security was behind locked doors, somehow it had found its way through those walls and was on the loose inside.

At the moment in which the tiger had been shot, it was crouching nearby, listening to the regular, methodical sound of Anna's firing, knowing exactly what those sounds meant and not fearing them, but only being sharply aware that it was alone, in a strange and fearsome place, and that men were hunting it.

It lay high on a narrow rafter that could not, one would have thought, have supported a cat in comfort. Its forelegs were stretched along the rough timber, its claws cutting sharply into the sides and its round head resting on the forepart of its arms. It's eyes were unblinking, fearless, understanding, and there was infinite menace in the perfectly relaxed yet high-strung looseness of its sleek muscles.

Somewhere in the room below it - it was a basement – a sudden light went on, casting a yellow beam across the rafters. Then, there was hardly a visible motion, but the leopard was gone, and if it could have been seen at all it would have been as a deeper shadow among the shadows of the open ceiling. Only the head was visible. All the long, graceful body was arched out of the way in darkness.

Looking down, hearing the soft pad of footsteps, it could see a man, ten feet below on the concrete floor. He was stopping to light a cigarette, and instinctively, knowing that this was one of its enemies, the leopard tensed and was ready to spring. And then it drew back as another man appeared, and watched as the two of them stood there, looking around them. One of them had his hand on the light switch and pulled it away to light his own cigarette, and for a while they stood there, chatting, oblivious of the danger above them. And then the second man, the one who had come in later, walked out again, closing the door behind him and leaving his friend alone.

The odds were easier now, and without further thought, the leopard sprang. There was one huge bound through the dusty half-light, the yellow bulb doing little more than causing a blurred shadow to fall across the ground at the moment he struck, and then the startled man was rolling on the ground with four hundred pounds of savagery mauling him, ripping quickly into his flesh with long white teeth and filthy, hollow claws. The man was dead in a few moments, and then the leopard went back to its perch on the rafter, waited a moment, and then wormed its way, licking at the blood on its lips, though a shaft where the air was warmer, and into another part of the building.

He came to an open window, and was about to investigate it when the unearthly sound of radio voices, floating past from a patrol car, sent him slinking back into cover, and then a door slid open silently beside him, and when he went inside to see what was there, it closed just as silently behind him and he was in a cage with solid walls that were too strong for his suddenly alarmed claws to rip through.

He snarled angrily, and spat, and pounced from one side of the elevator to the other, looking up and seeing a small open trapdoor and wondering if he could reach it, and then there was a whirring sound and he tensed as he felt the ground under him rising, rising, rising.

Had he been capable of fear, this was the moment at which he would have been most frightened. But as von Abart had said, this was a wise and old leopard, and one who had been hunted before and had seen many strange things, so he held his crouch, and waited. His heart was beating fast, but he knew that something was going to happen and that he would be ready for it. All the ancient heredity of the hunter, older than man himself, taught him this.

Above him, three floors higher, the woman who had pressed the button of the elevator was waiting for it to come up. She was straightening her dress, making ready to go out, and watching the indicator that showed the elevator's steady ascent.

Behind her, a door opened suddenly, and a man in shirt-sleeves came running out and clutched at her and pulled her back into the room, and as she stared at him angrily, he said, stuttering at her, "The—the radio. There's a leo—a leopard. Out on the—the...On the streets."

Her eyes were wide with disbelief. "A leopard? Have you been drinking again, Hans?"

"N-no. A leo—leopard. The radio said s-so. They s-say to s-stay in-indoors."

"A leopard? In München?"

"From the - from the Zoo."

"Oh. Oh, I see." She shrugged her shoulders resignedly and took off her coat again, saying, "Then why did I get up? I could have stayed in bed."

Outside in the narrow corridor, the elevator came to a stop. The doors slid open, and in a flash the leopard was out of his cage, knowing his readiness and taking instant advantage of it. He slipped along the silent corridor, not making any sound at all, slinking along without fear, looking for a way that would lead him higher to where, he was sure, lay safety.

A little farther along, he paused and snarled at a big tabby cat that was raising its hair and spitting at him, and then he went on his way, paying it no further attention, and as soon as he was out of sight round the bend, the tabby cat still spitting and snarling its hatred, a door opened and a little girl, about seven years old, came out of one of the apartments. She was clutching a huge bundle of laundry, staggering under its weight, and a doll was tucked under her thin arm.

She took it to the laundry chute at the end of the corridor, strained her frail form and tipped the bundle into the opening, and then stood looking at the tabby cat and saying, "*Kom, katzchen, kom. Puss, puss puss puss.*"

She wondered why her cat's attention was so hatefully riveted on something round the corner of the corridor, on something she could not see, and she squatted down on her haunches, her bony knees sticking out and the frail white of her legs showing above the black stockings, crouching down and saying, "*Puss puss puss puss.*"

Suddenly, the cat was gone, spinning round and racing off in the other direction, and the little girl went to the door of her apartment and opened it, and then, on the threshold, paused and clucked her tongue and went back to the laundry chute to retrieve the doll that she had left there, and as she turned back to her room, the leopard came stalking round the corner behind her, standing still and watching her move away. It turned its head to look at the cat that had found a safer place to spit from, watching it contemptuously for a moment, and when it turned back the little girl had reached her apartment and had gone inside.

The leopard followed. And when it reached the door it pawed at it curiously, scratching lightly at the woodwork.

Inside, the woman who was sitting by her sewing machine looked up, wondering what the noise was, and her husband put down his pot of beer and said, "It's the cat. Let him in, *liebchen*, before he scratches all the paint off. So much trouble from the landlord."

The little girl put down her doll, ran over to the door, and flung it open. She just had time to scream before the leopard was in there with them, moving so fast that the eye could not follow it, streaking from one of them to the other, and in a few moments the last moan from the dying woman turned to the rasping sound of escaping breath as, trying to crawl across the floor to her *liebchen*, she could not quite make it and died before she could touch the fragile white hand that was curled, claw-like, as though to grasp the sudden cold staff of death.

Outside, on the street, the darkness had set in and the wet stones of the road were gleaming in the police searchlights.

A kind of terror was settling over the town, a terror out of all proportion to its reality. At first, the news of the animals on the loose had brought little more than excitement, edged with the lip-drying knowledge that the tiger had made its kill within a few moments of escaping. Those at the scene or near it had felt the immediate danger, but once they were behind their locked doors and, through the upper windows, could watch the Volkswagens and BMWs of the police touring the area, there was only the excitement again.

Some of them, through half-closed shutters, the lights behind them extinguished, had seen the stalk of the tiger, with the young German girl and the American hunter moving in from opposite ends of the streets, and there had seemed, to these watchers, a very solid competence about the manner in which they had worked together, a competence against which, surely, no wild animal from the jungle could stand for long.

And then there had come the first announcement over the radio. A man had been discovered dead in a cellar, and the finder of the grisly corpse had called the Radio Station instead of the police, hoping to get a few marks for his trouble. The radio announcer had broken into his program to tell a waiting citizenry that all efforts to find the leopard had failed. Said the announcer with relish, "He is stalking us now."

When the news of the broadcast was brought to Auer, he had spoken angrily to his headquarters about it, but there was little the police could do, even in Germany, to suppress the news. And as he had been about to switch off his set and move out on patrol again, the static-cracking voice at the other end had said, "Wait. A new report coming in."

Auer had listened, his face set, and then he had turned to Stanton and Anna, who were standing by the car looking out into the darkness. His lips were thin and his face was angry, the face of a young and earnest man who knows that all his efficiency is not enough for the problem he is facing.

He said slowly, "It's in an apartment house. It has just killed a whole family. Three of them - a woman and a man and a small child. What are we going to do, Mr. Stanton? No one ever sees this animal except its victims. What are we going to do?"

Stanton passed a hand over his face, feeling the stubble of his beard. "An apartment house? He'll make for the roof." He turned to Anna, accepting her as his equal. "Don't you agree?"

She nodded. "He's on the rampage. He'll go as high as he can. Wherever there's a stairway, a fire escape, anything to take him up."

Stanton turned to Auer. "Can we seal off the apartment building?"

"It is being done now, Mr. Stanton. They are doing it now. All the people there are being told to stay in their rooms— those who have radios. Some men are going through it room by room."

"Then let's get over there..."

They climbed back into the car and as it shot off with a

burst of speed, swinging round the corner, he said, "Flares, can we get flares?"

"I can get a flame-thrower, Mr. Stanton. It seems rather...is it not rather a lot for just one animal?"

"It might be the best thing. This isn't the Malayan jungle - we're at a disadvantage here. We have to fight with whatever tools we can get. If you can send enough men through, floor by floor, a lot of men, as many as you can find, work up from the bottom room by room."

"It was in the basement that the first man was found. The one on the radio."

"The same building?"

"The same one."

"And these other people? How long ago?"

"Fifteen minutes, no more."

"In fifteen minutes he can be a dozen blocks away."

"I do not think, Mr. Stanton, that he would so easily get out of a building once the doors were shut. When the first man was found, they closed off all the exits, even the windows. I think it is quite possible that he is still there. The only question is, how may we drive him where we want him? And where, precisely, is that?"

"On the roof," Anna said promptly. "If we can both get up there...and you can drive him up to us."

Auer looked across at Stanton, and Stanton said, "It's the only way. We start firing high-powered rifles inside a building full of people..."

When they drew up outside the apartment house, he was startled at the numbers of police there. They had been reinforced by National Guardsmen, and there must have been more than a hundred of them gathered in the street. An officer came running over to Auer and said excitedly, "He's still in there. He was seen, just a few moments ago. He was moving up the stairway."

They stood for a moment peering up at the skyline,

looking at the grotesque baroque statues that stood around the cornice of the roof, their white stone catching the reflected light and shining in the rain. Stanton said, "The doorway to the roof?"

"It is closed," the officer said promptly. "I was there myself. There is no way out of the building, and all the doors inside are shut."

"Then he's in one of the rooms."

The officer shrugged. "I have as many men as we can use. We will have to make a search, room by room. If you will tell us what to do when we see it. I do not like to let my men fire inside the building, and yet..."

"Let them make as much noise as they can," Stanton said. "As much noise as they can drum up. Stamp their feet, shout, sing - I don't give a damn what they do as long as there's plenty of noise. If they could get some empty cans of some sort."

"Some saucepans, perhaps?"

"Anything like that. All the noise they can make. He'll run from noise. It's the only thing he will run from."

"All right, I will see to it.

"And the flame-thrower?"

"It will be here in a few moments."

"Then let the man who's handling it stay out in the front as you move up from floor to floor. If there's enough noise, he won't come near you, but to be safe, let him stand in the front and be ready to push that button in a hurry. And I mean in a hurry! How many men have we?"

"More than a hundred, Mr. Stanton, right here. If you want more..."

"No. Once a floor is cleared, leave a group of five or six men at the foot of the stairs, and take on the next one above. He might try to sneak back down once he realizes what we're doing. And for God's sake let them make all the noise they can?"

Someone came hurrying out of the building with an armful of pots and pans, and the men took them, some sheepishly, some grinning, some soberly realizing that a few of them could be dead before the night's work was over. When an Army Jeep came screeching up with a flame-thrower, Stanton said, "All right, let's go." He turned to Auer, "You know what to do?"

"I will clear the building floor by floor, room by room. I will drive him up to the roof."

"If there's room for a mouse to hide, a hole too small for a household cat, if it can hide a collar-button, he'll make use of it to elude you. You won't hear him, and you might not even see him. All you'll have is the smell. And don't forget, as much noise...Keep the upper floors quiet, keep the noise below him."

"I understand, Mr. Stanton. You can count on it."

Looking at his eager young face, Stanton said, "Yes, I believe I can. All right, the Fräulein and I will take up our positions on the roof. Do we know that he's not up there already?"

The officer was holding up a key. "It is closed. It has been closed for a long time. You will need this, and if you will permit me, I would like to accompany you."

"No, I'm sorry. Just the two of us. Anyone else will get in the way."

"All the same, Mr. Stanton," Auer said, "I will accompany you to the roof and leave you there. If you will allow me."

"Good!"

Auer called forward a squad of men, and with their rifles at the ready, as though a phalanx of troops were waiting for them, they advanced up the steps to the entrance hall, pushed the button for the elevator, and waited. A score of men came in behind them, holding an odd assortment of skillets and metal pans, and when the elevator came they went up to the top floor and then climbed the short stairway that led to the roof.

The rusty key turned with difficulty in the lock, and

Stanton muttered, "Good, at least we can be reasonably sure he's not here yet."

Auer said, diffidently, "May I at least be permitted to inspect the roof with you?"

Stanton smiled and nodded, feeling an affection for him. They walked slowly round the edge of it, noting the skylight covers and the wooden cupboards which had been built to house the elevator machinery and the heating ducts. They stopped to look at the fire escape and saw with satisfaction that it was only an iron ladder set into the stonework, at least as far down as the top floor itself. Feeling self-conscious about the question, Auer said, "He cannot, of course, climb that?"

"No, he can't climb that." Stanton could feel that the overpowering respect for their enemy was turning into a kind of awe. He said irritably, "Goddammit, it's just another bloody cat!"

Aver said nothing. Anna, close behind them, was staring at the next building and gauging the distance between them. She said slowly, "Just too wide for him to jump, I think. But perhaps he can. What do you think?"

Stanton looked down into the chasm of the street below them, "That's a thirty-foot street down there. We shall have to make sure he doesn't get the chance."

"If I were to put some men across there, Mr. Stanton?"

"No, let's not confuse the issue. The killing-ground will be here, right here. If it's to be anywhere at all. And once he's through that door and on to the roof, someone must close it, and lock it, and then keep away until we come down, is that clear? We don't want to chase him down there again. He'll try anything once he sees his escape's cut off, so I want that door shut tight. All right?"

"All right. So..."

"You'd better get back to your men. Start your drive as soon as you're ready."

At the doorway, Auer turned and held out his hand in a self-conscious gesture. He said, "Good luck, Mr. Stanton...Fräulein. A lot of people have been killed already. I hope..."

"Well do our best. Watch out on the way down. He's lurking there, waiting for you. Get down to the basement as quickly as you can and then work your way up."

"Good luck."

He signaled his men and they trailed down the stairway after him. A moment later, Stanton heard the whine of the elevator and knew that now they were alone. He turned to Anna and said, "We'll have a long time to wait. It'll be a snap shot as he comes through that door. Don't wait for me. Just fire. We'll both fire."

"The neck shot."

"He's got to come through there."

"What do you think happened to Otto, Harry?"

Stanton put a hand on her arm, showing a conscious affection. He said slowly, "He tried to kill us, Anna. If we hadn't jumped..."

"Yes, I know. He was drunk."

"He probably still is. And it's our fault, you realize that? At least, it's my fault. I should have kept away from you. I nearly did."

"Did you?"

"Yes. I'd made up my mind after Cora. I said never again, never."

"You can't live forever without a woman just because one of the species hurt you."

"You can try. Just the occasional...Well, you know what I mean. I determined that no woman was going to destroy me. Does that seem silly?"

"Not if you were hurt badly enough."

"No. That's just it, I wasn't. Only my ego was. She was

cold and beautiful and completely devoid of passion. She just wasn't good enough in bed, and that's not a very nice thing to say about anyone, or, come to that, about myself. It shouldn't be that important."

"It must be, Harry. And it is."

"Perhaps you're right."

"I know I am."

"What about Otto? What are we going to do about him?"

For a long time she did not answer. She said at last, "There's bound to be an inquiry. Into the wreck, I mean. They will have found out already that someone pulled the pin from the coupling. No one knows it was Otto, except us."

"And you want us to keep quiet about it, is that it?"

"That's what I want, Harry."

"Even though he tried to kill you?"

"He was only hitting back at us. You just said as much."

Stanton sighed wearily. "I suppose so." He knew that, despite all his determinations, he was inextricably entangled with her for the rest of his life. Looking at her now, he wondered if that was as bad a thing as he had always tried to persuade himself. He thought, *Perhaps I can still get out of it when this is all over.* And he knew, looking at her body, remembering it as he had seen it, that he would do anything to feel the touch of her flesh again.

Far below them, they heard a drumming start up, a raucous, tinny sound that alarmed them with its incongruity. It was a brass band, and it was playing an Offenbach march, with the drums and the trumpets and the cymbals working overtime in the confined space of the hall below.

His eyes wide, Stanton looked at Anna and raised his eyebrows. She listened for a moment, her lips beginning to smile, and she said, mocking him, "Well, you asked for plenty of noise. They've taken you at your word."

"For God's sake, a brass band!"

"The fire brigade band, by the sound of it. Can you think of anything more likely to frighten an honest leopard?"

The sound of it went reverberating through the empty corridors, searching out a cunning animal and seeking to frighten him into submission with the oldest weapon known to man. Like the gorilla's savage drumming on his chest, this was the ape's first attempt to drive away the predatory evils that threatened them.

The incongruity had grown into a menace. He said, "We'd better split up. It might be any minute now."

She nodded. "There are too many obstructions up here. If he gets through the doorway alive, it will not be easy."

"If he does, we'll have to stalk him. As long as the door is shut again, it's only a question of time. I'll go over by the housing of the elevator, and you take the opposite side. Mind you don't get in my line of fire."

"All right. We'd better be out of sight or he'll try to back down again. Someone's coming up behind him to slam the door, remember."

"Yes, I know."

She broke off, staring over his shoulders.

Stanton swung round, his rifle ready, thinking in a moment of panic. *The fire-escape. I don't believe it. No animal could get up that ladder.* The movement there almost caused him to fire, and it was only the urgent need for a killing shot, a sure shot, that made him hold.

Then he lowered his rifle as the form took shape in the half-light of the distance. It was von Abart.

The great bulk of the body came slowly over the parapet, ludicrously slow, as though time were momentarily suspended. His jacket was torn and his tie was loose, and the blond hair hung down lankily over one side of his forehead. He stumbled over on to the parapet and stood there swaying. He was clutching at his rifle.

As Stanton stared, von Abart saw him. He peered into the darkness, rubbing a hand across his eyes and leaning back against the cold stone of the wall. He was drunk, so drunk that he could barely stand on his feet, and in a moment of bewilderment Stanton wondered how he had found the stability to climb up there. He looked across at Anna and saw that in the light reflected up from the beacons below her face was hard, alert, anxious. He turned back uncertainly, beginning to move forward, and then von Abart shouted, his voice thick and hoarse and hesitant, "Stanton. Stanton? Are you there? I'm going to kill you, Stanton."

As he watched, he saw von Abart jerk up his rifle in a lightning movement that he would not have thought possible in a drunken man, and he threw himself sideways and to the ground as the bullet hit into the wall where a moment ago his body had been. He heard Anna shout wildly, "Take cover, Harry, take cover!" He heard her running, and as he scrambled to the shade of a projection, the blare of the approaching music stopped and in the silence he heard the heavy door to the roof slam shut and for a moment he wondered what had happened. It was a short instant of time before he realized what it was, and then he knew.

The leopard was up there with them, too. The roof was theirs now, a killing-ground to be shared by the four of them. The rest of the world was a long way from them.

CHAPTER 17

Down below, there was a silence now, and anticipation.

The orchestra, disappointed that its work was over so quickly, was already dispersing to tell their wives the glad news that they had been driving a leopard, chasing it with the cacophony of their music from floor to floor in the big apartment house, driving it up on to the roof where the hunters were waiting. It would be something to talk about for weeks to come, and some of them were already rehearsing the stories they would tell, brightly illuminating them with the fantasies of their imaginings.

The police were gathered together in quiet, orderly groups, smoking their cigarettes and casting occasional glances at the Captain, Auer, whose eyes seemed riveted on the stairway that led to the roof.

Mendel had come in, and they were talking together, talking quietly as befitted the occasion.

"And the door is shut on them? There's no other way out?"

"No, Herr Mendel. It is almost over."

"I hope so. So many people killed. In München. It seems impossible."

"A pity that he could not have been captured. I was told that it is an excellent specimen."

253

"Beautiful, beautiful. But I fear it is not possible. In Malaya, yes, but in the streets of the city, it cannot be done."

"None the less, it is a pity. If Herr von Abart were here..."

Mendel did not answer. He was wondering, uneasily, what had happened out there in the bush that had brought them home so sullen, so silent, so worried. He made a mental note to ask the Fräulein about it when this was all over. Had they quarreled? Had von Abart tried to assert too much of his old authority? Had his resentment flared up under the impetus of the loneliness and the struggle and the hardship? And what, in heaven's name, had happened to von Abart since? Had he, assuming the responsibility himself, gone off to drown his sorrow somewhere? He said to Auer, "I suppose the police are looking for him?"

Auer shrugged. "They went to his house. He was not there. I think, perhaps, when he saw what had happened...Perhaps he went off to get drunk. This is what I would do. But I do not know, I can only guess. I do not know von Abart the man. I only know the picture we have always had of him as a great German."

"Yes, yes, of course. I wonder how long this will take them? He is an expert shot, Mr. Stanton."

"And the Fräulein, too, he tells me."

"Oh, really? I didn't know. I suppose she must have learned a great deal from von Abart. Competence, I feel, is highly contagious. Wouldn't you say so?"

"Yes, perhaps you are right."

Cradling their rifles loosely in their hands, the men were sitting down on the stairway to wait.

Up there, Stanton was waiting, too.

He had found a place of immediate cover, a rough outcrop of boarding that concealed some electric cables. He was acutely conscious of the danger now, knowing that he was watching for von Abart's gun and for the leopard at the same time; watching, too, for Anna, not knowing where she was and knowing that she would be too preoccupied with his safety to think sufficiently about her own danger.

Forcing himself into the darkest recess of his corner, he called out, "Anna? Anna?"

She did not reply. He called out angrily, "Von Abart...Otto. The leopard's up here. He's hunting all of us."

Only the silence answered him.

A dark shadow fell across the concrete just ahead of him, and he swung round and raised his rifle at once, but it was gone immediately and only the lingering smell told him that it was the leopard. There was no sound. Then a small piece of masonry, a tiny pebble, rolled into his line of vision, and when he looked at the direction in which it had come he could see Anna, on the far side of the roof, under the overhang of part of the housing. Her finger was at her lip, and when she was sure that he was looking at her, she pointed across to the other side.

He moved out a little to see what it was, ready for either of them, and saw that von Abart was standing there, out in the open, his feet wide apart and his rifle ready.

He stepped out and called, "Otto! The leopard's up here - watch out!"

He was ready for the reply, and was back under cover the instant he had seen the arm go up. A bullet sounded by him, a ricochet off the stonework, and he cursed and called out again. "Don't be a fool, for Christ's sake pull yourself together!" He debated for a moment, wondering whether a carefully placed bullet would send the rifle from his hands, wondering if he could get in such a precise shot without running the risk of showing himself too long. And then he decided that he could not, and that, if he could, it would not be safe to leave von Abart without a weapon, knowing the acute danger that lay in his altruism, but accepting it as a relief from his guilt. Peering out from his cover, he saw that von Abart had lowered his gun and was drinking from a metal flask. He ran from his hideout and scuttled across the roof to where Anna was, and as he ran he heard the clink as the flask dropped and knew that an instant later there would be a shot, and when it came he was already slithering on his belly into the shadows at Anna's feet. They pulled deeper back under cover, and he whispered angrily, "The bloody fool."

She looked at him and said, "We'll have to kill him, Harry. We'll have to."

She was frightened now, and he stared at her in dismay. He said, "No, don't be a fool. If we can disarm him, if we can get the leopard..."

"Where is it?"

"It's up here somewhere. There's not cover enough for a beetle, and yet it's hiding out."

"And so is Otto."

He stared out into the darkness. The place where von Abart had been was empty, and in a moment he saw him creeping along the wall close to the parapet. As he watched, wondering whether to chance the shot he had been thinking of, the leopard came momentarily into his line of sight, a split fraction of a second as it moved with incredible speed across the roof, and he flung up his rifle and fired, knowing at once that he had missed, knowing that the target had gone before he even squeezed the trigger. And as he watched, three shots came back at him in rapid succession, the bullets spattering the masonry, and he heard von Abart taunting him, "You'll have to do better than that, Stanton! Or was that your Anna firing? Was it? Are you leaving it all to her, too?"

Close beside him, she whispered savagely, "We'll have to kill him, Harry. It's the only way. The only way."

He put his hand on the barrel of her rifle, gently. He said quietly, "Watch for the leopard. That's where our danger is."

"He tried to kill us before, and he'll try to kill us again."

"I know. There's nothing we can do about it."

"Harry, we must. We can't just wait here to be killed."

"He's drunk, good and drunk. He's firing all over the place."

"Not so drunk that he can't shoot straight when he wants to, Harry."

Her insistence saddened him. He said, "He's loved you for ten years, Anna. This isn't the way to end it."

"No?"

"No."

"At least let me disarm him. A snap shot at his rifle. He frightens me, Harry."

Her voice was low, controlled. He could find no trace there of the fear she spoke of. He said, touching her hand, "It's been building up inside him a long time, a very long time. He's been biting the nails of his mind. When he sobers up, he'll have to accept the inevitable. And all we have to do is wait. And keep our eyes open."

She stared at him, trying to be sure that she knew just what the inevitable was. He said abruptly, "I'm going to get that damned leopard."

Now the fear that he had not found before was in her voice. "Harry, be careful. Be careful of both of them."

"Cover me. Keep calm and cover me."

Slowly, he edged his way into the open, knowing that he was exposing himself and fearing the shot that would come, knowing that even a bad marksman, even a drunkard, could not miss at this distance, and worrying, too, that under the influence of drink some of the old skills might have returned to make von Abart a more formidable opponent than he was when he was sober. He looked carefully round him, wishing there were more room to maneuver, and then he saw von Abart and the leopard at the same split second, and as he threw up his rifle, praying for that instant of grace that would enable him both to fire and to get back under cover at the same time, he heard the shot, followed by another so fast they sounded like one.

He saw von Abart stumble, drop his rifle, and clutch at his arm, and he did not know whether her shot had been to protect him or to solve the problem that was vexing her, knew, too, that this was something that, whatever happened now, he would never know. And when the moment of confusion had gone, the leopard had gone, too, and he was back under cover, touching her arm and forcing himself to believe what she was going to tell him.

She said slowly, almost fearfully, "His gun was aimed straight at your head."

He did not hesitate. "Yes, I know. We'll just have to keep under cover. And we still keep hunting the leopard, we hunt it until it's dead. And we're a team, remember? A team. Just like with the tiger."

"With the tiger, we didn't have a drunken egomaniac shooting at us."

"Nothing can destroy us, Anna. Nothing. You must believe that."

"I can't believe it. I can't believe anything so unlikely."

"You must."

"If Otto were dead I could believe it. I hate him for what he's doing to us."

"Try to remember what he's done for you in the past. Remember only what you told me about him."

"I was fourteen then, a child. Now, I'm a woman."

"Promise me—no more firing. At least, not at Otto. You've already hit him, you know. In the arm. Did you know that?"

"I was aiming at the rifle."

"Can I believe that, Anna?"

"Is it important to you to believe it?"

"Yes."

"I aimed at the stock of the rifle. It was moving fast

across his body." She started to smile again. "I never was much good with a snap shot. I've got to have time."

"So no more? You promise?"

"No more."

He wished she sounded more convincing. He said, "As soon as we've got the leopard, Otto will be easy."

"I don't think we'll get the leopard while he's out there firing."

"We will, I promise you. Sooner or later it's bound to show itself."

"All right. If you say so."

Outside and below them, on the street, the raucous sound of the loudspeaker on the radio car came up at them. The voice was Auer's, anxious, worried, hesitant. It said, "Mr. Stanton...Mr. Stanton. If you are all right, fire two shots." The message came up again, louder, and Stanton said grimly, "They've heard at least a dozen shots from up here. They must think we're a fine bunch of hunters."

He pointed his rifle up to the sky and fired twice, rapidly.

"That ought to keep them quiet."

"Where is he now, Harry? Do you know?"

"Otto? He's over on the other side, somewhere near the fire escape."

"And the leopard?"

"God knows! We'll find him. I wonder if I could get close enough to Otto to disarm him - to take his rifle away."

"And then? The leopard?"

Not understanding what she meant, he said glumly, "That's the point. If he'd stay with us, nice and quiet and not making any fuss, we could get on with the job. But he wouldn't. And I can't leave him without any sort of defense. I've no great love for Otto, but I don't want to see him torn to pieces. And this is all my fault, remember. All of it."

"Are you sorry, Harry, for what we started?"

"No. No, I'm not sorry. I don't know how this will all turn out, but...No, I'm not sorry."

She pressed herself against him and he knew that the excitement, the hunt, was stirring her just as it was stirring him. He could not think of anything more dangerous than relaxing his vigilance even for a moment. He gripped her arm and said, "We must be careful. Cover me."

Alarmed, she said, "Where are you going?"

"Over by the parapet. I can keep in the shadows for more than half the way round the roof. Keep an eye on me as much as you can, and whatever you do, don't move from this spot." She nodded, gripping her rifle more firmly, and he said, "Remember, don't move from this place. Remember, too—it's only the leopard you shoot at."

He moved out, not waiting for her reply. He had seen that look of cold efficiency on her face again, the same look that had so impressed him when they were hunting the tiger together, when she had moved slowly down the street firing her rifle like a professional beater, not stopping for anything and being afraid of nothing. He ran quickly to the shelter of the surrounding wall, wondering why no shots came after him.

And then, in the angle, he saw it. It was crouched in the open, where the shadows of the two walls joined and were at their darkest, and as he saw it, it sprang, and as it sprang he dropped to one knee and raised his rifle, quite calmly, knowing that this was the essential moment, knowing that it was already in the air on its vicious way to him, its forepaws outstretched. He fancied he could even see the claws reaching for his eyes. The long soft underside of its belly was exposed, sleek and smooth and beautiful, and for an astonishing moment the sleekness of its widespread legs, muscular and taut and efficient, impressed themselves on his mind and he knew that he was thinking of Anna. In that dreadful delay he knew that he was too late for his shot, and he rolled backwards and pulled the trigger, and when he leaped at once to his feet there was blood on his face, her blood it seemed, and the leopard was gone.

He shook himself and felt for the wound, and then he knew that it was not his own blood that was tasting in his mouth but a spurt of blood from the animal he had hit, and he said to himself, *A wounded leopard. Now we're in trouble.*

When he looked to see where it had gone, von Abart was there, on the far side of the roof, shouting at him, and he saw the rifle go up again as he ran fast for cover. The voice was harsh and raucous. "You're no good, Stanton, you're no good! Set your Anna on him, let her have a shot at it. She's better than both of us, didn't you know?"

A slug hit the ground by his feet and another went over his head and he knew that in his drunkenness von Abart was firing in a wide, irregular pattern. He was under cover again before the third shot, and he did not even hear the whine of the bullet. Anna pulled him to his feet and said, "I was just going to shout, I saw the leopard at the same time. I was afraid to spoil your shot."

She broke off, staring at his face. "You're wounded."

"No. It's not my blood. He went over my head and I hit him, in the belly some place, I think. The blood must have been coming fast."

"In the belly?"

"I think so. It doesn't mean a thing. He can still fight. It might not even have been as bad as that. He was close, very close. I could feel the warmth of his body."

How could he tell her that it was the warmth of her own body that had held his fire? He said grimly, "It was a pretty lousy shot. Where's Otto gone?"

"He went back to the other side. He seems not to care a damn about the leopard, and yet it doesn't touch him."

They heard von Abart's mocking answer coming to them out of the darkness, knowing that their voices could clearly be heard right across the roof. He shouted, "He knows, Stanton, the leopard knows better than to go for me. The supremacy of the strongest animal, he knows it. That's why he won't touch me, Stanton, he's frightened of me! It's you he wants! It's you and Anna! And he'll get you, both of you. Even if I have to do his killing for him. So say your prayers, Stanton, if there's any prayer left in that heart of yours. Or is it all prayed out, Stanton, like a country that's been hunted over too often? Is that it?"

Stanton whispered, "If he's drunk, I'm a bloody Dutchman."

Anna's hand was tight on his arm. She said savagely, "He's drunk, Harry. Very drunk. And like that he's more dangerous. I'm frightened of him."

"Don't be. Be frightened of the leopard. Now that he's wounded..."

"He may be badly hurt. Too badly."

"You know better than that. He'll still fight with his guts strewn clear across the rooftop. Like a chicken with its head cut off. Or a rabbit with a heart full of pellets. You can't stop them. Sometimes it's frightening the way they go on struggling."

He was suddenly losing patience, losing patience with himself because he knew that, but for that one split second of time, except for that momentary image that had come to him of Anna—he knew that except for that the leopard would now be lying dead at his feet. He stood up abruptly and said, "I'm going out to finish off the job. If Otto tries to interfere, put a shot through his shoulder. A careful shot, in the upper arm, the right arm. You understand?"

He did not wait for her to reply. He went out of the shadows and stood there, his feet braced wide, knowing that he was exposing himself dreadfully, but knowing, too, that Anna would be watching over him, protecting him from the lesser evil while he went out to cope with the greater.

Not trying to hide himself, he strode forward, his rifle

ready, looking carefully into the shadows, moving cautiously and listening for the slightest sound in the silence, forcing upon himself the utmost awareness of sight or sound or scent.

Looking round, he saw that Anna had left the shadow, had moved forward a few inches so that the light from the beacons below had put half of her body in whiteness. He saw that her rifle was carefully levelled, the barrel steady and motionless, incredibly so, without even a trace of the slightest weaving. There was a moment of alarm as he waited for the shot, freezing, and when it did not come he looked in the direction of her target and saw that von Abart was standing there, far across on the other side of the roof, saw, too, that the upper part of his body, the vital area, could not be in her line of fire.

He knew then that she was waiting—waiting for a movement that would bring the aging torso into the deadly sights of her rifle for the killing shot, the heart shot, the neck shot, the break-the-spine shot.

He was trembling. When he saw that he was wrong, and that she could see von Abart clearly, he knew that he was forcing himself to believe what he wanted to believe. And in that moment he knew too that his love for her was a hypnotic fascination that would drive any glimmerings of wisdom from him. It meant nothing to him now that she had said, "Kill him, Harry. If you don't I will."

He wished that the habit of analysis were deeper in him, wished he could close the gap that lay wide between him and an understanding of her, knowing that all that had brought them together had been coldly and competently engineered. And yet, knowing that all this had been done because she wanted him, there came to him a knowledge of his supremacy over her, a knowledge at which he clutched with a desperate disregard of its specious logic.

And in that precise moment, he saw the leopard hit.

He saw the shadow of a motion, and he yelled hoarsely as

he saw that von Abart had sensed it, too, and was throwing himself forward. It was a black, savage motion of darkness, in which only the eyes and the open mouth had any color, and it seemed to hang in the air, almost motionless, poised over von Abart. And knowing that he could not fire without hitting both of them, he shouted harshly to her, "Now...at the neck! For God's sake, at the neck!" There was no answer from her.

He ran forward then, seeing the dreadful claws as they slashed an inch-deep incision across the base of von Abart's neck and tore the spinal cord right out of its column; he saw the face torn open and a biceps ripped out. There was time, too, to see the open wound in the leopard's belly where its blood was flowing with the blood of its victim, and then Anna came forward, quite slowly and gently, with an almost delicately unhurried motion, and fired three shots into the animal and waited till it rolled over, dead. Then she looked at him, staring at him wide-eyed and saying nothing, and the last thing he heard was a sudden wild scream that came inexplicably to them both and then stopped short because von Abart was dead.

They stood there for a while, looking down at the broken body that had been von Abart, close together, looking at the leopard, and then Stanton put out a foot and gently pushed its yielding body, and he looked at Anna, and when she would not take her cold, tearless eyes from von Abart's bloody remains, he walked to the door of the stairway and flung it open.

A yellow beam of light flooded the roof from the hallway, and he stood there for a moment, his hand on the lock, looking back at her, wondering.

Then Auer came running up from below, followed by Mendel and a dozen of the others, and they crowded round the bodies that lay there, the old man and the leopard, looking and saying nothing and feeling frightened because they were face to face with the resolution of something they did not fully understand. Mendel put out his hand and touched Anna on the shoulder, and she shivered and looked across at Stanton, and then she walked slowly over to him, waiting for him to accept or reject her, and perhaps not knowing which he would decide to do.

The whispered sound of the others came to them, and the noises from the street below. And somewhere, as if all the danger were now gone, the loud clanging of a streetcar sounded.

They stood together now, apart from the little crowd up there, feeling detached from them. And when he spoke to her, he glanced over his shoulder to make sure that they could not hear what he was saying. They were far away now, the two of them alone, and the group at the other end of the roof was huddled about the bloodied flesh on the damp concrete that was all that was left there. He found he was trembling, not with fear anymore, because the fear was now far behind him, but with a kind of savage emotion that he would have called, had it been weaker, apprehension. It was an excitement, as though the hunt were beginning again.

He was not accusing her; he was making a purely academic point, doubting in his mind if he were right, throwing the matter open, as it were, to debate. He said, "You could have hit the leopard. The neck shot."

She looked at him steadily, and there was a clarity in her eyes that had not been there before, as though for her, too, the hunt was on again and this was the moment of decision, just as it had been with the tiger. It seemed to him that she was marking his comments almost with respect, a pupil absorbing a lesson from the new teacher but ready to argue the point because she was skilled enough in this trade to tell him, if necessary, that he was wrong.

"No, Harry. Not to be sure."

There was a kind of despair settling in him. "I wish I could believe that. I wish I could be sure."

"You must be sure. It is the truth."

"I want so badly to believe you, Anna. Believe that I want to."

"You must believe me!" She said again fiercely, "You must!"

He looked across at the others, listening to the muffled sound of their voices, curiously hushed. He said sadly, "The end of a legend."

"No! Not a legend!"

He looked back at her in surprise, startled by the sudden vehemence, but she turned away and made as though to leave him. Not understanding, he clutched at her arm and said, "No. Don't go. Now you must stay with me. Forever, Anna."

She did not look at him. She said, very quietly, "You believe that I destroyed him, and yet you want to stay with me? Is that wise, Harry?"

He said somberly, "It is hard to be in love and to be wise."

For a long time she waited, and then she turned to him and he saw that she was close to tears. She said steadily, "I did not kill him, Harry, not even by omission. If I had fired just then, then I would have killed him. But I was sure that...Can you believe this, Harry? I was sure that he would win. Even wanting, perhaps—wanting that he would die, I was sure that he would not, because of the image that was in my mind. An image against which nothing could stand. Nothing."

"A legend."

"No! A myth. That's not the same thing, Harry, is it? I was thinking, *This is the man, nothing can conquer him.* And while I was watching, knowing that nothing could destroy him, I saw him destroyed. And in that moment I knew that he was not a legend after all, but that he was only a myth. Perhaps I should have known it before. I lived with him for a long time, Harry and still...You knew it, too. I told you, out there in the jungle, I told you that all he had done for many years was a lie, nothing more.

I told you that he had lost his competence, and yet—yet you still think of him as he used to be before you even knew him."

"Yes, I know. I was hypnotized. Is that the right word? That is why I called him a legend. I could not believe that he could ever be killed by an animal."

She said gently, "Invincibility is very vulnerable, Harry. Perhaps we should have known that. Both of us."

Both of us. He knew now that she was right, and the dismay was gone from him. He pulled her close to him, using his strength on her, gripping her tightly as though fearful that she would pull away. He took her by the arm and went with her down the stairs, closing the door behind them and leaving the world up there to the living who were gaping at the dead.

When they reached the street, the cars were already beginning to move again, and the town was slowly bursting open once more to become the big, bustling city that it had always been.

THE END

ABOUT THE AUTHOR

Alan Lyle-Smythe was born in Surrey, England. Prior to World War II, he served with the Palestine Police from 1936 to 1939 and learned the Arabic language. He was awarded an MBE in June 1938. He married Aliza Sverdova in 1939, then studied acting from 1939 to 1941.

In January 1940, Lyle-Smythe was commissioned in the Royal Army Service Corps. Due to his linguistic skills, he transferred to the Intelligence Corps and served in the Western Desert, in which he used the surname "Caillou" (the French word for 'pebble') as an alias.

He was captured in North Africa, imprisoned and threatened with execution in Italy, then escaped to join the British forces at Salerno. He was then posted to serve with the partisans in Yugoslavia. He wrote about his experiences in the book The World is Six Feet Square (1954). He was promoted to captain and awarded the Military Cross in 1944.

Following the war, he returned to the Palestine Police from 1946 to 1947, then served as a Police Commissioner in British-occupied Italian Somaliland from 1947 to 1952, where he was recommissioned a captain.

After work as a District Officer in Somalia and professional hunter, Lyle-Smythe travelled to Canada, where he worked as a hunter and then became an actor on Canadian television.

He wrote his first novel, *Rogue's Gambit*, in 1955, first using the name Caillou, one of his aliases from the war. Moving from Vancouver to Hollywood, he made an appearance as a contestant on the January 23 1958 edition of *You Bet Your Life*.

He appeared as an actor and/or worked as a screenwriter in such shows as *Daktari*, *The Man From U.N.C.L.E.* (including the screenwriting for *"The Bow-Wow Affair"* from 1965), *Thriller*, *Daniel Boone*, *Quark*, *Centennial*, and *How the West Was Won*. In 1966-67, he had a recurring role (as Jason Flood) in NBC's *"Tarzan"* TV series starring Ron Ely. Caillou appeared in such television movies as *Sole Survivor* (1970), *The Hound of the Baskervilles* (1972, as Inspector Lestrade), and *Goliath Awaits* (1981). His cinema film credits included roles in *Five Weeks in a Balloon* (1962), *Clarence, the Cross-Eyed Lion* (1965), *The Rare Breed* (1966), *The Devil's Brigade* (1968), *Hellfighters* (1968), *Everything You Always Wanted to Know About Sex* (*But Were Afraid to Ask)* (1972), *Herbie Goes to Monte Carlo* (1977), *Beyond Evil* (1980), *The Sword and the Sorcerer* (1982) and *The Ice Pirates* (1984).

Caillou wrote 52 paperback thrillers under his own name and the nom de plume of Alex Webb, with such heroes as Cabot Cain, Colonel Matthew Tobin, Mike Benasque, Ian Quayle and Josh Dekker, as well as writing many magazine stories.

Several of Caillou's novels were made into films, such as *Rampage* with Robert Mitchum in 1963, based on his big game hunting knowledge; *Assault on Agathon*, for which Caillou did the screenplay as well; and *The Cheetahs*, filmed in 1989.

He was married to Aliza Sverdova from 1939 until his death. Their daughter Nadia Caillou was the screenwriter for the film *Skeleton Coast*.

Alan Caillou died in Sedona, Arizona in 2006.

DON'T MISS ANY OF MICHAEL KASNER'S HARD HITTING MILITARY NOVEL SERIES

BLACK OPS

Formed by an elite cadre of government officials, the Black OPS team goes where the law can't - to seek retribution for acts of terror directed against Americans anywhere in the world.

3 BOOK SERIES

Armed with all the tactical advantages of modern technology, battle hard and ready when the free world is threatened - the Peacekeepers are the baddest grunts on the planet.

4 BOOK SERIES

CHOPPER COPS

America is being torn apart as criminal cartels terrorize our cities, dealing drugs and death wholesale. Local police are outgunned, so the President unleashes the U.S. TACTICAL POLICE FORCE. An elite army of super cops with ammo to burn, they swoop down on the hot spots in sleek high-tech attack choppers to win the dirty war and take back America!

4 BOOK SERIES

FROM CALIBER BOOKS
www.calibercomics.com

CALIBER
BOOKS

DON'T MISS ANY OF NEIL HUNTER'S NOVELS FROM CALIBER BOOKS

Reporter Les Mason is completing an expose on the Long Point Nuclear Plant. But before he can finish he dies an agonizing death. The doctors are baffled—and there are similar cases to follow...Chris Lane, his girlfriend, and organizer of the Long Point Protestors, discovers Mason's notes, and decides to find out for herself what the plant has to hide.

2 BOOK SERIES

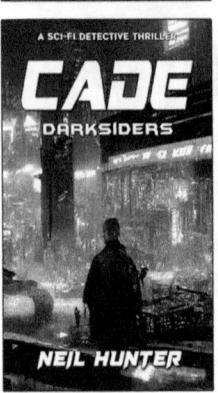

In middle of the 21st century America – over-populated decaying cities are ruled by hi-tech gangs pushing every vice and wastelands are controlled by bands of mutants. Ordinary citizens are oppressed and face a hopeless future. But Marshal T.J. Cade is a new breed of law enforcer. Teamed with his cyborg partner, Janek, Cade takes on these criminals and works in the gray areas of the law to get the job done.

3 BOOK SERIES

The village of Shepthorne England wasn't being gripped, but strangled by a winter's blanket of heavy snow and Arctic temperatures. The trouble began innocently enough with a massive pile-up of autos on frozen roads leading to and from the village. Then, from the sky, a military transport plane with its top secret cargo of devastation crashed down towards the center of the village. Hell was just beginning to touch Shepthorne and its unsuspecting citizens...

FROM CALIBER BOOKS

CALIBER BOOKS

www.calibercomics.com

CALIBER COMICS GOES TO THE EDGE!
Science Fiction and Horror themed graphic novels

FROM AWARD-WINNING COMIC WRITER AND ARTIST
WAYNE VANSANT
COMES TALES FROM WORLD WAR II

An action/adventure tale of the French Legionnaire soldier, Battron, who is involved with the liberation of a freebooting French ship, the Martel, from a heavily guarded Vichy French port during WWII. The Allies want the ship destroyed; the Germans have sent serious resources and firepower to save it. But a critical security leak in British intelligence could jeopardize not only the mission but Battron's life. The key is the beautiful former mistress of the Martel's captain, enlisted in the hope she can convince him to join the Free French movement with his ship. But has she told the Allies all she knows? And can Battron and his skillful commandos complete their dangerous mission in time under the luming shadow of the pending Allied invasion of North Africa?

Collection of tales involving the German Waffen SS from acclaimed creator and comic artist Wayne Vansant. These stories deal with the German Panzer troops during World War II and collects the highly acclaimed Battle Group Peiper story, Witches' Cauldon saga, along with three short tales. Knights of the Skull covers the war experiences of young German troops on the Eastern Front to the massacre of American troops near Malmedy Belgium to the harsh conditions of a crushing winter and engagements against an unrelenting Soviet troop onslaught.

The epic and incredible telling of the early days of the United States during the Second World War. Days of Darkness covers the darkest days of WWII for the US, when the country went from the tragedy of Pearl Harbor to the triumph at Midway. Covering in detail is the attack of the US Naval base and the devastation of the fleet in Hawaii, then the action moves to the evacuation and fall of the Philippines to the horror of the Death March of Bataan, and finally to the dramatic Battle of Midway which stopped the Japanese juggernaut in the Pacific.

"Heavy on authenticity, compellingly written and beautifully drawn." - Comics Buyers Guide.

WWW.CALIBERCOMICS.COM